*The Dog Sitter Detective
Takes the Lead*

By Antony Johnston

The Dog Sitter Detective
The Dog Sitter Detective Takes the Lead

The Dog Sitter Detective Takes the Lead

ANTONY JOHNSTON

Allison & Busby Limited
11 Wardour Mews
London W1F 8AN
allisonandbusby.com

First published in Great Britain by Allison & Busby in 2024.
This paperback edition published by Allison & Busby in 2024.

10 9 8 7 6 5 4 3 2 1

ISBN 978-0-7490-3025-4

Typeset in 11/16 pt Sabon LT Pro by Allison & Busby Ltd.

By choosing this product, you help take care of the world's forests.
Learn more: www.fsc.org

Printed and bound by
CPI Group (UK) Ltd, Croydon, CR0 4YY

For rescue workers and foster carers everywhere

CHAPTER ONE

I missed the first phone call from Crash Double because I was upstairs trying to dig myself out from under my mother's old clothes before I suffocated under a pile of wool and plastic.

Honestly, Monday mornings.

My phone was on the kitchen table and set to silent because I wasn't expecting anyone to call. With a couple of hours to spare until rehearsal, I was determined to make a start on my mother's seemingly endless wardrobe. She had never been an extravagant figure, and I didn't remember her wearing half of the clothes I now stood facing. But there they were, row upon row of dresses and blouses and skirts and more, gathering dust and packed so tightly they threatened to burst out of the wardrobe in this third-floor spare room. There could have been a passage to Narnia back there and I wouldn't have seen it. After she died, my father could never bring himself to discard her clothes, so he simply shrouded them in plastic. I sometimes thought he expected me to wear them but that was about as likely as me twirling down the King's Road in a tutu.

So I reached in to remove a dress from the rail, because if I've learnt anything from fixing up the house I inherited it's that you have to start somewhere, and they did. Burst out of the wardrobe, that is. With me underneath.

As I clambered out from under the squeaking plastic, it was becoming clear that sorting out this tailored abundance would take more than a quick hour or two. I abandoned it with a promise to return when I had more time, because today I had an important rehearsal to attend.

Not that all rehearsals aren't important, but this was to be my first major role since coming out of retirement. I'd given up acting to care for my father, and assumed I'd never go back. But when he died after a decade of illness, it turned out he'd burnt through all the money he'd made in the City, and there was nothing left. I'd have to resume working, which was easier said than done for a sixty-year-old woman who hadn't been in front of a camera or audience for ten years. Nevertheless, I was determined to give it a go, and since landing a new agent I'd had several auditions. Mostly for the role of 'quiet grandmother who has one good line if she's lucky', admittedly, but work is work. And now I'd landed a meaty part: Melanie, frustrated daughter of Margory and long-suffering mother to Michelle, in a new play at the Sunrise Theatre called *Mixed Mothers*.

After freshening up and changing into a standard rehearsal outfit of pullover, slacks and flat shoes for comfort, I returned downstairs to gather my things. That's when I finally picked up my phone and saw a call from an unknown number.

I didn't think much of it. There had been a time when my friend Tina was the only person I could reliably expect to call my mobile, while calls on the house phone had invariably been doctors or officials discussing my father's care. Those calls ceased with his death, and I'd considered removing the landline altogether because now everyone lives on their mobiles, don't they? I did, especially as I'd also begun dog-sitting to make ends meet (auditions are all very well, but they don't pay). My number had quickly spread through the dog owners' grapevine and now calls from strangers weren't unusual.

Normally, though, they left a voicemail. No such luck here, so I assumed it was a scammer and tossed my phone, keys and purse in my handbag.

I hadn't yet worked out how to get the towering piles of old *Financial Times* in the hallway to the recycling, so I stepped carefully around them and checked myself in the hallway mirror. Still short and grey, but not in bad shape considering. Then I stepped out onto Smithfield Terrace where a fresh spring breeze blew down the street. I took a sweet breath and smiled, my mind on nothing but making a good impression at rehearsals.

Which is why I jumped several inches in the air when

a familiar sharp voice behind me called out, 'Guinevere, my dear. Are you well?'

The black-clad Dowager Lady Ragley, my next-door neighbour and stalwart defender of Chelsea house prices, had somehow left her house and approached me without making a sound.

'Very well, thank you, my lady,' I said, forcing a smile. 'In fact, I'm going to first rehearsal for my next role. I'm appearing at the Sunrise, you see.' It was a small theatre, to be sure, but the Dowager was easily dazzled by celebrity. I lived in vain hope that she might one day be impressed enough by my career to stop badgering me about house repairs.

'How lovely,' she said, the information immediately dismissed. Instead, she gestured with a thin, white-cuffed wrist to my house. 'I wonder if you've given any further thought to your façade.'

I fought to stop my eyes rolling and stepped back to take in the frontage. Really, it didn't need that much work. OK, some of the window frames were a little worse for wear; yes, the guttering and drainpipes needed attention; sure, there was missing ironwork on the basement stair. But it was hardly threatening to collapse onto the pavement.

'All on my list,' I reassured her, tapping my head to indicate where said list was stored. 'Don't worry, I'll get to it before—'

A piece of first-floor render chose that moment to succumb to the spring breeze and claim its freedom. In silence (mine aghast, hers triumphant) we both watched it break away and skitter down the stone, to land on my front step as if mocking not just my words but my very thoughts.

The Dowager faced me with a silent, stony glare. I almost would have preferred her to be smug.

'I'll call someone right away,' I said quickly. Unable to resist, I added, 'Unless you can recommend a builder personally, of course.'

Her nostrils flared, offended by the suggestion that she might deign to fraternise with tradesmen. She turned on her heel and said, 'I have full confidence you'll deal with it, my dear,' then disappeared inside her house, somehow slamming her door in silence.

Suitably chastened, I pulled out my phone and prepared to call a builder. Except, of course, I knew no more builders than Lady Ragley did. I'd have to seek a recommendation.

Trudging toward Sloane Square Station, the spring breeze seemed to have turned sour.

CHAPTER TWO

I arrived at the Sunrise ten minutes before rehearsals were due to start, yet somehow still felt late. Finding the communal green room empty, I dropped my bag and coat on a free table and hurried through corridors towards the stage. Voices sounded from out front. Had I got the time wrong? Being late to first rehearsal wouldn't make a good impression.

I weaved past stagehands in the wings and emerged to find the principal cast huddled with the director, Simon. He had his arm around the shoulder of a young woman, and everyone smiled while she took a group selfie on her phone. I was still very much on the outside of acting scene gossip, having ignored it altogether for the past ten years, so I had no idea if this was Simon's daughter, his latest wife, a PA, or whatever. But they were clearly on good terms, so I decided I should make an effort.

Ted, the actor playing the eternally patient husband Martin to my harrassed mother Melanie, noticed me step on stage and discreetly cleared his throat. The others turned like a pack of startled meerkats then parted so I could approach Simon and his blonde companion.

I took the initiative and walked forward confidently. 'By my watch I'm early, but seeing you all here makes me wonder,' I laughed, and before anyone could contradict me, I put out a hand to greet the young woman. 'Good morning. You've met everyone else, so you might have already guessed I'm Gwinny.'

'Oh yeah, of course,' she smiled, handing her phone to Simon. 'This is so good of you, thank you. I'm Violet, obviously.'

'. . . Obviously,' I agreed, envying the confidence of youth. She probably had a million followers on social media, so why wouldn't it be obvious?

(I know what social media is, I'm not a Luddite. My new agent had suggested I create a profile and get involved, to let people see 'the real Gwinny'. But when I spent an hour looking around, it seemed what people *really* wanted to see was either beautiful young people posting pictures of themselves in sunny locations, or angry old people arguing with each other about today's tabloid frenzy. I doubted there was an audience for back pain, varicose veins and house renovations.)

'Let's begin,' said Simon, clapping for attention. 'Places, please.'

I reached for my lines then remembered I'd left my bag backstage. Ted and I weren't on until scene three, though, so I'd have time. As everyone scurried to position,

I passed him in the wings and whispered, 'I need to get my lines from the green room. Cover for me, I'll be back in a minute.'

Before he could reply, a stagehand handed me a stack of pages. I thanked her and flipped through to scene three, only to find it wasn't there. 'Darling, I think you've got these mixed up,' I called after her. 'These are for—'

'Places, Gwinny, places!' Simon bellowed from his seat facing centre stage. 'Get with it, you're in scene one now.'

Confused, I turned back to the opening pages and scanned in vain for my character. Had there been rewrites already?

'Sorry, Simon, I don't see Melanie in the opener. Are these definitely the latest sides?'

'What? No, you're Margory. Violet is playing Melanie.'

I was so still I could have won a prize. Vaguely aware that everyone else had frozen too, I glanced over at Violet. She stood in the wings, suddenly fascinated by her own script.

'Say that again?'

The director sighed theatrically. 'You're playing Margory now. The grandmother. Violet is playing Melanie, the mother. For heaven's sake, didn't anyone tell you?'

Blood rushed to my cheeks. I fought to keep my voice steady as I walked downstage to the footlights and said,

'Who, Simon? Who exactly would have told me? You're the director.'

'Yes I am, and that's why I've made the decision to recast with someone closer to the character's age. Now don't fuss, Gwinny. Find your mark and let's go.'

I did, and proceeded to stumble my way through unfamiliar lines and an unfamiliar headspace for the first run-through. I kept reminding myself that I was no longer a star, or even much of a recognisable character actor. I should have known that landing a central role so soon was too good to be true. This was what I'd dreaded most about resuming my career: having to start back at the bottom of the ladder, like a struggling young actress all over again but with several decades of accumulated aches, pains and wrinkles to contend with.

I didn't blame Violet. Assuming she wasn't sleeping with Simon, she'd done nothing more than be a pretty *ingénue*. Yes, she was twenty years too young for the part, but make-up could take care of that. In her position I would have done the same.

At lunch break I found a private area and called my agent, 'Bostin' Jim Austin.

'Bostin Agency,' he answered in his thick Brummie accent. *Bostin* was a nickname he'd acquired at school in Birmingham, apparently local slang for *brilliant*. It takes all sorts.

'It's Gwinny. What the hell's going on with *Mixed Mothers*? They want to recast me!' Furious, I related what had happened while Jim patiently tutted in all the right places.

'Believe me, I would have told you if I'd known about it,' he said when I finally paused to breathe. 'But I don't think there's much I can do.'

'Surely it's a breach of contract,' I sputtered. 'Margory has a quarter of the lines Melanie does. Are they at least going to pay me the same?'

He hesitated. 'Now there's an idea. Leave that with me. The thing is, do you really want to cause a fuss?'

There was that word again. 'I'm hardly being an unreasonable diva. I was cast in a role, and I expect to play it.'

'I get that. But now you've been *re*-cast, and a woman of your experience knows that sometimes happens on small productions. Especially when they can suddenly get a big name from TV.'

'She's practically a teenager. How has she been around long enough to be any kind of name?'

'Are you serious? Didn't you watch *Eastenders* last year?'

'Last year I was somewhat busy caring for my dying father.'

After a pause he said, 'OK, I apologise for that. But if we're going to work together, I need two things. First, you have to take more of an interest in the business. Second, if I can be frank, remember that you're basically starting over from scratch, and with a handicap. You don't want a reputation for making trouble.'

I seethed quietly at being called a troublemaker when none of this was my doing. But I knew exactly what 'handicap' he meant. There was no shortage of older women vying for stage parts, thanks to the lack of decent roles on TV. If word got around that I was difficult to work with, or even (gasp!) *ungrateful*, I'd be consigned to the do-not-hire pile.

'Five minutes,' came a shout from the corridor.

I pushed my anger deep down inside, took a long, slow breath, and said, 'All right, deal.' Struck by sudden inspiration, I added, 'By the way, I don't suppose you happen to know any good builders? My house needs a bit of work.'

'I do, actually. Just had our loft done, and quite reasonable too. I'll text you his number.'

Before I could ask whether Bostin Jim and I shared a definition of 'quite reasonable', he ended the call. I threw down my phone and reread grandmother Margory's lines.

At ten past four I stepped out of the stage door and was assaulted by a black Labrador. Thankfully it was a loveable attack, all wagging tail and lapping tongue, so I crouched to greet him and fuss his ears. 'Hello, Ronnie,' I said between licks.

Ronnie belonged to my friend DCI Alan Birch, retired, formerly a senior detective in the Met and presently standing behind his dog as it tried to drown me. Seeing Birch there, stoic and grounded, it struck me how like a faithful Lab he was himself. We'd become friends by tripping over a murder case, when Tina had been accused of killing her husband-to-be. With Birch's help I uncovered what the police had failed to, unmasking the real murderer, and through it all his loyalty had never wavered. Tall and wide-shouldered, with grey cropped hair and a full moustache, he couldn't look more like an ex-policeman if he tried. But beneath a firm brow he had the most delightful bright blue eyes, and wasn't to be underestimated.

Nevertheless, glad as I was to see a friendly face, it was a surprise. 'I don't recall telling you when I'd finish today,' I said. I wasn't entirely sure I'd mentioned rehearsals at all.

'You didn't.' He tapped his nose and winked. 'Asked one of the staff.'

'Once a detective, eh?'

'Guilty as charged. How'd it go? Did you knock 'em dead?'

I almost laughed at his turn of phrase. There had been several times today when I'd have gladly knocked someone dead. 'To be honest, I'd rather not talk about it. Can we discuss something else?'

'Sorry, didn't mean to pry. Lesson learnt.' He looked like a scolded schoolboy, and I relented. Like most people who've never seen behind the showbiz curtain, Birch would never understand how mundane it is ninety-nine per cent of the time. If all you see is the final film cut, the TV broadcast, or the two hours spent onstage,

18

it's natural to think the entertainment business is, well, entertaining. But behind the performances lie hundreds of unseen hours of planning, auditions, rehearsal, logistics, administrative blather, bad food, more rehearsal, more logistics, worse food . . . not to mention the simple tedium of sitting around waiting for someone to shout '*go*' so you can finally walk on set and do your job.

Don't get me wrong, it's hardly digging ditches for a living. But the life of a jobbing actor is not filled with jet-set glamour.

'Tell you what,' I said, falling into stride beside him as we walked away from the theatre, 'if you promise not to interrupt, I'll regale you with the whole sorry story. Now, where are we going? St James's?'

'Right enough, then if Ronnie needs more, maybe over into Green Park.'

We continued on, and as promised I told him the whole story, from being buried under my mother's old clothes to my surprise recasting. I could practically feel him shaking with outrage on my behalf, wanting to interject. But he held it in, directing his grunts and gruff outbursts at Ronnie instead as the Lab pulled this way and that, sniffing at every square inch of his surroundings in case they were edible.

I finished my tales of theatrical woe, and admittedly felt better for having shared them with someone else.

'So that's my day,' I said. 'Please tell me yours was more normal.'

'Nothing but, ma'am,' he said briskly. 'Breakfast,

walk, lunch, walk, *Escape to the Country*, and here we are.'

Nobody would accuse Birch of being loquacious, but after forcing him to hold it in for so long I'd expected a verbal uncorking, not an appointment schedule.

'Who'd you have lunch with?' I asked, trying to get a little more out of him.

He responded with a confused look. 'Ronnie, of course.'

I sighed. After a lifetime in the Met, he was much better at asking questions than answering them. Much like how he couldn't stop addressing me as 'ma'am', because I apparently reminded him of his old detective chief superintendent.

It was nice that Birch didn't speak unless he had something to say, but it meant that I still didn't know much about him. He was a widower; he enjoyed the theatre; he lived in a modest, orderly house in Shepherd's Bush, over which his late wife Beatrice cast a long and enduring shadow; and that same shadow kept his wedding ring firmly on his left hand.

'Tell me something I don't know,' I said.

Without hesitation he replied, 'Most people think CID coppers automatically outrank uniform, but that's not true. For example, a desk sergeant is superior to a detective constable regardless of plain clothes.'

I laughed. 'I asked for that, but it's not what I had in mind. Tell me something about *yourself* I don't know.'

'Oh,' he squeaked. 'Um, well . . .'

Before he could answer, my phone spoilt the moment by ringing.

I pulled it out of my handbag to silence it, and recognised the same unknown number that had called earlier. 'Scammer,' I explained, showing Birch the *Unknown Caller* display on the screen. 'They already called me this morning—hey!'

Before I could protest, he took the phone from me, jabbed the Answer button, and growled angrily, 'Look here, this is DCI Birch of the Met. Delete this number immediately or there'll be trouble.'

Birch wasn't averse to occasionally using his old rank when it could be helpful, but I was in two minds about this response. On the one hand, even if he was tilting at windmills asking a phone scammer to care about the law, it was a gallant gesture; he all but puffed out his chest as he spoke, which I wasn't complaining about. On the other hand, he'd snatched my phone without asking and assumed I needed him to fight my battles, which is precisely the sort of thing I will happily complain about.

'Oh, very funny,' he continued. 'Pull the other one, sunshine.' Then he ended the call and handed my phone back.

'What on earth did they say?' I asked, curiosity winning out over annoyance.

'Claimed to be Crash Double. You know, Bad Dice singer. Classic band.'

After deciphering Birch's habitually clipped phrasing, I did indeed know who he meant. Bad Dice was an Irish rock group from the 1970s, all long hair and loud guitars. Crash Double, their lead singer, was a notorious hip-swinger whom I'd briefly met once or twice at showbiz parties long ago. I realised this was something I did know about Birch. During a previous visit to his house, I'd noticed a collection of rock music records in his lounge, which had surprised me because to look at him you'd think he listens to nothing but marching bands.

'They still tour, don't they?'

'Absolutely. Saw them the year I retired. Great show. Not cheap, mind.'

'Why on earth would a scammer pretend to be an old rock star—*oh*.' Even as I said it, I came to my senses. 'Did it sound like Crash Double's voice? On the phone?'

'Oh, yes. Excellent impersonation.'

'And is Mr Double by any chance a dog owner?'

Birch shrugged. 'Unknown. Can't say I've seen him about.'

I was about to call the number back and find out when my phone buzzed again, displaying the same number. Staying well away from Birch's kleptomaniacal hands, I answered the call and wondered if I should ask for *Crash* or *Mr Double*. Fortunately, he spoke first.

'Look, is this Gwinny Tuffel or not?' asked a deep voice with a light Irish accent. 'I took this number on good faith, but if I've been set up for some kind of prank—'

'Not a prank, I assure you. Gwinny speaking, and I apologise for my *presumptious* friend.' I glared at Birch, but he'd already turned away to focus on pulling Ronnie out of a bush. A squirrel popped out of the top and scurried up a nearby tree, completely unseen by the Lab.

'He's a nutcase, is what he is. Said he was a copper! Anyway, my name's Crash Double, I sing in a band called Bad Dice.'

'Yes, I know who you are, um . . .' I still didn't know how to address him. 'What should I call you?'

He laughed. 'Crash is fine. Listen, I need a dog sitter for Ace. Got a gig over the weekend, so I'll be away for a few days. Normally I'd ask my wife, but she went and got herself a boat cat.'

'I'm sorry, did you say *boat cat*?' Birch shot me a baffled look. No doubt, hearing only one side of the conversation must have been confusing. Mind you, I could hear both sides and wasn't much the wiser.

'Yeah. You know, a cat. On her boat. A boat cat. What would you call it?'

Fair enough, he had me there. Although what her boat had to do with it, I couldn't guess. I shook confusion from my head and asked, 'What dates, exactly? And whereabouts do you live?'

'On . . . a . . . boat,' he said slowly, as if talking to a child. 'In Little Venice.'

CHAPTER THREE

I've never been what you might call a water person. Some people long to cruise the world or imagine living out their days on a yacht. My father was a little that way; it's why he and my mother are now both scattered in the Tegernsee. But the most time I've ever spent continually on a boat was when that French musician came over in the nineties to perform at Docklands and I was invited onto a VIP barge for a close-up view. Naturally, this being London it promptly rained and blew a gale, and we could barely hear over the plastic rustle of our promotional rain ponchos supplied by the record label. Was the fact they had them prepared in advance sensible or suspicious? I could never decide.

Anyway, suffice to say I won't be joining my parents in a Bavarian lake. Bury me under a tree, at least that's useful.

So when Crash Double said he lived on a houseboat on the Regent's Canal, I wasn't as impressed as I think he hoped. But I could use the money, and after Thursday morning's rehearsal *Mixed Mothers* paused for the bank holiday weekend anyway. I caught the Tube to Warwick Avenue Station and from there followed Crash's directions, walking a short distance to the main bridge junction at Little Venice.

To my right shone the triangular Pool where three canals meet. Tourist barges moved to and fro on the water but what caught my eye were the dozen or so narrowboats lined up side by side against the canal path, their occupants busily hanging bunting across their roofs. I had a sense of *déjà vu*, having seen something similar on my one previous trip to Little Venice many years ago.

Turning left took me onto Blomfield Road, then past the junction house and down to the canal path, finally to stand before a tall locked gate declaring this part of the canal for residents only.

I was a few minutes late, but so was Crash, assuming he was the tall, rangy man sauntering towards me along the path. Actually, *swaggering* is a better description; he had the confident gait of a singer, born of being worshipped for two hours onstage every night. Besides an occasional picture in the paper, I hadn't seen him for more than twenty years. I'm not much of a music person either, you see. It all tends to go in one ear and out the other.

Crash Double (Birch had told me with a tap of the nose that his real name was Shaun Donnelly, 'But even his family calls him Crash,') wasn't a conventionally handsome man. Heavy eyebrows, a long nose, pointed chin and hair that had long ago flown the coop, for which he compensated with a white goatee. He was all bones, with barely a scrap of meat on him and, I couldn't help noting, no bum whatsoever. Flat as a billiard table. Nevertheless, he had the same bright-eyed presence as a good leading actor and a charisma that swept aside concerns about photogenic looks and made the simple t-shirt, scarf and faded jeans he wore seem like designer clothes. Come to think of it, they probably were.

Dog and owner were well-matched. By his side, collared but not on a lead, padded a dutiful Border Collie with a rough tricolour coat, mismatched brown-and-blue eyes, and asymmetrical ears. *Eine poppen, eine floppen* as my father would have said in deliberately comedic bad German. In a breed competition, Ace's non-standard features would only win a wooden spoon. But in combination with his canny expression, effervescent tail and enthusiastic grin, they somehow made a very charming dog.

'Gwinny,' said Crash with a smile, taking a key from his pocket to unlock the gate. 'Actually, have we met?'

'Many years ago, darling. Parties.' I slipped inside and crouched down to greet Ace as Crash locked the gate behind us. The Collie sat of his own volition and extended his nose to sniff me out – or more precisely the small bag of treats I'd brought in my handbag. 'Nothing wrong with your sense of smell, is there?' I looked to

Crash for guidance. 'Any allergies?'

'No chance. This one's a canine Hoover.'

I held the treat in my open hand and offered it to Ace. He was practically drooling for it, but didn't take it until I said, *Good boy, go on.* Then he scooped it off my hand with his tongue and swallowed it immediately. 'Did you even taste that? It hardly touched the sides!' I laughed and fussed him behind the ears. He fixed me with his bright blue eye, and grinned to give me an unexpectedly close and comprehensive look at his teeth. They were in excellent condition and his warm breath smelt fine. 'How old is he?'

'Six. Prime of his life, like us.' Crash winked and turned to lead me along the canal towpath. Ace forgot all about his ear skritches, hurrying to catch up and fall in alongside his owner. I wasn't surprised. Thanks to my father being a soft touch with the local rescue, our family had owned or fostered a full house of dogs over the years including a Border Collie named Daisy he'd brought home, enthusing about the breed's sharp intelligence. As if to prove him right, Daisy quickly divined that the ranking member of our household was in fact my mother and from then on hardly left her side.

'You don't keep him on-lead?' I asked.

'Never needed one,' said Crash. 'He's collared and tagged, but that's to keep the warden away. Ace would never run off.' We reached the first houseboat along the path, a large black structure. Crash stopped and turned to me. 'So, have you not been to Little Venice before?

You sounded unsure on the phone.'

'I attended the Canal Carnival once, years ago. That was very jolly, all the boats and bunting. Is that what they're doing over in the Pool today?'

'Bingo,' said Crash with a curled lip. 'You're about to attend your second Carnival, and you're welcome to it.'

'Not a fan?' I recalled the event as loud, colourful and happy. All the narrowboats had been strung with flags, buskers and street entertainers passed round the hat, fast-food vans kept everyone fed and many boats were opened to the public to educate them about this quintessentially British way of living.

'I hate every minute. Tourists everywhere, screaming kids, people gawping in your home. Luckily the bank holiday is the anniversary of our first proper gig in Dublin. So, every year we play two nights at the Olympia to celebrate, mostly fan club tickets. It's a great vibe and it gets me away from here while all this crap is going on.'

I had a sudden recollection of a past interview with Bad Dice on TV. 'Don't I remember you saying you were doing your last ever tour twenty years ago?'

'What can I say? It's a long tour.' He adopted a lopsided grin that had no doubt broken many a girl's heart.

'So these Dublin shows aren't your only concerts?'

'God, no. You must understand, sales aren't what they used to be, even for a so-called classic band like us.

28

It's all I can do to keep my head above water, pardon the pun.'

'Then you must go away often,' I said, alert to the possibility of a repeat client. 'Who looks after Ace normally?'

Crash gestured along the canal, lined on both sides with permanently moored houseboats. 'My wife's along there. She's always been up for it before but now she's got Lilith. The boat cat.'

I remembered the confusing phone call earlier but still felt unenlightened. 'Can we go back a few steps? You and your wife live on a boat, and you have a dog, but she's also gone and bought a cat? I'm not really a cat person, so you'll have to leave instructions for me while you're away.'

He looked puzzled, then laughed heartily. 'Ha! OK, we've got our wires crossed here. First of all, we don't live together. This is mine.' He rapped his knuckles on the side of the large black houseboat. 'She's my third wife, you see.' He smiled expectantly.

'Um, congratulations?'

'No, no,' he laughed. 'She's my third wife . . . and my first, and my second. Get it?'

The funny thing about fame and notoriety is that when you have it, suddenly everyone knows the intimate details of your private life. It's intrusive, and you wish they'd leave you alone . . . but it also means you can assume everyone you meet knows those details.

Of course, eventually the papers and gossip columns

lose interest and they really do leave you alone. Then you regain your private life, but at the cost of a serious blow to your ego.

Despite his fame, though, all I knew about Crash Double was that he sang in Bad Dice. I tried to let him down gently.

'Darling, I've been off the scene for too long. Caring for family, you understand. Indulge me.'

He produced a set of keys from his pocket. 'We're on our third go-around, for old times' sake. But if we tried living together again, we'd be onto the third divorce instead, you know?' I didn't, having never married let alone divorced, but nodded politely. 'I'm down here, she's up there, and she can't be looking after Ace any more. I'll introduce you later.'

The black houseboat occupied prime position at the head of the canal, and was also the largest. To be honest it barely resembled a boat at all, being a boxy shape and twice the width of a normal narrowboat. It was also twice the height, thanks to an unusual second-floor section along a third of its length. Crash saw me look up and shrugged.

'Eighteen months of fighting with the residents' association that took. Worth it, though. Grand views.'

He unlocked the front door and led me inside (or should I say *on board*?). It struck me that I'd never set foot inside a proper houseboat before. I'd been on a regular narrowboat once or twice, but this was on a different order of magnitude.

The most immediate and obvious difference was the front door, which opened from the side facing the path, and this narrow entrance hall into which we'd stepped, with stairs leading up to that second floor. But then Crash led me into the lounge (which he explained boaters call a *saloon*) and I gasped. First, because there was more space to move about in here than in the whole of a normal barge. Second, because you couldn't actually move about for the mountains of paraphernalia. Records, CDs, old videotapes, band memorabilia and more filled the room, threatening to trip anyone unwary enough to put a foot wrong.

A somewhat worn-looking sofa sat against one wall, while against another stood an upright piano, watched over by framed gold discs mounted on the wall. Facing it was a spirits bar with a polished wooden counter. In one corner stood a single bookshelf whose contents alternated between wellness guides and historical biographies: Churchill, Napoleon, Mandela, the usual suspects. There was no TV, I noted, so I resolved to bring a jigsaw puzzle with me for entertainment.

Opposite the sofa, tall French windows dominated the centre of the wall facing the canal. To one side of them was a stereo that looked worth more than my house. On the other side lay Ace's bed, on which he'd flopped down as soon as we entered the saloon and where he now methodically tore up pieces of cardboard.

'Every few days I get a box from Choudhury up the road,' Crash explained. 'When I go out, Ace dismantles and shreds it to cope. Did you know collies can have autism? I can't be sure if it's that, but he definitely suffers from separation anxiety. Pity I can't give him a Xanax, you know?'

I nodded in sympathy. Separation anxiety is a hard thing to deal with, especially in Border Collies, who need mental stimulation as well as physical exercise. I noted with approval that Crash kept a plastic box of toys next to Ace's bed, including flying discs, ball launchers and even some puzzle feeders.

'Better he destroys a cardboard box than your sofa, eh?'

'Exactly. He loves having a job to do, and it gives him something to focus on instead of worrying. I'll walk up to Choudhury's and get a new box tomorrow morning to occupy him until you get here.'

Beyond the spirits bar lay an open-plan kitchen (the *galley*, apparently) where a chrome-top stove gleamed. Was Crash an assiduous cleaner or just someone who never cooked? The pitifully bare cupboards suggested the latter, holding little more than dog food, multipacks of crisps and energy bars.

Further on, a corridor led first to the bathroom and then Crash's bedroom. I braced myself for silk sheets and a mirrored ceiling, but to my pleasant surprise I found cosy rumpled bedclothes with a thick woollen throw, a spartan wardrobe and a second dog bed for Ace. On reflection, black satin probably didn't go well with a rough-coated tricolour dog. A dresser stood by a window overlooking the water, piled high with male grooming products. Wedged into its mirror frame was an old paparazzi photo of Crash with a young woman on his arm. She looked familiar. A late-night Channel 4 presenter, perhaps? I didn't feel I knew him well enough to ask.

Finally, we returned to the entrance hallway, and I realised along the way that no windows faced the path. Aside from the front door, every view outside faced the water, presumably to maintain his privacy. So as we climbed the stairs to the second floor, where he'd boasted of 'grand views', I anticipated easy chairs, a sun lounger, perhaps even a yoga mat to fit my impression of him so far: an ageing rock star who left the business end to other people while he walked his dog, basked in gold discs and nostalgia, and did yoga every morning to feel better about takeaway the night before.

Don't get me wrong, I didn't begrudge him. He'd earned it, and God knows I wouldn't turn it down if it came my way.

But my expectations were confounded when I entered what appeared to be a hi-tech recording studio. Synthesiser keyboards lined the room, all hooked into one of those big recording consoles bristling with knobs and switches. Two large speakers stood on either side of what I assumed was the main desk, with a large computer monitor, a keyboard and more dials and buttons. Beside them sat a large mobile phone, in a photo case printed with a picture of Ace. Underneath the desk stood a huge metal-cased computer and in front of it an expensive Aeron chair. Finally, a dozen different microphones stood around the room on adjustable stands, ranging from old-fashioned crooner models to the kind of high-precision 'shotgun' mics I was familiar with from TV.

'Are you sure you have enough equipment?' I asked cheekily.

Crash smiled. 'You can never have enough.' He pointed out a series of small mesh circles embedded in the walls. 'There are mics hooked up around the room, too, for when inspiration strikes.'

'I'll be sure not to sing in the shower, then.'

He laughed. 'Don't worry, they're not permanently recording. But it's an easy one-touch control. See?' He pressed a button on the desk to demonstrate, but nothing happened.

'I'm sorry, was that supposed to do something?' I asked.

'Oh, it did. Watch.' He pressed another button next to it, and suddenly I heard my own voice asking, *'I'm sorry, was that supposed to do something?'*

As I took all this in, Ace padded up the stairs, deftly squeezed past me and walked over to his third and final bed, nestled under one of the synthesiser stands, from which he watched us and lazily wagged his tail.

Crash laughed. 'Here, you'll enjoy this. Take a seat.' He gestured for me to sit in the Aeron. I did, watching him carefully as he leant over me to wake the computer with a password, then tap and click on things. The desktop was a jumble of files, and when he started using some music software it all went entirely over my head. But Crash whizzed around the screen, very familiar and comfortable with it all.

Suddenly a traditional Irish reel began playing from the speakers. Crash stepped away as Ace's ears pricked up and the dog practically leapt off his bed to meet Crash halfway. He sat, waiting for a signal . . .

And then they danced.

Well, that's being kind and seeing it through a dog-lover's eyes, I suppose. But as I watched, Crash led Ace with a gesturing hand, turning around and weaving the dog between his legs, all in time to the rhythm of the music. It was a long way from Crufts, but it was delightful nonetheless and got even better when Crash began singing along in Gaelic. Neither he nor Ace missed a beat.

Abruptly the song stopped and Crash knelt down to give Ace a ruffle around the neck and ears. The Collie panted with delight but clearly could have gone for another song or ten. Crash gave him a treat, smiling all the time. Then he leant over me, put the computer back to sleep and picked up his phone.

'Something new I've been working on. All these years and I never did anything traditional, you know?'

'So you miss Ireland?' I asked as we returned downstairs.

'God, no,' he laughed. 'Miserable, cold, damp place.

I couldn't wait to get away. But the nostalgia kicks in as you get older. You'll see.'

I could have reminded him there was only a decade between us but whether he was merely being polite or really did think I looked younger than my age, I wasn't about to contradict him.

After seeing that mess of files on his computer, the state of the lounge made more sense. At least an agile dog like Ace could easily navigate the precarious towers of memorabilia. Crash unlocked the French windows with a key and pulled them open; they looked directly out onto the canal through an exterior guard rail.

'This room would be great for parties if you tidied up a bit,' I said. 'Do you have a cleaner . . . ?'

'Sure and I'll just call Bono round for dinner. No, I'm flattered, but my partying days are over and I like the place as it is. Although I should get that rail removed.'

'I assumed it was to stop Ace from jumping in the canal.'

Crash laughed. 'I suppose that's a bonus, but actually it was to stop idiots like Johnny from getting hammered and falling in.'

Presumably he meant the Bad Dice guitarist, Johnny Roulette. I remembered Birch enthusing about him after Crash had called me in the park.

'Has that actually happened?'

'More than once, until I had the rail installed. But like I say, those days are over.'

'The partying, or Johnny's drinking?' It was a

36

mischievous question, but I'd known enough actors who fell prey to the bottle over the years to understand the problems it could cause.

'Both.' He looked troubled for a moment, then his easy smile returned. 'Let's show you round the walk.'

We left the house with Ace in tow, and Crash looked up the path towards the Maida Vale bridge. Further along, a woman stepped off a boat painted in patchwork rainbow colours. Potted plants covered its roof and hung over the sides. She did something with a rope on the towpath, then saw us and waved. Crash waved back, and as I raised my hand to join in, Ace sprinted down the path. In the blink of an eye the dog was sitting obediently at the woman's feet while she stroked his fur.

'Your wife, presumably?' I said. 'I still can't get over the idea that you live on separate boats. Do you, um, alternate—?' I considered what I was about to say and stopped myself. 'Sorry, none of my business.'

Crash laughed anyway. 'The spirit is willing but the flesh is weak, Gwinny. No scheduling complications there.'

I felt my cheeks flush. It really wasn't my business, but Crash had so readily put me at ease that I felt I was chatting with an old friend, not someone I'd barely met before today.

'Can't live with 'em . . . can't live with 'em,' said a voice behind us, chuckling.

A man who wouldn't have looked out of place on a

picket line approached along the towpath. His square-shouldered coat was festooned with button badges, he wore a flat cap atop a wide head, and his jeans ended in two-inch turn-ups over heavy boots.

'I'll thank you not to cast aspersions on my good wife, now,' said Crash, looking the man up and down. I couldn't say why exactly, but this new arrival didn't look like a resident. I wondered how he'd got in through the gate and what he wanted with Crash. There was a tension in the air, like one of them might throw a punch. Both men looked about the same age, but I'd have put my money on Mr Picket Line any day.

Then they laughed and embraced in a half-handshake, half-hug movement and I felt foolish.

'This is Johnny,' said Crash, turning back to me. 'Johnny Roulette, meet Gwinny. She'll dog-sit Ace while we're in Dublin.'

'Sure and you're Gwinny Tuffel,' repeated Johnny, smiling. 'I remember you from the telly. Looking good, pet, are you well? D'you have your health? Course you do, you're grand. What brings you out here? Don't let this one play games with you, now. How are you?'

I wasn't sure which of this barrage of questions to answer first, or if he even expected an answer. Crash saved me by asking, 'What's the tale, Johnny? Early for you, isn't it?'

'That's a fine thanks for me making an effort. It's the big one, you know it gets me all excited. Have you been rehearsing your words? We don't want Live Aid all over again.'

'For God's sake, that was forty years ago. Have I ever dropped a lyric since?' Crash stage whispered to me, 'He's showing off. One sniff of a girl and Johnny Roulette reverts to a spotty fourteen-year-old.'

Johnny gamely ignored this ribbing, while I made sure to keep Crash between the guitarist and me to prevent any such sniffing. Luckily by now we'd reached Crash's wife, who stood on the path fussing Ace as we approached. When she looked up in greeting, I had two sudden revelations. First, that I was looking at Fox Double-Jones, whose gardening programmes had been a guilty pleasure during the years of caring for my father. That explained all the plants on the boat's roof. Second, I saw now that she was the woman in the photo on Crash's dresser. She had indeed been a late-night TV host, young and glamorous, but unlike most of her contemporaries Fox had successfully reinvented herself as she aged out of the party girl bracket. She'd now been a celebrity gardener for decades longer than she'd been a starlet.

While watching her dig up borders and plant hedgerows, it had never occurred to me that Double was her husband's name (especially as it wasn't even his real name) or that she was a rock star's wife, thrice married to the same man. That's showbiz.

'Morning, boys,' she said brightly. A black cat poked its head out from the houseboat's open door behind Fox as she offered me a hand. 'You must be—'

But our pleasantries were interrupted by sound and fury as Ace spied the cat and gave chase, barking furiously and scrabbling down the stairs into Fox's boat.

'Oh, no! Lilith, run! Ace, stop it!'

A frantic *meow* sounded from somewhere inside.

CHAPTER FOUR

'Ace, no! Leave!' Crash shouted, giving chase with Fox following close behind. Johnny and I looked at each other, then he shrugged and strolled after them with no sense of urgency. Rather than remain outside on the towpath like a spare wheel, I brought up the rear.

It took me a moment to get my bearings as the interior of Fox's houseboat was unlike anything I'd seen before, including Crash's place moments ago. This boat only had one floor but that was far from the main difference.

In some ways it was more like my own house, filled to the brim with what other people might call clutter but I call evidence of a life. Not that I don't intend to clear some of it out, but the minimal lifestyle holds no appeal for me.

Fox's house wasn't filled with books and jigsaw puzzles, though, or even piles of music memorabilia. Instead, it was full of plants. Plants in pots standing on the floor, plants in pots balanced on stools, plants in baskets hanging from wall brackets, plants in troughs lined up on shelves. Even a large glass display cabinet was filled with yet more pots and plants of all shapes and sizes.

I could barely see the walls behind all this greenery, which may have been a blessing in disguise because they were a gaudy clash of purple and orange. Somehow it suited this crazed interior rainforest.

We found Ace standing on a hippy-chic sofa that, at first glance, I took for a pile of duvets. Back feet on the seat and front paws on the chair back, he gazed unblinking at Lilith the black cat. She hissed at the Collie from behind a plant pot, safely out of reach atop a shelf unit, protected by cacti.

'Ace, get down! *Heel*!' Crash called. The dog looked at him, looked back at Lilith, then realised he was on a hiding to nothing. Ace jumped down from the couch and returned to Crash's side.

In most other dogs I might have been surprised to see them give up so easily, but despite his wonky features, Ace was a Border Collie through and through. Our family house in Chelsea was as far from the herding-sheep farm lifestyle as a dog could get, but Daisy had also been capable of snapping from playful family pet to obedient working dog in a heartbeat. I handed Crash a dog treat from my pocket which he gratefully took and gave to Ace.

Then he took a bottle from his own pocket, unscrewed it and removed a pill which he swallowed dry. 'Anti-anxiety,' he said with a wink.

I was about to suggest he clip a lead on Ace, then remembered he didn't have one. To be fair, it didn't seem necessary; the dog now sat patiently at his owner's side, appearing to ignore the cat completely. I doubted that was truly the case but as long as he didn't act on it there was no harm. Lilith, for her part, remained atop the shelf, carefully grooming herself behind a spiny cactus while keeping one eye out for opportunist dogs.

'As I was saying, you must be Gwinny,' said Fox, sitting on the many-layered sofa. 'Crash told me you're looking after Ace while he's away. Have we met before?'

'No, but we were almost certainly at some of the same parties years ago.' I gestured to the array of plants. 'I watch your show, though. It was a big help to me over the past ten years.' I explained about my father and she took my hand.

'I'm sorry, but I'm also glad I could help. So you're a gardener too?'

'Heavens, no,' I laughed. 'Strictly wildflowers and a badly mowed lawn. But I like watching other people do it. Like those shows where a foolhardy young couple build a house halfway up an Italian mountain. I admire their ambition but preferably from the safety of my living room.'

'Sure and you've got a fan, Trips,' laughed Johnny.

'Why don't you give her the tour?' Crash added. 'Get some practice in for the weekend, like. Johnny and me need to talk about the gig.'

This was news to Johnny. 'For what? After thirty

years we can do it in our sleep. You probably have.'

'Ah, come on. Give the ladies some privacy.' Crash put a hand on Johnny's arm and guided him back to the door, taking Ace with them.

'"Trips"?' I asked when they were out of earshot.

'A silly nickname. Married three times to a man called Double, so Johnny says I should change my name to Triple-Jones. Cheeky sod, but it's his way.'

'I suppose being married to Crash for so long, you must have known Johnny all this time too.'

She laughed. 'They come as a pair, right enough. Don't you worry, I give as good as I get. Now let me show you around.'

The tour took in her whole boat, apart from a spare room which she said contained personal items. Every other room, and almost every flat surface, featured plants of some kind, from exotic bromeliads to common tulips and everything in between. Even with my layman's interest it all blurred together.

'I'm amazed you can keep track of what's where,' I said. 'You sound as if you've given this tour a hundred times before.'

'I have. During the Carnival I open the boat to visitors and take families around. I often practise on the residents, too.'

'Ah,' I said, understanding. 'That's what Crash meant about preparing for the weekend.'

'Not that I need it, but yeah. Kids always love these in particular.' She gestured to the glass cabinet I'd noticed earlier, which I now saw was locked. 'My poisonous collection,' she explained. 'Deadly nightshade, monk's hood, burning bush, and so on. Always gets their attention.'

'I assume the key is safely hidden away?'

'Of course. Well, it will be.' Her glance flicked to a brightly painted jug on a shelf with a pair of gloves poking from its mouth. 'Don't worry, tomorrow morning I'll put that away in a cupboard, far from little hands. Do you have children?'

'Not even married,' I said. 'Although, these days one doesn't necessarily follow the other. You?'

Fox smiled. 'Just Ellie, but she's long flown. Lives in Tokyo now, married to a government minister. Her own form of rebellion, I suppose.'

'She didn't feel the pull of show business?'

'I think seeing two divorces and plenty of smashed crockery over the years put her off. But then, loving someone means giving them ammunition to hurt you, doesn't it? Anyway, she's happy. That's all I care about.'

I've seen enough eternally on-again-off-again showbiz partnerships not to pass judgement. Instead, I changed the subject.

'So you're a fan of the Carnival, I take it? Crash tells me he can't wait to get away.'

'That's because he's a miserable old sod,' she said. 'I've told them, they should get the band to put on a show, play on a barge in the Pool. People would love that, and it'd smooth the waters between him and Lucy.

But he won't miss the anniversary concert. Every year, like clockwork.'

'Who's Lucy?'

'The Carnival organiser. It's so silly, they're always at loggerheads.'

I thanked Fox for the tour, said goodbye to Lilith the black cat, and left with flashbacks to the rain-soaked Docklands concert running through my mind. Dublin anniversary aside, I couldn't blame Crash for not wanting to trust the British weather.

Climbing the steps to the deck, I heard low voices talking. Actually, more like arguing, in the quiet and urgent way people do when they don't want to be overheard. To my surprise the voices belonged to Crash and Johnny, standing close together on the path with their backs to me. I saw Johnny take something from his pocket but couldn't see what it was.

Then Ace noticed me and barked, the traitor. Both men turned hastily, now smiling and relaxed. There was no sign of whatever it was Johnny had been holding.

'How'd you like the tour?' asked Crash.

'Delightful,' I said. 'I'm sure lots of people will enjoy it during the Carnival too.'

He grimaced, earning a hearty laugh and a slap on the shoulder from Johnny. 'She's got the measure of you, Crash. Gwinny, a pleasure. You'll be here when we get back, won't you? Of course you will. Maybe you can get us a ticket to your next show, that'll be grand.'

'Do you live here on the boats as well?' I asked. Was

half the canal related to Bad Dice?

'Not at all, the water's not for me. I'm on the Crescent, a hop and a skip away.'

A thought formed in my mind. 'Then I wonder if you could recommend a good builder?'

I'd spoken briefly to Bostin Jim's man, a local tradesman called Darren who, in a stroke of uncommon luck, could actually fit me in on the condition he started early next week. He still hadn't supplied an estimate, though, so I wanted to have at least one fallback.

'Actually, I—' Crash began then stopped himself. 'Yeah, yeah, he probably does. Johnny?'

'Sure, and I had some people in last year. Give me your number, pet. I'll text you.'

'Hold on,' I laughed, 'I'll need to look it up. I can never remember my own mobile number.'

Crash rolled his eyes. 'I've got it, Johnny. I'll send it to you later. Go on, now.'

'Grand,' said Johnny. 'See you in Dublin.' He bent down to fuss Ace. 'Take care of the old man, now. Make sure he learns his lyrics, you hear?' Then he walked away down the path chuckling to himself.

'Shouldn't you unlock the access gate for him?' I asked Crash.

'Just watch.'

The guitarist reached the gate, gripped its railings, hauled himself up, and easily climbed over it. He made it look effortless.

'Told you he's a show-off. Runs around like he's still

twenty years old. And speaking of . . .'

I followed his gaze a few moorings down to a lovely, traditional-looking boat. It was another one twice the width of a regular barge but unlike Crash's was shaped in the traditional English style. It looked very well maintained, as did the man who stood on its deck and waved to us.

'That's Howard Zee,' said Crash. 'Not his real name, of course. He's . . . actually, I'll let him explain. He'd prefer that.'

Howard Zee was tall, athletically built, and proud of it. As we watched he lifted a heavy gas bottle and lowered it into a trapdoor, showing off his chest and arms under a fitted sleeveless vest. He wore a bulky computerised watch on one wrist but no other jewellery, and was completely bald with a bushy white beard. The overall effect made it hard to guess his age which I imagined was the point.

He closed and locked the trapdoor, wiped his hands on a rag, then reached for a plastic jug of dark green liquid perched on the roof. He swigged from it and smiled at us, leaning against the boat in a studied, languorous pose.

'Afternoon, Howard,' said Crash. 'This is Gwinny, she'll be looking after Ace for the weekend.'

'Gwinny Tuffel, of course,' he said, dazzling me with a made-for-TV smile. 'I didn't recognise you with the grey hair. It suits you well.'

'You've nothing on today?' Crash asked.

'Plenty, but I'm between sessions,' Howard replied. 'I did three this morning and I resume at half four for the evening. Can't start too early, they all want to have time with the children after they're brought home.'

'Brought home?' I asked. 'What do you mean?'

'Howard's yummy mummies aren't going to sit in school traffic themselves for an hour,' said Crash playfully. 'That's what nannies are for, isn't it?'

Howard took the ribbing in good humour. 'Those "yummy mummies" are some of my best-paying clients. Probably yours, too. Who do you think is paying three hundred quid for your VIP tickets, Crash? It's not a struggling teenage mother collecting her dole, is it?'

By now I was thoroughly confused, and frankly hoped I was getting the wrong end of the stick. 'Clients for what, Mr Zee? What do you do?'

'Howard, please,' he said, his expression turning serious. 'I'm a body and mind wellness guide. Don't you think today's modern world demands so much of us, Gwinny? It saps our ability to focus on the truly important spirit of our inner self and it's our collective responsibility as superconscious human beings to say "No!" The world is dying of thirst, but if we don't take time to replenish our own well, how can we offer water to others? I help seekers find their own unique path through yoga, relaxation and mental reassurance, guiding them to inner fulfilment and contentment.'

I waited for this well-practised spiel to end, then

asked, 'And how much does inner fulfilment go for, these days?'

'Eighty pounds per group Zoom session, or two hundred and fifty for a personalised guided experience on board,' he said without hesitation. He swigged more of the green liquid, which I guessed was some kind of health drink.

'But the first is always free, isn't that right, Howard?' said Crash, nudging me. 'Maybe you should sign up, Gwinny.'

'I'm perfectly content, thank you.' The truth of that could be argued but I had no desire to pay someone for the torture of having my limbs twisted into yogic knots.

'I don't think I could anyway, Gwinny. I only take clients over forty years old.'

I almost gagged at this transparent flattery, particularly after he'd already recognised me. 'You're too kind,' I said, and quickly changed the subject. 'This boat is lovely. Quite traditional compared to most of the other residents.'

'Which is ironic seeing as Howard's the new boy on the block,' said Crash. 'But you're right, she's a fine craft. Aqualine, isn't it?'

Howard ran a loving hand across the boat's lacquered exterior. 'She's my saviour, really.' He turned to me. 'Crash has been so welcoming, as has everyone else. This is such an intimate community. Are you considering life on the water, Gwinny?'

'The water's not for me,' I demurred, echoing Johnny's

response, 'but I can appreciate a good-looking boat. Crash, don't you think we'd better move on before Ace gets restless?' In fact, the Collie was happily lying on the path to watch ducks paddle by on the water, but he was a convenient excuse.

'Absolutely. We need to get you a set of keys, anyway. See you later, Howard.'

Howard beamed his smile again, parting the thick white beard and deepening his telltale crow's feet. In the afternoon light I now saw that even his baldness was fake. Stubble marks betrayed a shaved head, presumably befitting a guru.

'A pleasure to meet you, Gwinny,' he said. 'Do stop by again.'

'Not without a chaperone,' Crash muttered as we walked away.

I laughed. 'I don't think Howard is my type. Or that I'm his, despite the sales pitch. Fancy doing yoga sessions from his boat!'

'To hear him tell it, he didn't have much choice. Laid off, divorced, lost the house, so he came down here a couple of years ago and spent everything he had left on the boat. As for you not being his type, you're in the right half of the population and that's normally enough for Howard.' He quickly added, 'Uh, not that you're – you know, I mean . . . well . . . you're a perfectly fine . . .'

I enjoyed watching him squirm in the wake of his *faux pas*, but eventually spared him. 'No offence taken. Believe me, I've met plenty like Howard Zee before.'

'I don't doubt that for a moment. Here now, let's get you my spare keys.'

Crash stepped inside his houseboat and took a ring of two keys from a sideboard; one for the front door, one for the French windows. Then he walked back out onto the towpath, gesturing for me to follow. Ace tried to come with us too, but Crash firmly told him to stay. The Collie obeyed, sitting and watching us as we stepped outside and closed the door.

The singer shrugged at my quizzical expression. 'I was burgled a while back, so I had the locks changed.' He quickly added, 'Don't worry, they were donkey's years old. I reckon someone got a key copy from an old set somehow and tried their luck. Besides, they didn't take anything. There's nothing worth lifting.'

'I doubt that,' I said. 'Your band memorabilia, the record collection . . . not to mention all that equipment upstairs. So the police didn't catch anyone?'

'Do they ever? Anyway, these modern mechanisms are great.' He locked the door, and I heard the reassuring heavy click of multiple bolts engaging. 'But I haven't actually tried the spare keys yet, so go ahead. It'll do Ace good to see someone else unlock the door and go in.'

He stood back as I inserted the main key and turned it to unlock. Through the door's small windowpane Ace eagerly watched my every move, his wagging tail banging a tattoo on the floor. I pushed the door open and walked inside, then rewarded the Collie with another treat.

'Perfect,' said Crash. 'Be here for eight, and take Ace

for a walk when you arrive. He'll be ready for it by then and you can feed him when you get back.'

'Wait, you won't be here?'

Crash shrugged. 'I'm an early bird. I'll take Ace for his usual dawn walk, then get a cab to the airport. As long as you're here by eight he'll be fine.'

'And when do you get back?'

'Gig nights are Sunday and Monday, and I'll be on the first flight home Tuesday morning.' He looked around, as if running a mental checklist. 'Now, I've showed you the food, towels, his toys . . . I think that's everything?'

It was everything to do with Ace, but he'd hardly shown me anything about how to live here for the weekend as a human. I'd have to buy in some groceries, for a start. That wouldn't be a problem, though. Little Venice's isolation is deceptive; walk half a mile and you're back in regular old London.

'Yes, I think that's everything,' I said. 'Don't you worry about Ace, I'll take good care of him. We'll have a fun time while he's off rock and rolling, won't we, boy?' The dog looked from his owner to me. With Border Collies it's easy to imagine they really do understand every word. As if to confirm this, Ace padded over, sat down beside me and leant his head against my leg.

I said goodbye and walked back to Warwick Avenue Station, smiling in the spring sun. Notwithstanding the sheer amount of exercise that any Collie requires, I looked forward to a nice relaxing weekend.

How wrong could a woman be?

CHAPTER FIVE

The next morning, I woke to find four waiting text messages that sent my mood on a rollercoaster ride. The first was from Crash, sent the previous evening to tell me he'd given Johnny Roulette my number. The next was a few minutes later, from an unknown number that turned out to be Johnny, with the details for a builder. I added both to my contacts. The third text was from Crash again, this time sent an hour ago, to inform me he was setting off for the airport and trusting I'd take good care of Ace. I smiled at his concern and sent a quick reply telling him to break a leg, assuring him Ace was in good hands.

The final message was from Darren, the builder recommended by Bostin Jim, sending me an estimated cost that quickly wiped the smile off my face. Did he think everyone who lived in Chelsea was loaded? Did he not understand the concept of 'property rich but cash poor'? These were things I would have asked him in no uncertain terms if he'd deigned to answer his phone, but after it rung out again on the third attempt I stopped trying and replied to the text using an emoji of a bundle of cash with wings flying away. This made me feel very modern and with-it, which cheered me up until I realised I'd have to continue gathering quotes and find someone I could actually afford. Thank goodness I'd had the sense to get a recommendation from Johnny.

Brushing my teeth, I wondered again if I'd have to take a pay cut on *Mixed Mothers*. If I was honest with myself, though, the indignity bothered me more than the money. Not that I hadn't been passed over for a younger face when auditioning before; every actress over thirty has experienced that. But to be replaced *after* casting was a new kind of embarrassment.

Still, I couldn't dwell on it now. Ace was waiting for me.

I guzzled some coffee, filled a tote bag with spare clothes, dog necessities and a jigsaw puzzle I'd bought for the occasion, then dashed out of the house. I locked up, popped the key in my purse and turned to find the Dowager Lady Ragley standing six inches away on my doorstep.

'Guinevere, my dear. You haven't forgotten the matter of the workmen, I trust?' She glanced upwards, as if I needed to be reminded of the crumbling render.

'It's a bank holiday, my lady,' I said, squeezing past her. I decided not to tell her about my failure to find someone so far, as it would invite further conversation.

'Oh, is it? How tiresome.'

'Don't worry, there'll be someone here to fix things before you know it. Must dash, bye!' And with that I rushed along the street towards the King's Road.

It was only when I arrived at Little Venice that I noticed the keyring Crash had given me didn't include a key for the residents' access gate. I called out, but nobody answered. Either they couldn't hear me, or nobody was yet awake. Or they were simply ignoring me.

But I couldn't stand there forever in the hope someone would emerge. Ace was waiting and it was now a couple of hours since the text from Crash to say he was departing. Remembering Johnny Roulette's antics the day before, I shifted the tote bag to put the weight across my back and gripped the gate railings. Then I hoisted one foot halfway up the gate, which for a shortie like me was no mean feat, and pulled myself up despite the metal jabbing painfully into my tennis shoes.

'Hey! What are you playing at?' shouted a man's voice behind me.

Startled, I lost my balance, tried to get a firmer grip, failed, and toppled backwards to the ground. Or I would have, if my inquisitor hadn't been so close that I actually fell on top of him instead. I both heard and felt the air being pushed out of him as he struck the paving, and I lay still for a moment trying to steady myself. Then I rolled off and pulled myself upright with the help of the gate, simultaneously explaining and apologising.

'I'm so very sorry, you startled me, and you see I'm actually house-sitting for someone whose boat is through here, but he forgot to give me a key to the gate, and hang on a minute, didn't I meet you yesterday?'

Howard Zee, the wellness guru, pushed himself into a sitting position and rubbed his winded stomach. He wore a hooded top, jogging bottoms and scuffed trainers, evidently returning from a morning run.

'I was pulling your leg,' he said weakly. 'Although I didn't mean to pull it on top of me.'

I helped him to his feet. 'I really am sorry. The only contact number I have for anyone on the canal is Crash himself, and obviously he's in Dublin. Or mid-flight by now, anyway.'

Howard unzipped a pocket in his jogging bottoms, removed a key, and used it to unlock the gate. After we passed through, he locked it again behind us. 'For all the good it does to keep people out, as you so aptly demonstrated,' he said. 'Listen, I've got a spare key at home. Why don't you borrow it for the weekend?'

'That's very kind. You're right, it's really not much security, is it?' Climbing the gate wasn't as easy as Johnny had made it look. The guitarist was bigger than me, undoubtedly stronger, and unlike my tennis shoes his heavy boots would allow him to clamber over without a second thought. But anyone determined and prepared enough could do it. No wonder the police hadn't been able to find whoever burgled Crash's boat.

As we walked along the path a procession of

narrowboats floated past us towards the Pool. 'Plenty coming for the Carnival, I see.'

Howard followed my gaze. 'If you're staying at Crash's, I warn you now that you won't get any peace. The price of being boat number one is you're within earshot of Rembrandt Gardens, just over the bridge, where they entertain the kids. Before Saturday's done, you'll be able to recite the Punch & Judy show from memory.'

I laughed. 'You're not a fan of the festivities either, then?'

'Heavens, no, I love it. Anything to bring some life to the area. The residents don't normally mix with the cruisers, you see.'

'But what's the difference? Surely you're all boaters?'

'Don't go saying that too loud around here,' he laughed. 'We tend to keep to ourselves . . . apart from during the Carnival.'

We reached Crash's houseboat, and through the door I saw Ace already lying in the hallway. 'New locks,' I explained to Howard as I opened the door. 'That's probably why the gate key isn't on this ring.'

I stepped inside and playfully shuffled Ace backward to make some room to walk past. 'Poor thing! Let me put these things down and then we'll go for a walk, OK?'

I thought that was a perfectly reasonable request, but Ace disagreed. He bounded past me, out of the door and onto the towpath, where he first cocked his leg up the bushes on the far side, then squatted down and unloaded a substantial poo on the flagstones.

Howard watched with bemusement as Ace stood up, shook himself, and proceeded to sniff enthusiastically at the guru's ankles. 'You're really not used to being on your own, are you?' he laughed, and reached down to skritch the Collie's ears.

I opened the tote to find a dog bag and grimaced upon seeing the 1,000-piece jigsaw I'd brought along. The box had been between me and Howard when I'd fallen on him and was flat as a pancake. I'd deal with that later. For now, I tore off a bag to collect Ace's business.

'There's a bin outside the gate,' said Howard. 'You're definitely going to need that key.'

Murmuring agreement, I tied off the bag and for the time being placed it on the path outside the door, where nobody would step on it. Then I led Ace back inside and began emptying my tote in the lounge. Removing the dog bags, a lead and the crushed jigsaw left only my spare clothes.

I heard the main entrance close and looked up to see Howard Zee leaning in the lounge doorway. Rather presumptious, I thought. But a close-knit community like this was probably the sort of place where people walked in and out without waiting to be invited.

Meanwhile, Ace had found a flying ring, the doughnut type with a hole in the middle, and held it in his mouth for me to take. Howard looked down and smiled. 'Too smart for his own good, that one.'

'Yes, well, that's collies for you. *Give*,' I said to Ace,

who obeyed and released the ring into my hand. '*Sit.*' He did, and I popped the ring over his head to rest around his neck. 'In my experience, a well-trained Collie will do absolutely anything you tell it to – unless that thing is "relax and take a nap", of course.'

My clothes could wait. I clipped on the dog lead I'd brought along – Crash might be confident enough not to use one, but Ace and I were barely acquainted so I wasn't taking chances – and it was then I noticed the tiny shreds of cardboard scattered on the floor around his dog bed. Crash wasn't kidding about Ace's separation anxiety; the dog had made very short work of that morning's box.

I turned to leave, but Howard stood in my way. 'Before you go running around the park, why not walk with me to my place?' He placed a hand on my arm and gently squeezed. 'I'll give you my spare key, and maybe we could—'

Whatever else he was about to suggest was interrupted by a knock at the door. 'That'll be the postman,' I said, unsure if the post even delivered here but using it as an excuse to slip out of Howard's grip.

The knocking was immediately followed by the sound of the front door being opened, and a woman's voice calling out, 'Crash? It's only me. I called last night but you must have been busy, so I—*aah*!' She saw me, Ace and Howard step into the entrance hall and recoiled, jumping backwards out of the door and onto the towpath, mercifully missing the filled poo bag.

Clearly this was no postal worker. Instead, standing

on the path but now poking her head back inside the doorway was a strikingly elegant east-Asian woman, forty-something, wearing tweeds, Hunters and a hiking gilet over a sweater. The ensemble gave her an air of somewhere between 'country manor lady' and 'local government official', though I suppose there's no law against being both.

'Hello, Lucy,' said Howard, immediately stepping towards her. 'Don't worry, we're all friends here.' He placed his hand on her arm, much as he had with me, and I began to wonder whether Mr Zee was touchy-feely because he was divorced . . . or divorced because of his wandering hands?

Lucy, though, returned the guru's smile. 'Hi, Howard. I'm sorry, I've come at a bad time. It's an impromptu visit, Crash wasn't expecting me.' She raised her voice and called past me, 'I'll come back later, OK? No worries.'

'He's not here, and he won't be here later, either,' I said, ushering everyone out onto the towpath and locking the door behind us. 'He's in Dublin for the weekend, performing.'

'Gone at the crack of dawn, as usual,' said Howard. 'Do you know one another, by the way?'

The woman looked me up and down as if assessing me, and from the expression on her face I didn't make the cut.

'My name's Gwinny,' I explained. 'I'm dog-sitting Ace while Crash is away.'

'Lucy Kwok,' she said in a tone implying I should curtsy. 'Carnival Chairperson.'

'Yes, Fox told me. So I imagine you two must have an interesting relationship?'

The question seemed to catch her off guard. 'What do you mean?'

'Only that I gather Crash isn't the Carnival's biggest fan.' I'd clearly struck something of a nerve, so smoothed it over with flattery. 'Putting on a big show while not annoying the residents must take quite a balancing act.'

She relaxed again. 'Yes, well, some residents are more accommodating than others.' She turned to Howard. 'Actually, perhaps you can help with a bind I'm in. Do you have any actresses among your clients?'

'Not that I know of. Why?'

'I'm a woman down thanks to flu. If I can't find someone to play Mother of the Waters in the opening ceremony play, I'll have to double up.'

Howard laughed. 'Then it's your lucky day, dear Lucy. Gwinny here is an actress. She used to be on TV all the time; don't you recognise her?'

She obviously didn't but I wasn't offended. The last time I was regularly working, Lucy Kwok would have been in her twenties.

'No, I don't think so,' she said, which I took as confirmation until I realised she was talking about my suitability for the role. 'The Mother needs to exude authority and dignity.'

Now, if I had any sense I would have let that pass me

by. But the humiliation of being replaced by a younger model in *Mixed Mothers* still burnt inside me, and something snapped.

I pulled myself up to my full height – which admittedly isn't much, but posture is everything – and said, 'Young lady, I have played Elizabeth at the Globe, and a recurring headmistress on *Heartbeat*. Whatever the role requires, I assure you I can deliver. What sort of costume does it involve?'

Lucy reassessed me. 'Not a costume, a headdress.' She peered at my head, looking at it from both sides. 'You and I are about the same size, so it should fit . . . All right, I'll bring the script round later. It's only four pages, anyway. The Mother is a minor character.'

Inwardly I breathed a sigh of relief. I'd begun to worry I'd signed up for an hour of tedium, but of course an amateur community piece would only be a few minutes long. I was certainly capable of learning half a dozen lines for a minor character overnight.

'Call it serendipity, then,' I said. 'When and where?'

'Noon tomorrow on the dot. Be at the exhibition barge ten minutes before. Now, I really must get on. Goodbye.' Barely giving Howard or I chance to return the farewell, she hurried off along the path and out through the access gate. I noticed she had a key, but given her Carnival role that made sense.

I let Howard watch her go for a while, then gently elbowed him to get his attention. 'Is she always like that?'

He laughed. 'She's just getting started. Now, about

that key.' We walked to his house, the traditional narrowboat I'd so admired the day before, where he invited me inside.

I hesitated. 'Perhaps I should wait out here with Ace. I don't want to risk tying him up if he's not used to it.'

'Nonsense, Ace is welcome too. He's been in here before.'

I relented and followed him inside, to be once again surprised by a boat's interior. Behind the traditional exterior, this one was even more ultra-modern than Crash's place.

A large TV hung from a wall in the wide saloon with a camera and shotgun microphone secured to its frame. A dozen wires connected the screen to a cluster of computers and technical systems on shelves beneath. From these, cables snaked out to more cameras in the room; two mounted on tripods, one on the ceiling. I could tell from my own experience on sets that they were all positioned safely; no camera would be visible in the frame of another, all wires and cables clipped safely out of view. Finally, several studio lights were positioned on stands to properly illuminate the room.

In front of the TV, in the cameras' focus area, was the set itself; an exercise mat, keep-fit equipment within easy reach, plus a couch and table facing the screen.

'This is a very professional set-up, Howard.'

He beckoned me to follow him through to the galley kitchen. 'Coming from you, I'll take that as a compliment. But you should see the kit some of the YouTube kids have got. I used to be an English teacher so this was all completely new to me when I started. Luckily there are lots of people online to explain how it all works and the signal strength around here is good enough to transmit out.'

'Crash with his recording studio, you with a broadcast set . . . what's next, does your neighbour run a mobile phone company?'

Howard took a spare key from a drawer and handed it to me. 'Were you expecting a bunch of hippies?' He selected fruit and salad vegetables from the fridge, then removed the lid from a large blending machine on the countertop. Ace immediately perked up, sniffing the air. I noted stacks of protein and health supplement packs lined up against the splashback.

'I wouldn't put it like that . . .' I said, even though 'a bunch of hippies' is exactly what I'd expected.

'It's OK, I did too before I moved here. But what I found was a community of independently minded people. It's true, some are anti-establishment but it's also a perfect lifestyle for an entrepreneur. Can I interest you in a smoothie?' He piled the fruit and greens into the blender, and I remembered that he'd been jogging. I was interrupting his morning exercise routine.

'No, I'll let you get on. I'm sure Ace is ready for a good runaround. Thank you for the key.'

'My door is always open, Gwinny. Well, except when I'm working, but you know what I mean. Feel free to drop in any time.'

Ace and I left, my emotions about Howard now mixed. He was clearly vain but was that surprising in a man who'd decided to become a keep-fit instructor? I still had misgivings about his touch-feely nature but he'd been consistently friendly and polite.

I unlocked the access gate with Howard's key, then took Ace across the bridge to Rembrandt Gardens, overlooking the Pool.

On my umpteenth throw of the ring for this tireless Collie, I remembered Lucy Kwok's expression when I'd asked about her relationship with Crash Double. His star may have faded but Crash remained a celebrity. If he wanted to, I had no doubt he could find a friendly journalist to write a hit piece about the Carnival. Lucy probably had to handle him with kid gloves, and my sympathies shifted a little in her favour.

I wondered, though, if her surprised look had been something else. Had she thought I meant her relationship with Howard? They were obviously friendly and, age gap notwithstanding, they'd make an attractive couple. She an elegant, professional woman; he a rough-hewn guru *artiste*. Heaven knows it's a common enough combination. But I'd also noticed Lucy wore a wedding ring, so if they were carrying on in secret their shared innuendo was understandable.

The canal community was proving to be a fascinating little microcosm. I wondered what other secrets I might learn during my stay.

CHAPTER SIX

When Ace was finally ready to rest, we returned to Crash's boat where I fed and watered him before unpacking my clothes for the weekend. Then I checked the galley kitchen again and found it still empty. Even the fridge contained little more than some cheese and butter. I'd have to nip to the local shop; if nothing else, I'd offered to cook Sunday dinner for Birch and it would pay to get familiar with the cooker. I wondered if it had ever been used.

In the saloon, I finally opened my new jigsaw puzzle. One thousand pieces now bent and warped thanks to Howard Zee. But I was relieved to see it wasn't as bad as I'd feared. The box was crushed and the lid needed flattening out, but only about a quarter of the pieces were affected. I examined the lid picture. It was a painting of Little Venice's Pool with narrowboats moored along its edges, ducks in the water and the grand white houses of Blomfield Road overlooking it all on a beautiful spring day. It had seemed appropriate when I found it in town, and a thousand-piecer would keep me occupied for at least a few days, though I was confident I'd be able to finish it before I had to return home.

Ace padded into the room, having finished his food. I sent him on his corner bed for a post-exercise nap while I sifted through the jigsaw pieces, folding bent lugs back into place. It was quite zen, really, and my mind began to wander. Perhaps that's why I finally noticed something I'd missed in my previous coming and going through the saloon; one of Crash's gold discs, mounted directly above the piano, was askew. I went over and stood on tiptoes to adjust it but somehow made things worse and had to catch it from falling altogether. Holding it in my hands, though, revealed why it had been wonky in the first place. Mounted in the wall behind it was a safe.

Never mind the value of the audio equipment upstairs. Surely this would be far more enticing to any burglar who knew it was here. But how would they? Crash hadn't mentioned it to me and I didn't imagine wall safes were a common feature in houseboats. It was the type found in a hotel room, shallow and wide with a keypad. Hardly Fort Knox but enough to secure important papers, like . . . a passport, of course. Crash must have taken his out in a hurry and failed to straighten the disc properly before he left. Satisfied at solving this mini-mystery, I hopped up on the piano bench for a bit of extra height and carefully rehung the framed disc.

Ace was now firmly in his post-meal snooze, and I knew I might not get a better chance to leave him here while I stocked up. According to my phone's map, Choudhury's was a short way past Warwick Avenue Station; I didn't know if it was technically the closest grocer, but it made sense to use Crash's regular shop. I left Ace sleeping, locked up and set off.

I was there in less than five minutes; Little Venice was proving to be a surprisingly compact place with everywhere only a short distance from anywhere else.

Choudhury's was styled like a boutique, all rustic untreated wood and handwritten signs, but it was still just a fruit and veg shop. I headed directly for the chilled section for a couple of pints of milk, then picked up some onions, mushrooms, a few apples . . . the usual necessities that Crash somehow did without.

A middle-aged Asian man, presumably Mr Choudhury himself, awaited me at the counter behind a beautiful old manual till with pounds-and-shilling pop-up numbers. It was for show, of course. A bleeping electronic touchscreen, mounted out of view under the counter, did the real work as he totted up my basket.

I was debating whether and how to introduce myself when he asked, 'Looking forward to the Carnival tomorrow?'

'Very much,' I said, taking advantage of the opening. 'In fact, I'm staying on Crash Double's houseboat, looking after Ace while he's away.'

'Ah! Such a well-behaved dog. How is he?'

'He's fine, though I think the oddity of the situation is making him more anxious than usual. He's already torn through the box you gave him this morning.'

Mr Choudhury looked puzzled. 'Not this morning. I haven't seen Crash since Tuesday.'

I chided myself for making assumptions. Ace hadn't been surrounded by tiny shreds of cardboard because he'd made short work of a new box; he was still tearing up Tuesday's box into ever smaller pieces.

'Crash planned to get a new box from you,' I explained. 'He must have forgotten entirely. Maybe that explains why the fridge is empty, too.'

Mr Choudhury suddenly dropped to his knees, rummaged under the counter, then popped back up, smiling and holding a sturdy cardboard box. 'I've been keeping this one back,' he said, placing my shopping inside it. 'Good, thick card. Ace will have his work cut out.'

'That's very kind, thank you. Does the Carnival bring you much trade?' I gestured at a small selection of premade sandwiches behind the counter glass.

'A little, but I mostly enjoy attending. Anything that brings the community together is always a good atmosphere, don't you think?'

I agreed, paid and thanked him again before returning to the houseboat. Ace had woken up in the meantime and once again lay in the hallway, but this time all thoughts of toilet were forgotten when he saw me carrying a cardboard box. He bounced up and down in circles, anticipating the destruction to follow, and his mismatched eyes watched my every move as I unpacked the shopping. Then I found a broom and dustpan to sweep up the old cardboard shreds, which he found equally fascinating. Finally, laughing at his eagerness, I carried the empty box through to the saloon and placed it on the floor.

Crash hadn't told me the normal routine but I assumed Ace was smart enough to correct any 'mistakes' I made. Sure enough, he gripped the box with his mouth, lifted and placed it on his bed then looked back at me for permission.

'*Go on*,' I said, nodding, and without further encouragement he ripped into it with claws and teeth, deftly dismantling it to a flattened state before settling down to tear and chew on the pieces. If nothing else, it reinforced that a wolf still lives inside every dog. Those teeth could just as easily have ripped someone's skin if Ace was so inclined. I let myself imagine Simon the director's face on the box for a moment, then tutted at myself for being petty.

After brewing a cup of tea, I sat at the coffee table and began searching for jigsaw corner pieces to make a start. After all, come the evening I'd be too busy learning my lines for tomorrow's opening ceremony. At least Lucy Kwok was willing to put her faith in me for a role.

CHAPTER SEVEN

That afternoon I walked Ace around Little Venice, getting to know the area and enjoying the sight of dozens more narrowboats entering the Pool to line up side by side against the path, ready for the Carnival. Everywhere I looked bunting was being strung and shouts of greeting between boats mixed with invitations to dinner and drinks. It was all quite heartwarming. I didn't see what Crash had against it.

In the evening I fed Ace, cooked myself dinner, then settled in to continue the jigsaw. The houseboat's lack of a TV struck me as odd. I wasn't a telly addict but I liked to have it on in the background while I puzzled and I'd certainly never before been in a home without one. Mind you, I'd never been on a rock star's houseboat either. Music appeared to be Crash's sole concern; the stereo was impressive and there were enough albums, CDs and tapes here to last for a very long time.

A chiming sound startled me from my thoughts, and

prompted Ace to shoot off his corner bed into the hallway. I hadn't known the boat had a doorbell, but it was obviously well used enough for the dog to recognise it.

I opened the door to find Lucy Kwok now wearing something more like a businesswoman's power suit, complete with heels, which can't have been easy to negotiate on the path's uneven flagstones. I wondered what she actually did for a living and resolved to ask Howard.

'Good evening,' I said.

She thrust a sheaf of papers into my hand, said, 'This is very good of you, thank you so much, got to run, lots to do, bye,' then turned on her precarious heels and left.

'. . . Noproblemthankyou?' I suggested to her dwindling back, unsure whether she'd heard me. I fussed Ace, who sat patiently at my feet. 'Lots to do, and all of it more important than talking to me, it seems.'

Back in the saloon, I settled on the sofa to read the script.

'The Welcome of Water': A Fable
The Opening Ceremony Dramatic Presentation of
the Canal Carnival
Written by Lucy S. Kwok
From a story by Lucy S. Kwok
Directed by Lucy S. Kwok
Copyright © Lucy S. Kwok

Half-expecting page two to be a credit for Lucy S.

Kwok's typing skills, I turned over. There were definitely more than three pages here. Had she given me multiple copies?

Before I could concentrate on that question, I was distracted by a pair of mismatched eager eyes in my peripheral vision. Instead of returning to his corner bed, Ace now stood by the couch staring at me. I looked at Crash's bookshelf of Great Men biographies and wondered if this was part of an evening routine; reading on the couch with Ace at his side. But he hadn't actually said whether the dog was allowed on the furniture.

Remembering the bedroom, I commanded '*Stay*,' and dashed along the hallway to quickly retrieve the cover throw I'd seen the day before. I needn't have worried; when I returned, Ace remained sitting exactly where I'd left him. I spread the throw over the couch, sat down, said '*Good boy, come,*' and patted the thick fabric beside me. He leapt up, thanked me with a lick on the cheek, then curled up in a position that allowed him to keep an eye on me. I picked up the script again, and this time turned straight to the back.

That's when I noticed *Page 35* in the top corner and groaned. I'd completely misunderstood what Lucy had meant. This wasn't a four-page script with two lines for the Mother of the Waters; it was a thirty-five-page script, with what I now saw was four pages of monologue for me to learn in a little over twelve hours.

Perhaps sensing my despair, Ace cocked a sleepy ear at me. I rubbed his head and began to read.

* * *

74

By ten o'clock my eyes were glazing over. The opening three pages were a narration monologue from my character to welcome the audience and set the scene. I didn't speak again until the final page, when I had another monologue to bid everyone farewell. It ended:

So as our story reaches its joyful and delightful end,
We bid you enjoy the waters' bountiful gifts, dear
friends!

It was all like that, but to be honest I've recited worse. *The Welcome of Water* was a broad-strokes fable celebrating water as the source of all life, with an allegorical cast: Mother of the Waters, the Husband of Brent (as in the river), the twin Springs from which the river flows, and so on. For some reason Lucy had composed the entire play in rhyming couplets which should have made it easier to learn, but choices like rhyming *canal* with *diurnal* and *water* with, well, *water* didn't help matters. Still, I was determined to show Lucy I could handle it, even if I now regretted volunteering at such short notice. Dodgy memory or not, I bet Crash Double never had to learn the lyrics to a brand-new song the night before a concert.

That did give me an idea, though.

I climbed the stairs to his home recording studio, followed by a suddenly very awake and curious Ace. Reaching the top, I looked out the wide windows and finally understood what Crash had meant about it being a grand view. From here he could look over and down the length of the canal, past the other houseboats towards the Maida Hill Tunnel. Moonlight reflected on the water, tree branches swayed overhead, and it was all very peaceful. But I could also understand why the other residents had fought him over building this second floor. It was high enough that, if not for their curtains, I'd have been able to see inside half the other boats. If I'd been in their shoes, I would have objected too.

I sat in the fancy Aeron chair and shuffled it toward the desk. Two small spotlights detected my movement and automatically shone on the computer keyboard. How very high-tech! A press of the spacebar lit up the screen . . . and then a box popped up, demanding a password.

I hadn't been deliberately watching Crash as he unlocked the computer the day before but it was hard not to notice that the first letters he'd typed were *e-q-u*. I tried *equine*, *equine123*, *equestrian* and more along those lines but nothing worked. I wondered if I was completely on the wrong track. Crash was a dog lover but he hadn't mentioned horses at all.

Frustrated, I took out my phone and called him. It was late, but surely a rock 'n' roll man like Crash would be awake. I began to concoct a story in my head about wanting to dance a jig with Ace but decided instead to be truthful. He might dislike the Carnival, but surely he'd understand.

He didn't answer, though, going straight to voicemail instead. I left a message reassuring him it was nothing to worry about but asking him to call me back as soon as he could.

Ace lay on his bed, his upright ear twitching at my every noise and movement. I've never known a Collie who could actually fully relax. I thought of sharks, who sleep while they're still swimming because if they stop moving they'll drown. Was that right? Or was I confusing them with the birds who sleep while they're gliding?

My mind was wandering and Crash hadn't called back. Feeling frustrated, I phoned Birch instead.

'Everything all right?' he asked sleepily. I pictured him dozing on the sofa with Ronnie while the TV quietly showed . . . snooker? A programme about steam trains? I really had to find out more about what this man did when he wasn't dog walking.

'Yes, don't worry. I wondered if you might be able to help me with a question about Crash Double seeing as you're a fan.'

'Delighted to. Fire away.' Now he sounded fully awake.

'Can you think of a word associated with him that begins with *e-q-u*? I assume he doesn't own a racehorse.'

Birch thought for a moment, then chuckled. 'His daughter. Of course.'

'No, that's not right. His daughter's name is Ellie. Even if that's a shortened form, "Eleanor" doesn't contain a q.'

'Ah, but it's not Eleanor. Her birth name was Equilibrium, if you can believe that.'

I groaned. 'I suppose I can. Who'd be a rock star's child, eh?' I typed *equilibrium* into the password field, and hey presto, the computer desktop appeared.

'Anything else?'

'No, thank you – wait, actually, yes. First, give Ronnie a fuss from me. Then tell me, what are you doing?'

'Oh. Um, well, now you mention it, watching an old *Classic Albums* I have on tape. About Bad Dice. Long time ago. Forgot I had it until this week, you know.'

Suddenly I felt sorry for him, in a way. Here I was sitting in Crash Double's home, but it meant nothing to me. Meanwhile, Birch would have been doing cartwheels but he was in Shepherd's Bush. I almost invited him over for the night then remembered there was only one bed. I hadn't even risked asking him for a kiss yet. Leapfrogging directly to an invitation between the sheets would probably give the former policeman a heart attack.

'Birch, why don't you come over tomorrow morning instead of waiting until Sunday? You can see inside Crash's house and we can walk around the Carnival together.' I suddenly had a brainwave. 'In fact, you could look after Ace while I'm performing in the opening ceremony.'

'Beg pardon? You're what?'

'It's a long story. But do come over, I'd love to see you.'

'Right you are. Good night.'

I clicked around Crash's computer, searching for a way to record myself. Like his house, the desktop was chaos; a jumble of files and shortcuts with cryptic names I didn't understand. Some had dates, some looked like abbreviations. Song titles, maybe? Without opening them I couldn't tell, and I didn't want to go snooping.

78

Then I saw one titled with yesterday's date and a familiar time. I prepared to kick myself and opened it up.

'*I'm sorry, was*—' My own voice blared from the room's speakers before it was suddenly interrupted by a burst of garbled digital noise. Then it returned, ending, '*do something?*'

I went ahead with the self-kicking, having forgotten all about the one-touch recording he'd shown me yesterday. Mind you, I was glad I checked; clearly something had gone wrong if it couldn't even record five seconds of speech properly.

Then I remembered that when Crash had played it back for me, it sounded fine. As an experiment I found the button on the desk, pressed it, and recited, '*All the world's a stage, and all the men and women merely players; they have their exits and their entrances, and one man in his time plays many parts.*'

A file immediately appeared on the computer with today's date and time; I played it back and this time it had recorded perfectly. How strange. Still, I couldn't trust it. If it went wrong again, I didn't have the time or knowledge to fix it.

Before I left the computer, though, something caught my eye; a folder in amongst the chaos of other files titled *Lucy*. I double-clicked it to open it and found myself faced with another box asking for a password. I typed *equilibrium* but it didn't work. I wasn't about to sit here and try to guess again so I closed the box and now saw three other similar folders; one each titled *Fox*, *Johnny* and *Howard*. I tried them all but they all required a password.

Even by my standards this was getting uncomfortably nosey, so I closed everything and turned off the screen.

Ace watched patiently from his bed. No doubt he'd spent many a late night up here with Crash, too. 'It's a wonder he hasn't got you on backing vocals,' I told him. He cocked his head, trying to understand, and I laughed. Most dogs lying on their bed would roll over and ask for a belly rub, but not collies. The slightest sound from a human and they assume it's time to go to work.

I got down on the floor and fussed him anyway. He really was an odd-looking dog but his constant eager grin more than made up for it.

From down here on the floor, I noticed something glint under Crash's desk. Not a light; a reflection. Thinking it might be a mislaid dog toy, I crawled over and used my phone's flashlight to peer under the desk. It wasn't a toy at all. One side of the computer was partly open, revealing wires, lights and metal parts. Some were disconnected but I had no idea if that was good or bad.

Was this why the recording was damaged? Had Crash attempted some computer DIY, messed things up and hastily left before going to Dublin? After all, he surely didn't expect a busybody like me to mess around with it.

Nevertheless, it gave me an idea. Originally, I'd thought I could use the computer to record myself performing the monologues as an *aide-mémoire*. I could use it to learn them by ear, almost like they were songs. I didn't trust the computer to do it properly any more, but in the spirit of DIY I could use my phone instead.

So I hauled myself up with the help of the desk, then propped my phone on the window sill and opened the camera to make a video recording. Standing in front of it, I held up Lucy's script and performed both monologues. Then I stopped the recording, pocketed my phone and led Ace back downstairs where I made a cup of tea, sat on the sofa, and played back the video.

I thought I'd opened the wrong recording. I could hardly see a thing. Then I heard myself talking, even though the picture remained dark. Finally, I caught reflected moonlight on water and movement in shadows and understood. I'd used the wrong camera. Instead of recording myself perform a dramatic monologue inside, I'd taped the scene outside through the window where I'd placed the camera. It looked directly down the canal path, past all the other boats and towards the Maida Hill Tunnel, and while it was a lovely nighttime scene, it wasn't at all what I'd intended.

'Silly old Gwinny, eh?' I mumbled to Ace, who groaned sleepily in agreement and pressed his back into my side.

Oh, well. I could still hear myself, which was the important thing. I went back to the start of the video, pressed play and turned off the screen to save the battery.

Two hours of recital later, I had it down. A night's sleep and a couple more practice runs early in the morning would properly fix it in my memory. Feeling pleased with myself, I nipped Ace outside for a final toilet then locked up for the night and climbed into my pyjamas.

Ace dutifully went on his bed while I brushed my teeth, but the moment I got under the covers he leapt up and stretched out beside me. I suddenly panicked, remembering the throw was still on the couch. Still, I'd intended to wash the bedclothes before Crash returned home anyway. A few dog hairs wouldn't make any difference. With one hand stroking Ace's soft fur, I held my phone in the other and played the video one last time in the dark.

But now, I saw something strange.

Because I'd made a mistake, I hadn't really been paying attention to the video that first time. But now, in the dark of the bedroom, I could make out things I hadn't seen before. Things like Fox, wearing a hooded top, emerging from her boat carrying a tartan-patterned holdall. Instead of walking along the path towards the access gate, though, she ran directly to the fence facing Blomfield Road, tossed the holdall over onto the path, then leapt the railings to follow it.

How very odd.

Of course, it was none of my business – but it was distracting enough that I hadn't been paying attention to my own voice. I started playing the recording again and switched off the screen.

CHAPTER EIGHT

I woke with a grunt to find Ace standing over me, licking my face. I shooed him off and sat upright, wondering what I'd heard falling over. Then I realised it was my phone hitting the floor because I'd fallen asleep with it on my chest as I listened to the recording over and over.

It buzzed as I blearily leant over to retrieve it, and to my surprise the screen told me Johnny Roulette was calling.

'Johnny? Can I help you?' I answered.

'I hope so, pet. Has he left?'

'Sorry, has who left what?'

I could almost see him pinch the bridge of his nose. 'I'm in Dublin, but there's no sign of Crash and he won't answer his phone. Are you sure he's not sleeping off a bender, now?'

'If he is, darling, I can assure you he's not doing it here. I've been on his boat since yesterday morning. Crash texted me early to say he was off and nobody's mentioned seeing him in Little Venice. Are *you* sure he isn't already in Dublin in a pub somewhere?'

'I wish I was,' he said. 'Listen, if you see that overgrown kid, tell him to call me immediately, understand? Christ, we'll have to charter a plane . . .'

He ended the call before I could retort, which was probably just as well given what I might have said in response to his brusque tone. Nevertheless, I hoped Crash was OK and simply sleeping off a hangover. If they did this same concert every year, by now it probably needed minimal input from the band themselves before showtime anyway.

Besides, he'd hardly be the first performer who liked a drink. If Crash was all that stable, would he be on his third marriage to the same woman?

I fed and toileted Ace, then myself, while deciding what to do with the bright spring morning. It was an hour until Birch said he was going to come by with Ronnie and a further hour until the opening ceremony. When I opened the French windows, though, the noise from the Pool made it clear the Canal Carnival had already begun. A small green tugboat drifted by with a giant orange contraption mounted on its front to scoop up leaves and floating debris from the water's surface as it went. It was all rather idyllic so I decided to have a look around the Carnival myself.

Ace still wasn't used to being on-lead, but he didn't complain. I led him out through the residents' access gate and under the junction bridge to the Pool.

The noise was as much from the boaters as the Carnival-goers. More had arrived overnight, filling every remaining gap around the Pool's edge. It was now a solid mass of boats and bunting with yet more flags still being strung up.

A queue of people waited at the permanent café boat for coffee and pastries. Next to it an exhibition barge, open to the public, offered families a chance to see inside a narrowboat and learn about the canal's history. Lucy Kwok was there, talking to a young man in a high-vis bib who stood on the rear deck taking payment and issuing tickets. She waved at me, so I waved back, then realised my mistake when she shouted something about cash floats and the bank, and a woman wearing a matching bib emerged from behind me to talk to her. Faintly embarrassed, I let my hand drop and moved on.

The beautiful boats gleamed in the sunshine. I imagined every owner had been hard at work cleaning and polishing before they arrived, and now they stood proudly on deck chatting to the public. Here was a woman my age, selling her paintings of the canal; there was a grizzled old man, demonstrating a tiller mechanism to three fascinated young boys; further on, a younger man sold straw hats from his deck.

'A boater selling boaters,' I said to Ace as we passed, chuckling at my own joke.

I was in quiet awe of the ease with which the owners moved about their barges; climbing up and over the sides, walking on the roof, shimmying around the edge. I stopped to watch one young woman, barefoot in a flowing skirt, hold the lip of her boat's roof with one hand while her toes gripped the gunwale, where the hull met the housing. With her free hand she reached down into the water. It was a little precarious for my liking and I wondered what she was doing.

Suddenly she plucked something from the water, pulled herself upright in a single move and returned to the rear deck with practised ease. I moved closer and saw she was another artist selling her work, but these were different to the landscapes and friendship bracelets others were flogging. Her pieces were sculptures of barges, made from bits of metal and plastic hammered and moulded into shape. In fact, what she'd retrieved from the water was a floating piece of plastic.

'My material source,' she explained. 'They're all made from things I find discarded in the canals.'

'How meaningful,' I said, admiring the striking sculptures. I was so absorbed I didn't notice a news reporter suddenly begin talking nearby.

'Now, look at this. Amazing creativity and the sort of thing that truly makes the Canal Carnival worth visiting. Let's take a closer look. Excuse me!'

That last was directed at me, or so I assumed from the reporter's subtle elbow jab in my ribs. I quickly stepped aside, but stumbled over a coil of mooring rope on the path and lost my footing.

I flailed, windmilling my arms in vain as I fell

backwards, and all I could think was that if I fell in the water, I must remember to let go of Ace's lead so I didn't drag him in with me.

But I was saved by a strong hand and a firm grip that caught me halfway and kept me mostly upright. I turned to thank my hero and was mildly surprised to see a short, broad woman with a stern face holding my arm.

'Are you all right, madam?' she asked. 'Have to be careful around here, all sorts of hazards about.'

'Yes, thank you. I tripped because I was trying to get out of the way of . . .'

I trailed off, finally seeing who had shoved me aside. It wasn't a news reporter at all; it was Violet, the actress who'd taken my part in the play! She held up her phone as if taking a selfie with the boat, yammering away like she was doing a field report and completely oblivious to me or anyone else around her. Violet was recording herself, I realised; and this was all that stopped me from giving her a piece of my mind there and then. Ace, however, had no such compunction and barked loudly at her.

Her smile fixed and her gaze never wavering from the camera, she said, 'Sorry about the noise you can hear, but that's life among the people! Not everyone can keep their dog under control.'

Camera or not, I wasn't having that. 'Or their elbows, eh, Violet? You nearly put me in the water.'

She stopped recording, lowered the phone, and turned to me with eyes blazing. 'You were in the way!

My followers don't want to see you, they want—hang on, do I know you?'

'Very possibly, considering we've been in rehearsals together all week,' I said, taking a deep breath.

Her eyes lit up in recognition. 'Glenda!'

'Gwinny.'

'Yeah. So great to see you, hold on.' She raised her phone again and tapped a button. 'Hey everyone, look who I met at the Carnival! This is Glenda Tubby, who's got a bit part in *Mixed Mothers*, playing the grandmother. Say hiiiiiii!'

'Gwinny Tuffel,' I said, leaning into the camera. I may no longer be able to compete with Violet's flawless skin and flowing hair but what I do have is decades of experience holding an audience's attention. 'Playing Margory. We're on at the Sunrise Theatre all next month, five nights a week, so don't miss it.'

'It's going to be so amazing,' Violet gushed, 'Proper theatre and everything. I play Melanie, a character who's really emotionally complex, yeah, and almost, like, traumatised . . .'

She wandered off into the crowd, still talking to the camera, having already forgotten about me, Ace and the boat sculptures.

'Friend of yours?' said the sculptress, laughing.

I sighed. 'If we'd had these phones forty years ago, I doubt I'd have been any different. Now I really must thank—oh.'

The good Samaritan who'd saved me from an

unexpected bath had done her own disappearing act and was nowhere to be seen. I decided to keep an eye out in case our paths crossed again, so I could thank her.

Suddenly Ace yanked on his lead, pulling me backwards. I half-stumbled, half-turned to see what had caught his attention, and for the second time in five minutes found myself held by a firm grip. This time, though, I was more than happy to find the hand belonged to Alan Birch.

'Steady on, ma'am,' he said. 'Dogs keen to say hello, that's all.' He nodded down at our feet with his bright blue eyes.

I would have gladly looked into those eyes for another minute or two but as this was the first time Ace and Ronnie had met we had to make sure they socialised properly. They happily sniffed one another, tails wagging upright as they moved in a circle and tangled their leads like a maypole.

'Well, I don't think we need worry about them,' I laughed as we unwound the leads. 'Come on, I'll show you Crash's boat.'

We made our way through the crowd and under the bridge towards the residents' area. The access gate was now open and crowds of people milled about on the narrow path, especially around Crash's place.

'Is it always this busy?' asked Birch.

I groaned. 'I forgot, they open it to the public for the Carnival. It's why Crash goes away every year, to escape this lot.'

Tourists stood against the singer's houseboat, alternately posing for selfies and trying to peer in through the door. One young man with a sculpted beard and tattoos stood at the back of the crowd, focused not on the boat but on a handheld gizmo with a telescopic antenna. A high-pitched whine sounded from above, and both Ace and Ronnie became agitated, looking up at the sky. I followed their gaze to see a small flying drone buzzing around the windows of Crash's upper floor studio.

Tapping the young man on the shoulder, I said, 'Is that thing yours? The noise is bothering our dogs.'

'Go away, then,' he said with a filthy look. 'I'm here for BuzzFeed.' I had a vague recollection that this was a website, and as he returned to looking at his controller I now saw it contained a screen. As I watched, the image panned over the boat's upper windows, looking into the studio. The drone had a camera.

'Problem?' said Birch, eyeing up the reporter.

'Just the usual celebrity gawping,' I said, ushering him away. 'Let's come back later, when the crowds have gone. Hopefully they'll lock the gate again—'

Suddenly someone grabbed my arm from behind, startling me. I was getting tired of this and turned on my harrasser with fury.

'For God's sake, what now?!'

Lucy Kwok faced me with an icy expression. 'The opening ceremony begins in ten minutes. Follow me.'

CHAPTER NINE

Birch graciously offered to take Ace, and my handbag, while I hurried after Lucy. She cut through the crowd with practised efficiency, leading me to the exhibition boat.

I'd anticipated a troupe of bored housewives, harangued into taking part because Lucy wouldn't take no for an answer, but I was wrong. The half-dozen people standing on a flat-decked barge next to the exhibition boat all looked happy and excited. A couple of housewives, to be sure, but also a middle-aged man, two teenage girls and a young boy. Each wore a piece of elaborate headgear to identify their character: the Girl of the Waters, the Husband of Brent, the two youthful Springs, and so on. The barge was decorated with water-themed scenery, behind which hid two trunks filled with props and a small PA system connected to speakers at the barge's corners.

'I say, she was telling the truth!' said the man, fastening his chin strap and looking wide-eyed at me. 'It's Gwinny Tuffel!'

The housewives turned to see and smiled in recognition. I don't get recognised often, as Lucy had demonstrated the day before, but she'd evidently told them I was taking part and some were old enough to remember me. It was a pleasant salve for my bruised ego. The youngsters hadn't the faintest idea who I was, of course, but they smiled politely.

'Hello, everyone,' I said. 'Thank you for inviting me to take part. Let's all break a leg, eh?' I wondered if the children might ask confusedly what I meant but they nodded and continued dressing. They start them young in Maida Vale.

Lucy picked up my headgear, a sort of helmet with metal prongs shaped like waves radiating out and a small microphone, presumably connected to the PA system. She was about to hand me the headdress, then thought again and rammed it directly onto my head. I steadied it with my hands while she fastened the chin strap. Lucy had the same stressed-out look all directors get five minutes before curtain-up and I knew in her mind she was running through a checklist of a hundred different things that could go wrong, hoping she'd done everything to ensure they wouldn't. Even rampant egotists get stage fright.

'Don't worry,' I said quietly, 'it'll be fine. I learnt my lines last night.'

'Of course you did,' she replied, giving me a strange look. I couldn't tell if she was complimenting my professionalism or couldn't conceive that I wouldn't do what she'd requested. It didn't matter. The show was about to begin.

'So,' I asked, 'do we gather everyone around on the path, or—*oh*!'

My question was answered by the ground, or rather the barge, moving beneath my feet. I grabbed its rail to steady myself as the man playing Brent held the tiller, guiding us to the centre of the Pool. Lucy retrieved a handheld microphone from behind the scenery and began welcoming everyone to the Carnival. People on the paths stopped to watch and listen. I spotted Birch standing at the water's edge with Ronnie and Ace, and Mr Choudhury from the grocer's stood nearby.

Lucy was a good speaker: confident, clear and well-rehearsed. I was especially impressed that she had no problem addressing people from a moving platform, because the barge was now turning circles around the Pool to ensure everyone got a view.

Then it was time. Lucy said, 'And now we present our dramatic presentation to officially open this year's Canal Carnival: *The Welcome of Water*. It begins with the Mother of the Waters.'

That was my cue. With one arm clutching the rail just in case, I swept the other in a grand, beneficent gesture to the audience.

> *'From fissures cracked low and springs gushing high,*
> *I bring you all clear flow and abundance of life.*

From everywhere, in everyone,
I am never the same, yet all as one.

I wander the land, but I am not aimless.
I have many bodies, yet I am shapeless.
I have no feet, and yet I run;
I am all life, yet carry destruction.

The water welcomes you—'

I thought it was off to a good start, but clearly someone disagreed because I was interrupted by a loud, piercing scream; all the more so for being both right next to my ear and broadcast through the barge speakers.

Startled, I turned to see one of the Spring-playing housewives screech in horror and point at my feet. No, not at my feet. I followed her panicked gaze down to the canal, where something long and pale had floated to the surface in front of the barge as we slowly circled. It bobbed and turned, rotating lazily, and then *everyone* screamed.

Welcomed by the waters, Crash Double's dead eyes stared up at the sky.

CHAPTER TEN

Needless to say, the show did *not* go on. I shouted for someone to call the police, forgetting I was hooked up to the barge's PA speakers. The entire Carnival heard me and now even people who'd shown no interest in the play ran over to rubberneck.

The Husband of Brent was on his feet, waving his arms around and shouting, 'Everyone stay calm! Stay calm, please! Everyone stay calm!' until it became so much background noise.

For her part, Lucy Kwok was so calm she didn't move. She stood at the edge of the barge, transfixed by the sight of the body. I removed my costume headdress so as not to broadcast to the world, gently shook her shoulder and said, 'Take us to shore, quickly.'

As if speaking from somewhere far away she said, 'Lakes have shores. Canals have banks.'

'Then take us to the bank, the path, dry land. I don't

care what you call it but make sure you give the body a wide berth.'

She took the tiller, and as we moved away I looked at Crash's upturned face. What on earth had happened here? He was fully clothed, even still wearing trainers. His hands were empty. His skin was deathly white and I saw no obvious injuries. How did he end up in the water? Why wasn't he in Dublin?

I was still watching the body when the barge bumped into the bank and a familiar voice said, 'Take my hand, ma'am, let's get you off there.' Hearing Birch's reassuring tones, I turned to face him with my arm extended – only to see him take Lucy Kwok's hand and help her disembark.

He then turned to me, but I'd already stepped onto the path unaided, and made a point of greeting Ace before him. The former policeman reddened slightly at his *faux pas*. I wouldn't make him suffer any further, though. There were more important things to worry about than my bruised ego.

'Birch, did you see anything before he floated to the surface?' I asked, retrieving my handbag. 'Did anything happen?'

'Nothing out of the ordinary. Rum do.'

'It certainly is, considering he was supposed to have caught a plane yesterday. Did you call the police?'

'No need. Fletcher was already here.'

A short, broad woman emerged from the crowd with a phone pressed to her ear. It was the woman who'd saved me from falling into the water, now wearing an even more serious expression. Not that everyone here wasn't suddenly serious, but most didn't know what to say or do other than opine how awful it was, and that perhaps they should try one of the boat cafés up near Paddington instead. The crowds drifted away, the Carnival over before it had properly begun.

The woman finished her phone call and turned to Birch. 'The cavalry's on its way, but as I'm already here and there's a celeb involved my boss has requested I handle it. Looking forward to it, if I'm honest. Work out some rust from the old gears.'

'Then it's in good hands,' he said, and introduced us. 'DCS Fletcher, Gwinny Tuffel. Fletcher's at the Carnival with family,' he explained.

'Not any more. Hubby and grandchildren have sensibly scarpered to get some peace. Still, the cream'll sour in a bottle.' I wasn't familiar with that saying but before I could ask she said, 'Tuffel, Tuffel . . . have we met?'

'You saved me from falling in the canal earlier. You left before I could say thank you.'

She shook her head. 'No, I mean the name's familiar. Are you another copper?'

Birch laughed, a little too quickly for my liking, and said, 'From the telly, ma'am. Gwinny's an actress. She was in *Midsomer Murders* once.'

'That was a very small part,' I said, embarrassed. 'I didn't even get a close-up, you wouldn't remember.'

'No, I've got it. I knew a Kraut called Tuffel when I was in Special Branch. Advisor type. We used to call him Kaiser Henry!'

'Henry Tuffel was my father,' I said, nonplussed. 'You do know there hasn't *been* a kaiser for a hundred years . . . ?'

'A harmless nickname,' she assured me, as if that made everything all right. 'Our guv'nor liked him a lot,' she added quickly.

It was no secret that my father had, well, secrets. I knew he'd done favours for the Foreign Office when called upon, and his funeral had been attended by a surprising number of politicians and City bigwigs. I made a mental note to press DCS Fletcher for details later, if she could manage it without invoking Dunkirk and 1966.

Then something clicked into place about this woman. 'Hang on – are you *Birch*'s old DCS?'

'Calls me "old", does he?'

'Sorry, I mean "former". He speaks well of you but I assumed you'd also retired.'

DCS Fletcher narrowed her eyes at Birch. 'Some of us aren't ready to hang up the uniform and be idle all day,' she said. 'Now, here come the woodentops.'

Uniformed police had arrived, directing some people away from the area while ensuring others stayed. They began erecting a white gazebo on a wide section of the path.

'See?' said Birch. 'Knew you two would get along.'

Personally, I thought the superintendent and I had got off to a rocky start but Birch was often oblivious to things *not* said. So this was the woman I reminded him of! Physically we had little in common; it's often said a strong breeze would blow me over, whereas Fletcher could probably withstand a gale force. But there was a certain flinty steel in her eyes that I liked, and chose to believe that's what he saw in us both.

'This is Crash's dog, Ace.' I held the Collie's lead and quickly explained the dog-sitting situation. 'What are we going to do about him?'

Fletcher looked down at Ace, who was busy trying to understand why the humans were idly standing around instead of doing something interesting like walking or throwing his ring.

'I suggest you carry on as intended, madam, until the deceased's family decide what to do. I'm sure they'll have a plan.'

I didn't share her confidence. A surprising number of people don't account for pets in their will, blithely assuming they'll outlive their cats and dogs. But the mention of family did remind me that someone important wasn't here.

'Has Fox been told?' I asked. 'She's been in her boat all morning, giving tours. She's along there in the residents' area in a rainbow-coloured barge with plants covering the roof. Someone should inform her before she hears it from the public.'

'A bird in the woods is the last to know,' said Fletcher

and began walking towards her colleagues. 'Please don't either of you leave, I'll want to talk to you later.'

'Perish the thought,' said Birch. We stood together on the path watching uniformed police and men in wetsuits pilot a barge to retrieve Crash from the water. 'Fletcher's a good one,' he reassured me. 'Talks nonsense, but she'll get to the bottom of it.'

Considering his comparison of us, I wasn't sure how to take that. 'You assume there's something to get to the bottom of,' I said.

'You think he might have slipped and fallen in?'

I hesitated, then said, 'No, actually, I don't. He'd lived here for years and seemed to know every inch of the place. Plus, he was still running around onstage, wasn't he? So even if he did fall in, surely he'd have been able to swim back out.'

'Heart attack, then? While walking the dog, maybe.'

I pictured Crash walking Ace by the Pool at dawn, suddenly clutching his chest and tumbling into the water. But one piece of that image didn't fit.

'Hang on, though. If he was walking the dog and fell in, how come Ace was waiting for me inside the houseboat when I arrived?'

'Smart dog. Could have squeezed through the gate, opened the front door.'

'What, and locked it behind him as well? Even the smartest Collie doesn't have opposable thumbs. So why was Crash out walking by himself after he'd already texted me to say he was taking a cab?'

Birch's moustache twitched. 'Texted you? When?'

'Yesterday morning, around six.' I took out my phone and showed him.

'Let's inform Fletcher. Significantly narrows down time of death.'

I agreed. We approached the gazebo, where the DCS was talking to Lucy Kwok.

'Sorry to interrupt, but I remembered that Crash sent me a text yesterday morning.' I showed her the message, and this time noticed something odd. 'Oh, look. I texted him back, but it says here my reply couldn't be delivered.'

Fletcher nodded, reading the screen. 'So the deceased texted you at oh-six-hundred but when you replied at oh-seven-ten the phone was offline.'

'I also tried to call him last night but he didn't pick up. He must have already been in the water.'

'Assumes the phone is still on his person,' said Birch.

In the Pool, police divers lifted Crash's body out of the water and onto the barge. Fletcher radioed them and asked but the answer came back negative.

'*Pockets empty. No phone, no keys, no wallet.*'

She looked at the text again, read Crash's number off the screen, then dialled it. There was no answer. 'Voicemail. Likely, then, that everything fell out when he submerged, but point of entry could have been anywhere along the canal so we may never find it. At least we know he died sometime after six.'

Lucy's hands flew to her mouth. 'Oh my god, I think I saw the killer!'

We all looked at her, waiting. She had a thousand-yard stare; I could almost see her mind working overtime to reassemble the memory.

'I live on Blomfield Road,' she finally explained. 'My bedroom overlooks the canal. I was coming out of the bathroom when I heard a cry. I looked out and saw someone climbing over the access gate, to leave the residents' path.'

'Is that unusual?' asked Fletcher, scribbling in her notebook.

'Of course. Residents all have keys. I assumed it was a thief, or burglar.'

'Crash was burgled recently,' I agreed.

Lucy nodded. 'So they came back to kill him then escaped over the gate! Oh, how awful!'

'Let's slow down for a moment,' said Fletcher. 'What time was this?'

'Six o'clock. I'm an early riser, especially during Carnival when there's so much to do.'

'Can you describe the person you saw?'

'Not really. There was a spring mist yesterday morning and all I saw was someone dressed in black.'

'Or it looked black through the mist,' offered Birch.

Fletcher nodded. 'The cry you heard: male or female? Did you make out any words?'

'No, just a cry of pain. I think it was a man but I can't be sure.' Lucy looked shocked again. 'Perhaps it was Crash! Oh, I heard him dying!'

'Slow down,' said Fletcher again with much more

patience than I could have mustered. For a woman who normally appeared so self-possessed, Lucy was dangerously close to losing her composure. 'You might simply have heard this person slipping and hurting themselves as they climbed over the gate, and the person in question could be unrelated to Crash's death.'

I suddenly remembered the video I'd accidentally taken last night of Fox jumping over the fence. But mentioning it would only throw suspicion on her and confuse matters. Instead I said, 'Besides, why wouldn't a killer simply hop over the fence into the road? It's a more direct route, not to mention a couple of feet shorter than the gate.'

Lucy looked at me with a strange expression. 'That doesn't matter. Whoever I saw *did* climb over the gate.'

'And around the same time Crash sent that text message,' said Fletcher. 'Thank you, Ms Kwok. We'll be in touch.' She handed Lucy off to a uniformed policewoman, who gave her a cup of tea.

'So someone might have killed Crash right after he texted me, then escaped,' I said.

The superintendent shook her head. 'There's no clear evidence that this was intentional. It could have been misadventure; a heart attack while walking the dog, perhaps.'

'I don't think that's very likely.' I explained that Ace had been locked inside the house when I arrived. 'Why would Crash be walking around by himself when he was expecting a car to drive him to the airport?'

'Perhaps he was meeting someone. Lot of people here this weekend.' Fletcher gestured at the assembled narrowboats with her pen as if I hadn't noticed them before. 'Or perhaps he was mugged, and things got out of hand.'

'Yet nobody saw him fall in the water? What about CCTV?'

'Road junctions only, I'm afraid. Nothing here on the canal.' She flipped her notebook closed in a gesture of finality. 'Leave it with us, Ms Tuffel, and we'll get to the bottom of it. We always do, eh, Alan?'

Birch nodded, clearly on the side of his old boss. Feeling betrayed, I turned on my heel and walked to the water's edge. The barge carrying Crash's body was being carefully guided back to the path.

I sensed Birch approach and stand beside me, but kept my gaze on the water. He didn't try to make conversation, to his credit, but that only made me more frustrated. I should have known police would stick together, no matter how flimsy their speculation.

Finally, I had to say something. 'It doesn't make sense, Birch. If he died out here, surely someone would have seen or heard something. And if Lucy is right, Crash was targeted. Why else would anyone go to the trouble of climbing over the gate?'

'It'll all come out in the wash,' he said, then quickly added, 'Um, so to speak. Fletcher knows what she's doing.'

'Really? She doesn't seem very willing to contemplate

that Crash might have been murdered.'

He was quiet for a moment, then said, 'Perhaps best if you don't stay in the houseboat any more. Potential killer on the loose, and all.'

I appreciated his concern, but it was misplaced. 'I don't think he died on his boat. There's no blood, toppled furniture, or any sign of a struggle. Besides, what kind of killer locks the door behind them when they're escaping?'

'To stop the dog from chasing?' Birch looked down at Ace.

The Collie keenly watched the police carry Crash's body off the barge and into the gazebo, which had been enclosed on three sides. I wondered if he could still recognise Crash's smell, even after a day underwater.

'Let's get out of here in case Ace smells something he shouldn't,' I said, suddenly feeling awful for the dog. 'In fact, why don't we go and have a look in Crash's houseboat? If I'm wrong and he was killed there before being thrown into the water, there's only one place it could have been done.'

Birch coughed. 'Been a while since I picked a lock. Besides, that was always in the line of duty. Breaking and entering is out of the question.'

I dangled Crash's keyring. 'Hardly breaking in when we have the key, is it?'

He grinned, and we ambled away slowly, trying not to draw attention to ourselves. We needn't have worried. The public was focused on the police, and the police were focused on Crash's body. I led Birch along the path and under the junction bridge to the residents' area. The access gate stood open and now I saw that not entirely everyone was watching the police. A crowd had gathered around Crash's boat, posing for pictures and calling their friends. I thought I heard a news reporter relating the story but once again it was an ordinary person recording themselves on their phone.

Birch walked ahead, gently but firmly moving people aside so we could get to the door. I sharpened my own elbows a little and the dogs also helped, with most onlookers retreating at the sight of Ronnie and Ace.

Finally, we reached the door. I unlocked it while Birch stood facing the crowd, dogs in hand to deter followers. Then he backed through the open door after me and I quickly locked it again. As if on cue the crowd surged forward, pressing against the door, trying to see who we were and what we were doing.

We entered the saloon, and Birch whistled at the untidy jumble. 'Looks like he was burgled after all.'

'No, it was already like this,' I said. 'I've been here since yesterday, remember?'

'Oh, yes. Of course.'

I let Ace off his lead and Birch did likewise with Ronnie, who let the Collie lead him to the water bowl on the galley floor. My stomach rumbled and it occurred to me I hadn't eaten since breakfast.

'I wasn't looking for anything untoward yesterday when I arrived, so it's possible I missed something,' I said, beckoning Birch to the French windows. 'Apart from the front door, all the house's windows are on the canal side and only these are big enough for a person to fit through. Crash even said he had those railings fitted to stop drunk guests falling in the water.'

'So if he was killed in the house and dumped in the canal, it would have to be here,' said Birch. 'Much simpler than dragging a body outside, then dropping it in the water. Are they locked?'

'Yes, but so was the front door – oh, hang on.' I weaved back through the piles of records and tapes to check the sideboard in the hallway. The crowd was still peering in but I ignored them and returned to the saloon. 'Crash's keys are missing. Perhaps that's why they weren't found on his body; the killer used them to lock up when they left.'

'If they were in here at all,' said Birch. 'Think you're right. No signs of a struggle I can see. No blood, nothing obviously knocked over.'

It would be difficult to have a fight in this saloon and *not* collide with a tower of records or a stack of DVDs. Even if Crash had been killed elsewhere, carrying a dead body through the room without disturbing anything would be impossible.

I unlocked and opened the French windows, then examined the floor and frame. 'I don't see any marks to suggest a body being dragged . . .' Leaning out to check the railing, I heard a high-pitched buzzing from above. A tiny drone descended, probably the same one from before. I would have swatted the nosey parker away, but it wisely stayed out of my reach so I ignored it and continued looking. 'Nothing on the railing either. No chipped paint, no fabric caught on the metal, nothing. Here, take a look.'

'Tricky,' Birch said from behind me, punctuated by barking from Ronnie and Ace. I turned to see him straining to hold both dogs back by their collars, as they tried to attack the buzzing drone outside.

'Get lost,' I shouted at the hovering contraption. 'Have some respect!' Not that I imagined the reporter could hear me over its infernal buzzing. I was about to retreat inside and close the windows, but saw Ace's box of toys by my feet and had an idea. I grabbed a plastic ball launcher, leant out over the window railing and smacked the drone with it.

I only wanted it to fly away but I must have hit it in a particular spot. Something inside the drone went *bang*, and smoke curled out of the top. It swayed from side to side, flipped over twice, then plummeted into the water with a splash.

'Well, serves them right,' I said, closing the windows. 'They shouldn't be poking their noses in.' Birch coughed quietly. 'Oh, shush. It's different; we knew Crash. Well, I did. Well, I did a bit.' Suddenly feeling awkward, I was glad the drone was no longer recording.

Then I had a brainwave. 'Follow me,' I said, walking past Birch into the hallway (where the crowd still pressed against the door) and up the stairs to Crash's studio.

'Stone the crows,' said Birch, taking in all the high-tech recording equipment. He put the dogs on Ace's bed while I sat at the computer. Then he watched me enter the password *equilibrium* and said, 'Ah.' It was amazing how many emotions he conveyed in that single syllable.

'I wanted to use it to rehearse my monologue,' I said defensively.

'Of course you did. No question at all,' he said in a tone implying there were in fact many questions.

I found the recording of me from Thursday afternoon and played it for him, garbled static and all, explaining what had happened. 'Now I want to see if he recorded anything after that,' I said, scanning the mess of files on the desktop. 'He may not have died here but you never know what he might have recorded. There could even be something from Friday morning.'

'Good thinking,' he said, peering over my shoulder.

Unfortunately, my hopes were in vain. Not that it was easy to find anything in the chaos, but I saw no files with Friday's date.

'Hang on, though. Here's another from Thursday afternoon, after I'd left.' I opened it, and we listened to Crash and another man talking. Unfortunately, this recording was also damaged:

[Static]
Crash: '. . . *could have phoned, you know.*'
Unknown man: '*Not likely. Listen, we just want to talk. She*—' [Static] '. . . *very generous offer*

to resolve this once and for all. At least—'
[Static]

Crash: '. . . *making your own generous offer to the likes of Vicki—'*
[Static]

Unknown man: '. . . *serious. Nine o' clock, all right? Don't be late.'*

'Well!' I said. 'What do you think that was about? Who was the second man?'

'Search me,' said Birch. 'Definitely not Johnny or anyone else in the band. I'd know their voice.'

'It didn't sound very friendly, did it? But that talk about "generous offers" makes me wonder. A recording contract? Someone who wanted to buy the boat? Hardly a recipe for murder.'

'Not to mention he wasn't killed until the next morning,' Birch reminded me. 'Let's pass it on to Fletcher.'

'For all that she'll care,' I snorted. 'Hardly convincing evidence of a murder, is it?'

That question would be answered sooner than expected because as I walked back down the stairs I came face to face with an angry DCS Fletcher, standing in front of the crowd outside and hammering on the door.

CHAPTER ELEVEN

There was no point trying to hide, so I let her in. Upon opening the door I was greeted by a wall of noise: shouting, jeering – a few people were even laughing for some reason. They all held up their phones to take pictures which I wasn't especially happy about, but they do say no publicity is bad publicity.

'Come in, Superintendent,' I shouted over the din. Then I turned to the crowd and said in my best dog-obedience voice, 'The rest of you, *stay*!'

To my surprise, they did. Fletcher and a uniformed policeman whom she introduced as Constable Wright slipped inside and I quickly locked the door behind them again. As I did, my phone buzzed with a call from Bostin Jim. On a Saturday? How unexpected. But I didn't have time to talk to him. I declined the call and ushered everyone into the lounge away from the gawping public.

We stood amid the piles of records and memorabilia. Sitting felt inappropriate somehow. Ace went onto his bed, while Ronnie took a great interest in Constable Wright and proceeded to sniff every inch of the policeman's legs.

'Don't tell me you carry sliced ham in your pocket too?' I laughed. The confused constable shook his head. Birch called Ronnie over and produced a strip of cooked meat from his own pocket which the Labrador greedily chomped.

'So this is where you whacked that young man's drone, is it?' said Fletcher, looking out of the French windows.

'How on earth do you know about that? It happened a few minutes ago.'

The DCS sighed and took out her phone. 'You've gone viral, Ms Tuffel.'

She played a video headlined 'Crash! Former Actress Goes Mediaeval on Our Drone in Dead Singer's Home!' I watched myself lean out of the boat's French windows, ball launcher in hand, and whack the camera. The shot swayed and flipped before plunging head first into the canal. That drone must have been transmitting live and the whole thing had been recorded. I was apparently the top-trending video on BuzzFeed.

'The owner has made a complaint and wants you to compensate him with a replacement as the equipment is necessary for his work. I'd say you don't have a leg to stand on. The film clearly shows you destroying his property.'

'His property?' I blurted. 'What about Crash's privacy? Those vultures have been buzzing around this place all day, and now he's dead there are twice as many.'

'Isn't that like the deer mocking the rabbit's tail? At least they're standing outside, while you've broken into the place for a sniff around.'

While I tried to piece together another of her garbled aphorisms, Birch spoke up. 'No breaking and entering needed, we have keys. Gwinny's dog-sitting for Crash, remember? Besides, not a crime scene. No evidence he was killed here.'

'Actually, it seems Mr Donnelly wasn't "killed" at all,' said Fletcher. 'Preliminary examination of the body reveals no signs of foul play. My first assumption remains that he slipped and fell into the canal, though we also can't rule out suicide.'

'He'd lived here for years,' I said. 'Now suddenly yesterday morning he falls in the water, but nobody sees or hears him, and he doesn't swim out to the nearest boat? There must be a hundred in the Pool this weekend.'

Fletcher nodded sagely. 'Unfortunately, everyone was sleeping off the night before. Apparently, it's tradition to hold parties most nights of the Carnival and Thursday was no exception. Come Friday morning, Mr Donnelly could have gone in the water or even cried out without anyone noticing.'

'Might even strengthen the case for suicide,' said Birch unhelpfully. 'He figured nobody would see him and attempt a rescue.'

I protested. 'If it's suicide, why not do it here in his house? Why bother hiring me?' I crouched down and fussed Ace, who was listening intently and waiting for words he recognised. 'Crash loved this dog. His phone case was a big photo of Ace, for heaven's sake. He wouldn't have gone without making arrangements to rehome him. Besides, where's the note?'

'Suicide notes are a myth,' said Fletcher. 'Even in very clear cases there often isn't one. As for going in the water, if he'd died at home he might not have been found for days. This way, as you point out, he knew his dog would be looked after.'

'I don't buy it. He had no reason to kill himself.'

The superintendent smiled sympathetically. 'In this country, the single group most at risk of death by suicide is men over fifty. The evidence, or should I say the lack of it, suggests Mr Donnelly may have been one more number in that sad statistic. You simply had your part to play.'

What she said made sense but I could hardly believe it. Could Crash really have hired me so he was free to kill himself, knowing Ace would be taken care of?

While we talked, Constable Wright had been rifling through the kitchen cupboards, then moved on through the rest of the boat. Now he returned from the corridor with a pill bottle.

'Found this in the bathroom waste, and there are at least half a dozen more in the cabinet.' He read the label. 'Xanax, private prescription.'

DCS Fletcher turned to me. 'Is that yours?'

'No, it's Crash's all right. He said he suffered from anxiety.'

'Interesting,' she said, taking out her notebook. 'I understand you also found the body?'

I didn't like where this was going. 'I was closest when Crash floated to the surface but that's a coincidence. There were several people on the barge.'

She consulted her notebook. 'The barge that was doing circles, yes?'

'That's right, and which was in full view of the public at all times,' I added with a certain amount of pique. 'Perhaps the barge stirred up the waters, bringing him to the surface. Crash wasn't even supposed to be here. In fact, their guitarist called me this morning because he hadn't turned up in Dublin and now we know why. He hadn't left Little Venice, let alone the country.'

My phone buzzed; Bostin Jim was still trying to call me. I declined again, hoping he'd get the hint and leave a voicemail. Much as I was delighted I now had an agent prepared to work hard to get me roles, the day's events put things into perspective. The police seemed so sure, I began to wonder if I was wrong. Had Crash really decided to end it all, even with all his fame, success and gold discs?

'What about his safe?' I said, suddenly remembering the disc above the piano. I pointed it out. 'That frame was askew when I arrived. I assumed Crash took his passport from the safe in a hurry, but maybe someone tried to break into it? He was burgled recently. You might get some fingerprints . . . *ah*.' I watched Fletcher put on a pair of gloves to remove the disc from the wall. 'Or not, because I wasn't wearing gloves when I straightened it. Sorry.'

'You weren't to know,' said Birch. 'What was taken in the first burglary?'

'Nothing, apparently. I found that odd, given all the expensive studio equipment upstairs.'

'Not to mention these records and tapes,' said Birch. 'Plenty here would fetch a bob or two from collectors.' He looked like he fancied a chance at them himself.

'So what if they were only interested in the safe?' I wondered. 'Who knows what's inside there?'

DCS Fletcher removed the gold disc, revealing the hotel-style keypad. 'Simple enough to find out. Standard model.' She ordered Constable Wright to fetch 'the gizmo' and to station another officer outside to disperse the crowd. Finally, she turned to me and said, 'Thank you for your help, Ms Tuffel, but now I must ask you to leave. Police business, you understand.'

I did understand but I wasn't done. 'Before we go, there's something I need to show you. Or rather, play for you. It's upstairs, in the studio I mentioned.'

With dogs in tow, Birch and I led Fletcher to the second-floor studio. I sat at the desk and woke Crash's computer.

'You know his password?' said Fletcher, surprised.

'He was very trusting,' I squeaked, trusting Birch to stay quiet. I explained the one-touch recording system, the damaged files and the disconnected computer cables. Then I found the file from Thursday afternoon, of Crash talking to an unknown man, and played it.

'The Irish voice is Mr Donnelly's?' Fletcher asked.

'Correct. We don't know who the other man is. Birch says it's not one of his bandmates.'

The former policeman shrugged at the surprised look from his old boss. 'Long-time fan,' he explained as we heard the police re-enter downstairs, followed by beeping noises.

'Perhaps the same person tried to break open the safe and then damaged these recording files,' I said. 'It must have been done after I left here on Thursday afternoon, you see.'

Fletcher didn't immediately dismiss the thought but I could tell she wasn't convinced. 'They could have been talking about someone owing a fiver for the biscuit tin, though. Without the full recording we'll never know.'

The beeping from downstairs stopped and was followed by a cheer. A shout reached us: 'Safe's open, ma'am. You'll want to see this, all right.'

CHAPTER TWELVE

Our expulsion momentarily forgotten, Birch and I crowded into the lounge behind DCS Fletcher to see what her officers had found. Unfortunately, everyone there apart from the dogs was taller than me, so my view was completely blocked. I stood on tiptoes, one hand on Birch's shoulder for balance, and could just make out the superintendent removing items from the safe. Constable Wright whistled, impressed.

'What's in it?' I asked.

'Passport, set of keys, notebook,' she said, while Constable Wright took notes. 'A substantial amount of money, too. That must be, what, a few thousand?'

'At least,' said the constable.

'So much for Crash protesting he was broke,' I said. 'All this time he had money stuffed away in his safe. No wonder someone tried to break into it.'

Fletcher opened the passport. 'This is definitely Mr Donnelly's. The keys look well used.'

'Probably his old house keys, from before he had the locks changed,' I said. 'What's in the notebook?'

The DCS flipped through it and shrugged. 'Poetry.'

'Poetry?' said Birch, his ears pricking up like a dog hearing a whistle. 'You mean song lyrics?'

'Well, Crash was a singer,' I smiled, nudging him. 'Surely that's not unusual?'

The former policeman shook his head. 'But there's been no new Bad Dice material for twenty-five years.' He gasped. 'A new album?' He said it with such wide-eyed excitement that I immediately pictured him as a long-haired young man, sitting on the floor and listening rapt to a hi-fi. Birch could be so gruff and, well, *old* at times that I hadn't imagined him as a young man before. It was a pleasant thought.

'Seems like overkill to put them in a safe,' said Fletcher. 'Mind you, it was his livelihood.'

'Could I see?' Birch asked. 'You, um, never know. Bit of knowledge can't hurt.'

Fletcher saw through this transparent excuse but passed him the notebook anyway. 'You'll never get to hear them now, so go ahead. Glove up.'

Birch donned a pair of latex gloves supplied by Constable Wright, then began to leaf through the pages. I thought of the studio upstairs and Crash and Ace dancing together. *Something new I've been working on*, he'd said.

The notebook was about half-full of lines and lyrics, all scribbled, scratched out, underlined and circled. There was no need to ask Birch if this was all new material; it was plain from his wide-eyed expression.

The police were understandably distracted by the more pressing matters of Crash's passport (the presence of which confirmed he hadn't been en route to the airport) and the bundles of cash, so I whipped out my phone, made sure it was on silent and started snapping pictures of the notebook. Cottoning on, Birch grinned and leafed through the pages, pausing briefly on each so I could take a photo. We reached the end of the lyrics and he turned over a few blank pages before flipping it closed. But as he did, I saw something and nudged him to open the back page again.

It wasn't like the others. Instead of scrawled lines and margin doodles, this page contained several lines of random letters and numbers, like '*JOW-1000T-434206913IAFCLSHER*'. Then underneath was the name of a management company and an email address. It meant nothing to me, but maybe it had something to do with his studio upstairs?

'Birch, how are you getting on?' said DCS Fletcher suddenly. I took a final hasty photo, then hid my phone behind my back as she turned to us and held out a hand for the notebook.

'Confirmed all new, as far as I could see. Damn shame.'

I wondered about the idea that the notebook was in the safe because it was Crash's livelihood. Were his lyrics really that valuable? Or was there more to this than met the eye?

Fletcher sealed it inside an evidence bag while I tried to ignore Ronnie licking my hand behind my back. He must have thought I was hiding a treat from him. Knowing Labradors, if I wasn't careful he might try to eat my phone.

'I really don't think he killed himself,' I said, pretending to look for a tissue in my handbag so I could surreptitiously slip my phone back inside. 'Crash was in good spirits. He was writing new lyrics, making new music and looking forward to the Dublin concerts.'

'It's a funny thing,' said the superintendent. 'Suicidal people are often said to have been in a good mood right before they do themselves in. The shrinks say it's because they've finally made up their mind and feel free of responsibility at last.'

'That's terrible,' I said. 'How depressed must someone be to think that way?'

She grimaced. 'By definition, enough to kill themselves. You can't get much more depressed than that.'

Ace had padded over to see what Ronnie was so interested in. Now I reached down to stroke his head, wondering what would become of the Collie in the long term. Fox couldn't take him in, not with her new 'boat cat'. Ace would have to go to a local rescue.

'You don't have pets, do you, Superintendent?'

Fletcher looked at me with surprise. 'What makes you say that?'

'It's hard enough saying goodbye to a family pet when it's their time to go. I can't believe anyone who's been through that would kill themselves without making arrangements for their dog to be rehomed.'

'In my experience, motivations are rarely so neat or clearly thought out. Whether or not this was suicide or an accident, I fear we may never know. But it will take a lot more than what we have so far to convince me it was anything else.'

Well, I do love a challenge.

CHAPTER THIRTEEN

After collecting Ace's throwing ring from the saloon, I led Birch and the dogs outside and over the junction bridge to Rembrandt Gardens, leaving the police to finish their work.

That morning the park had been full of people but now it was deserted. The Punch & Judy tent stood empty and unoccupied; there would be no more shows today. I looked out over the Pool and saw a few people milling about, but it was nothing compared to the earlier crush and most of the boaters had retreated inside. If I'm honest, I was a little surprised it wasn't more lively precisely *because* a celebrity had been found dead.

We let Ace and Ronnie off-lead, and Birch kept an eye on them while I finally returned Bostin Jim's call.

'Gwinny,' he answered, 'I've been trying to get hold of you. Is it true you're at Little Venice? Where Crash Double turned up dead?'

'Correct on all counts, Jim. How did you—oh, you've

seen that video, haven't you? I can explain . . . '

He laughed. 'Save it for the agency who just called me. They saw it online and want you to play a crotchety old woman in a new campaign.'

'A campaign for what?'

'No idea. Don't think they know themselves, but that's not the point. Got to strike while the iron's hot, haven't we? If we can keep your profile up I might book you some panto this year too.'

First a crotchety old woman, now an ugly sister? 'Darling, I'm a serious actress.'

'With serious cashflow problems. Listen, if it's good enough for Priscilla Presley it's good enough for Gwinny Tuffel, know what I mean?'

I mulled over this unexpected comparison and watched Ace try to herd Ronnie, who remained completely oblivious. This naturally only made the Collie more determined. Ronnie was a lovely dog, but like most Labs he had no more brains than the sheep Ace so fervently wished he was. Birch ran after them, waving his arms in vain as he tried to calm them down.

'I'll want to see what the agency is advertising, first. But so long as it's not a stairlift or incontinence pants, I'll consider it.'

'Can't say fairer than that. I'll get details. Any joy with Darren, by the way? The builder I sent your way?'

'Oh, I'm afraid he was too rich for my blood. Thanks, anyway.'

I ended the call and related the news to Birch, who by

now was red-faced and out of breath.

'Sounds like it's all going to plan,' he said between gasps. 'This time next year you'll be in *Les Mis*.'

I grimaced. 'I sincerely doubt that. Nobody wants to hear me sing.'

'All the same.'

His belief in me was charming, even though it was mostly based on what he'd seen of me twenty-plus years ago on TV. I laughed as Ace, presumably seeing my hands empty, ran up and nudged at my leg.

'On the other hand, someone definitely wants to see me throw a ring. All right, boy.' I took it from around his neck and prepared to toss it, but Birch held up a hand in defeat.

'Think we'll pass,' said Birch. 'Ronnie's tuckered out.'

To be honest, they both looked ready for a lie down somewhere. I sympathised. Even a boisterous dog like Ronnie couldn't match the energy reserves of a Border Collie. Then I remembered that Ace would soon have to go into rescue for rehoming and felt sad all over again.

'Birch, put your copper's head on for a moment—'

'Never off.'

'No, I suppose not. What do you think to this suicide theory?'

'Not impossible. Empty pill bottle's suggestive. Lack of witnesses is significant either way. Whether suicide or murder, someone troubled themselves to make sure it wasn't seen.'

I considered that again. 'If you were going to end it

all and didn't want witnesses, wouldn't you do it at night rather than waiting until daylight? I do wish there were cameras on the canal itself.'

'Mmm,' he murmured and gestured back towards the road. 'CCTV on junctions and crossings, though. Be easy enough to see anyone coming and going from the area, even at night.'

'If Fletcher bothers looking.' I fussed Ace, who sat eagerly waiting for the humans to finish making noises and start throwing things instead. Once again I thought how unlikely it was that Crash would leave his beloved, kooky-looking dog with an uncertain future. I made up my mind and said, 'After I've run Ace for a while, I'm going to pay Fox a visit. She knew Crash better than anyone, and seeing Ace might raise her spirits a little. It's probably better if I go alone, anyway.'

'Right you are. Dinner's off tomorrow, then? Sure you won't need a hand taking things back to Chelsea?'

'Oh, rats. In all the fuss I'd completely forgotten about dinner, sorry.'

I also hadn't considered where I'd be sleeping, but Birch was right. The police wouldn't take kindly to me staying at Crash's place any more. I'd have to return home and take Ace with me until his fate was determined. I hadn't made any preparations for Birch to eat at my house.

'Can we postpone? How about we do our usual walk and I'll buy you lunch at the café instead?' We'd fallen into the habit of meeting at the Kensington Gardens bandstand on Sunday mornings to walk Ronnie. It was where we'd first met – and where I'd given Birch a thorough ticking-off for not keeping the Lab under control.

'Right you are. See you at eleven.' He was obviously disappointed, but it's not like I could have anticipated a dead body wrecking our plans.

I watched him leave the park, taking his tired dog up the low ramp instead of the steps, until Ace nudged my leg again. I dutifully threw the ring but was so distracted I completely messed up the throw. Instead of sailing the length of the grass, it hooked to the left and got stuck on a bush halfway down. Ace chased it anyway, trying to jump for it, but it was too high. After a couple of attempts he lay down on the grass, looking alternately at the ring and me.

Annoyed with myself, I stomped over to retrieve it. As I stood on tiptoe and reached up, I heard a familiar voice speaking quietly from the other side of the bush.

'. . . wondering if he left any instructions? No, I don't mean his will, I understand you can't disclose that yet . . .'

I leant forward a little to peek through the branches and saw Lucy Kwok standing on the narrow path between the Gardens and the Pool, shoulders hunched as she spoke on her phone. What on earth was she doing there? During my Friday walkabout I'd tried that path but found it narrow and treacherous, used solely by boats moored on this side of the Pool. It was much easier and safer to walk through Rembrandt Gardens, which had exits to the canal at either end. Besides, Lucy's own exhibition boat was less than a hundred yards away.

She continued, 'You know . . . any *other* instructions. In the event of his death. Well, he has a dog. Yes, *had*, sorry. So I thought there might be some provision for that, and maybe some other . . . I see. No, I understand. Of course. Thanks for your time, Mr Patwari.'

Suddenly Ace barked, startling me. I turned to see what had set him off but trying to crane my neck while still leaning into the bush wasn't my best idea. I stumbled, slipped, and fell over in a tangle of limbs and branches. The impact dislodged the throwing ring, which fell from its adopted branch and landed on my chest. Ace pounced on it, knocking the wind out of me, and ran off with the disc in his mouth.

Breathless, I looked up to see a large-chinned man with big, fuzzy white hair looming over me. Then I realised I was looking at Howard Zee but upside-down, like everything else from this angle. Beside him was a young, dark-skinned woman I didn't recognise.

'Gwinny,' he said in a level voice. 'May I ask what you're doing down there?'

'I was wondering the same thing,' said Lucy, leaning in from the other side.

I sat upright and took a moment to replace the air that had been knocked out of my lungs, as well as my dignity. Forcing a smile I said, 'I was retrieving Ace's ring,' and gestured at the Border Collie now doing laps of the Gardens with it in his mouth. 'But he promptly stole the evidence. If you've ever wondered why dog owners keep separate "dog-walking clothes", you're looking at the answer.'

'How are you holding up, Lucy?' asked Howard over my head. 'Such a terrible business. If there's anything you need, anything I can do before tomorrow evening, don't hesitate to ask. I'm only over the road.'

I stood up and brushed myself down. 'Yes, such a shame about the Carnival,' I said. 'All that hard work you put in, wasted because of this tragedy. You had event insurance, I hope?'

Lucy looked at me like I'd grown two heads. 'On the contrary, tomorrow morning we'll resume as normal. I'm sure the police will be out of our hair by then, considering Crash apparently killed himself.'

'But you said you'd seen his killer. On Friday morning, remember?' I was taken aback by this cold change of heart.

'Oh my God, really?' said the young woman accompanying Howard. She had a fast-paced American accent. 'Who was it? What did they look like?'

'Hang on,' I interrupted. 'What's happening tomorrow evening?'

'My last ever session with Howard, not that it's any of your business,' said Lucy. 'Now I must be getting on.' She walked away along the narrow path, back towards the junction bridge.

Ace bounded up, ring in mouth, to ask for another throw. Howard's American companion flinched and moved to put him between her and the dog. He smiled and reassured her, 'Nothing to worry about. Ace is perfectly friendly.'

I quickly threw the ring, to my relief managing a straight flight this time. 'He really is, don't worry,' I said to the woman. 'Howard, you haven't introduced us.'

'Of course, how rude of me. Gwinny, this is Latesha Michaels. My new business partner.'

Latesha waved rather than offered a hand, keeping her distance as Ace returned the ring. 'I'm with Zabok+ in LA,' she said, as if I should know what that meant. 'We're pivoting to streaming on-demand wellness and Howard will front our P1 strand.' I understood most of that, though, and wondered if she'd descended into TV lingo to bamboozle me, or if it was how she always talked. You can never tell with executives.

'So your lovely boat's going to be famous,' I said to Howard.

He laughed. 'Goodness, no. We're off to LA this week to begin production, and I doubt I'll be back. I feel the universe pulling me to California and who am I to resist?'

Especially with a large cheque and a pretty girl waiting for you, I thought, but who could blame him?

'Crash's death brings things into focus, doesn't it? *Carpe diem*, as they say. So have you already sold your boat?'

'It's in hand,' he said, putting an arm around Latesha. She gave him a dazzling smile in return.

'What do you think he was doing out there, Howard?'

I said, throwing Ace's disc again. 'From what I saw, Crash barely left the house without his dog. Why would he go for a walk alone, right before he was due to catch a flight?'

'Didn't that woman say the cops called it suicide?' said Latesha. 'There's your answer.'

'I don't accept that. I think someone killed Crash.'

'What do the police think?' Howard asked. 'Are they looking into it?'

'No,' I admitted. 'Apparently there are no injuries on the body, so they're not looking for a suspect.'

'They can look somewhere else, anyway,' said Latesha. 'I know how cops work, always trying to pin something on somebody. But Howard was working Friday morning and we've got video to prove it.'

That took me by surprise. 'Why?'

'The live streams are automatically recorded,' she explained. 'After the show launches, we're going to pull second-strand material from them. So you tell the cops he's got an alibi, OK?'

'That's not really how it works . . .' I began, but she was already walking away, offended at any suggestion that her golden ticket might be tarnished.

Howard turned to follow, then stopped and turned back. 'Gwinny, remember that you only met Crash for a few hours. People on the canal have known him a lot longer, and . . . well, we all have our darker side, don't we? I tried to help him focus on his inner light. So did Fox, as much as he'd let her. But this isn't a huge surprise to the community. You know yourself what it's like being in the spotlight for years, only to have it fade away.'

He hurried after Latesha before I could respond to such an offensive remark, although I couldn't deny it. Even before I retired to care for my father, work had been drying up for a while as I aged. When Fox had faced a similar problem she'd successfully switched from young starlet to an older, friendly face. But it was too late for me to do the same, and besides, I didn't have useful skills like her. I doubted audiences would run home to watch *Gwinny Solves Jigsaws* on BBC2.

It was time I paid the widow a visit. If Crash really had committed suicide, surely Fox would know why better than anyone.

CHAPTER FOURTEEN

The residents' access gate was now locked again and Constable Wright stood guard outside Crash's boat. I nodded politely as Ace and I passed but kept walking towards Fox's boat.

As we neared the unmistakeable rainbow-and-plants combo, Lucy Kwok emerged from within looking harassed.

'Are you still here?' she demanded, seeing me. Remembering her panicked distress that morning at the thought she might have seen Crash's killer, I wondered how much of it had been an act for the police's benefit.

'I've come to see Fox,' I explained. 'How is she?'

'She's fine. Goodbye, Gwinny.' Lucy turned to go and I remembered something else: she didn't live on the canal but in one of the lovely, white-painted houses on Blomfield Road overlooking it.

'Which is your house, by the way?' I asked.

'Why do you ask?'

'I hoped you could recommend a builder. I need some work doing but I'm at something of a loss.'

She blanked for a moment, blindsided by the change of subject. 'Um – yes, I suppose. Number thirty.' She pointed to a house back towards the junction bridge, then thought better of it and said, 'But don't call. My husband wouldn't like it. I'll look up the number for you later.'

'If he's anything like you, I wouldn't like it either,' I murmured as Lucy strode away.

She turned back. 'Sorry, was there something else?'

'No, nothing. See you soon.'

I wrapped Ace's lead around my hand to make a short hold, then stepped on board Fox's boat. 'Fox?' I called out. 'It's Gwinny. Can I come in?'

There was no answer. Which wasn't a definite 'no', so I decided to take is as a 'yes' and walked down the steps.

'I've got Ace with me but he's under control,' I called out into the gloom. 'Where are you?'

'In here,' Fox replied quietly, then sniffed and blew her nose. I threaded my way through the towers of foliage and found her on the duvet-slash-sofa, clutching a tissue to her red-rimmed eyes. A low table held a cup of tea and a tray of cookies. Lilith looked balefully out from the shadows of a bookshelf, pinpoints of light reflected in her cat's eyes. Through the lead I felt Ace tense up but trusted he could tell she remained out of reach.

The room's only other seats were wooden stools being used as plant pot stands, so I sat next to Fox on the sofa. Ace immediately flopped to the floor between us and rubbed his furry head against Fox's feet, which made her smile. She reached down and fussed him.

'How are you, Gwinny?' She took a cookie and delicately bit into it.

It struck me that she was the first person to actually check I was OK. But much as I appreciated her consideration, it felt wrong that Fox of all people would be the one to ask after my well-being.

'Never mind me,' I said, 'how are you coping?' I took a cookie then thought to ask, 'Is there chocolate in these? I'm sure Ace would love one.'

She smiled ruefully. 'There isn't but best not anyway. It'd make him ill.'

I decided to keep it for myself instead but, despite my hunger, I dropped it in my pocket for later. I wasn't about to put her to the trouble of making more tea.

'Thirty-five years,' she said, gazing out at the water. 'That's how long we'd been together. Sounds a long time, doesn't it? But it feels like we met yesterday.'

'At a party, I assume?'

'No, he invited me to the Royal Albert Hall when they played. Apparently, he used to watch me on TV.'

'Crash had green fingers?' That took me by surprise. He hadn't really seemed the type and I hadn't noticed any plants on his houseboat.

Fox laughed, sniffed, then blew her nose again. 'This was before the gardening shows. No, he used to watch *me* on TV. Short skirts and long boots, you know the sort of thing.'

There was no easy way to ask but I couldn't think of a better time, so I plunged in. 'Fox, is there any reason you can think why he might kill himself? Was he ill?'

'What, mentally? He's a lead singer, Gwinny. They're all a bit special.'

Many would say the same about actors but it wasn't what I meant. 'No, physically. Cancer, perhaps? Something terminal?'

She munched on her cookie. 'Not as far as I know. I mean, whatever was going on in his mind, I guess you could call that terminal. But I didn't – I never thought . . .' She trailed off, holding back tears.

'He told me the Dublin concert was the highlight of his year.'

'It was. He'd never admit it but the older he got, the more he missed the place.'

I took a deep breath. 'Which is why I don't think he killed himself. Or that it was an accident.'

'No, no,' she said, looking puzzled. 'The police said it was.'

'Fox, nothing fits. Why would Crash text me to say he was leaving for the airport, then lock Ace in the boat and jump in the water? How come nobody saw or heard him? Who was the stranger climbing over the gate at six in the morning?'

She sat up a little straighter. 'The what? What stranger?'

'Lucy saw someone from her bedroom window. She couldn't tell who it was, but if they had to climb over the access gate, then it obviously wasn't a resident . . .' I suddenly remembered what I'd seen on the phone video I'd taken accidentally. 'Although not everyone uses the gate, do they? Why did you jump over the railings last night?'

Fox reeled, her expression turning to outrage. 'I beg your pardon? How is any of this your business?'

I'd pushed too far but there was no going back now. 'Well, for a start it looks like I'm the one who'll have to rehome his dog. You can't take Ace on, not with Lilith here. Why did you go and get a cat right before the Dublin concerts, anyway?'

She leapt to her feet. 'I will not sit here and be interrogated! Get out!'

I got up too, followed by Ace, his head ping-ponging back and forth between us. 'But don't you see? If someone murdered Crash, they're still out there. They must be stopped.'

'You're the one who has to stop! It's bad enough he's dead, but you want to run around shouting murder? How dare you!'

'Now, what's going on here?' said a man's voice from behind us. I turned to see Johnny Roulette descend the steps into the saloon. 'Fox, I flew back as soon as I could. Come on, pet.' He approached her with open arms and Fox gratefully collapsed into them, sobbing. Johnny frowned at me over her shoulder. 'What's this nonsense you're talking to upset her?'

'I'm sorry. But I don't believe Crash killed himself,

and if I'm right then someone has got away with murder.'

Johnny opened his mouth to say something, then decided not to and closed it. 'Maybe you'd better leave.'

I did, leading Ace through the plants and up the steps. The afternoon was getting on but the day was still bright and pleasant, and by Collie standards the poor dog had barely exercised. I decided to give him another run around before collecting my things from Crash's boat and heading home with my own tail between my legs. Lucy wanted nothing to do with me, Howard thought I was naive, I'd upset Fox, and Johnny understandably took her side.

Besides, I hadn't been inclined to argue with him. When he'd wrapped Fox up in his long arms, the guitarist's sleeve rode up to reveal a sticking plaster on his right forearm that hadn't been there on Thursday. Somewhere between then and now, Johnny had cut himself.

CHAPTER FIFTEEN

People were returning to Rembrandt Gardens, though the half-dozen families sitting on benches were a sorry sight compared to how full and lively the park had been that morning.

I threw Ace's ring over and over, thinking about Crash's death and wondering: was I wrong? Had he really decided to end it all? Or had he fallen in? No matter how hard I tried, I couldn't convince myself of either possibility.

If I was right, though, it posed an even more difficult question: who would murder Crash, and why? A random mugging at six in the morning was unlikely, and surely even people sleeping off a hangover would have been woken by a cry for help.

Did Crash have a stalker? Crazed fans, who feel somehow betrayed and decide that if they can't have you nobody can, are more common than you might think. But wouldn't he have warned me, in case they'd turned up at the houseboat? Besides, most stalkers stab or strangle the objects of their obsession, not shove them in a canal. Perhaps that part of it could have been an accident. Crash argued with his stalker, they fought and he fell into the water. But then why didn't he swim back out?

'I think he's waiting for you, pet.'

Startled, I turned to see Johnny Roulette approaching. Then I saw Ace, sitting at my feet with throwing ring in mouth, patiently waiting while I'd been lost in my thoughts.

I tossed it for him and said to Johnny, 'I really didn't mean to offend Fox.'

'She'll be fine. It's a shock, you know? For her, me, everyone. Crash had his moments, sure we all do, but this is out of the blue. Then you come along and cry murder, so it's no wonder she lost her rag. Who wouldn't? What makes you think that, anyway? The police are positive it's either suicide or an accident. And there's no proof either way, so best let it rest. Don't you think?'

I waited for him to finish this characteristic wall of blarney, wondering how much I should say. I wanted to ask about the plaster on his arm, not to mention the argument I saw him and Crash having on Thursday. But I didn't want to risk Johnny walking away in a huff as well.

'You're right,' I said, 'We'll have to wait for the police's final verdict. Hopefully I'm barking up the wrong tree . . . which reminds me, do you know if Crash had any plans for Ace if he died?'

The guitarist puffed out his cheeks. 'Now that's a good question. He didn't mention anything to me.'

Standing there, throwing discs in the park for the second time today, I remembered Lucy's phone call and decided to take a chance. 'What about Mr Patwari?'

'His solicitor? How would he know?'

'Owners sometimes write a letter of wishes in addition to their will,' I explained, feeling pleased with myself that I'd guessed the mystery man's role correctly. 'It states what they'd like done with any surviving pets. My parents always updated theirs as dogs came and went in our house.'

Johnny shrugged and took out his phone. 'Worth a try, isn't it? Hold on, now . . . here you go. Not sure if he'll be working Saturday.' My phone buzzed as he texted me the number.

'Oh, I have a feeling he already is,' I said. 'Would you keep Ace occupied while I call him? No time like the present.' I stepped away, leaving Johnny to dutifully throw the dog's ring.

Mr Patwari answered himself, sounding harrassed.

'I'm sorry to bother you,' I said. 'My name's Gwinny Tuffel and I'm currently looking after Crash Double's dog. I wondered if he left any instructions in the event of his death?'

'His dog? That's a new one. Where are you, the *Mail*?'

'No, I promise you, I really am his dog sitter. That's why I'm calling, to find out what happens to Ace.'

The solicitor sighed. 'I really don't think Mr Donnelly

expected to die before his dog. You're by no means the first to ask if he left any special instructions and I'll tell you what I told all of them: none whatsoever. However, there is the will and the matter of his estate and properties which I expect will be protracted. So I'm sure you can imagine I have a lot to do. Unless there was anything else . . . ?'

'Wait, hang on, yes. You said "properties", plural. But I thought Crash only owned the houseboat in Little Venice. Did he have a holiday home as well?'

'No, nothing like that. A small concern on Penfold Mews that he rents to a boutique management firm. Actually, thank you for reminding me as I'll have to inform them. Good day.'

He ended the call and I let my brain run in circles for a while as I watched Ace do the same. The dog obviously adored Johnny, but then they'd probably spent a lot of time together.

Questions swirled in my mind, a morass of puzzle pieces in search of a connection. Why had so many callers asked if Crash had left instructions in the event of his death? Why did Crash tell everyone he was broke when there were thousands of pounds in his safe, and now it turned out he also collected rent on a second house?

High-pitched shouts and cries shook me from my thoughts. On the far side of the Gardens, several children shouted and screamed while Ace ran around them and Johnny tried in vain to call the dog to heel. The children's parents yelled at him to 'call off his vicious dog', threatening all sorts of lawsuits and recriminations.

It was naughty of Ace to herd children but it was also pretty normal behaviour for a Border Collie. I ran over, putting myself between them so the dog couldn't avoid eye contact and called out, 'Ace, *stop*!' with a sweeping gesture of my hand. He paused, eyeing me warily, so I stepped away from the children – but not towards him, to show that he was the one who had to approach – and pointed down at my feet. '*Come. Heel.*'

His eyes flicked between me and the oh-so-tempting children, but I held his gaze and waggled my hand again, to keep his attention. Finally, he slunk over to me, tail drooping and sat by my side. I quickly clipped on his lead and turned to the children.

'Ace was just playing,' I reassured them. 'He wanted to pretend you were sheep, that's all. Collies will be collies.'

They stared at me for a moment, before one wailed and burst into tears. The others immediately joined in. Dealing with children has never been my forte.

'You're the mad woman from that video!' One mother jabbed a finger at me as her weeping daughter clung to her legs. 'It shouldn't be allowed!'

'What shouldn't, exactly?' I protested, confused. 'Did you miss the part where I brought my dog under control?'

But, like an angry audience on opening night, I'd already lost them. Other parents followed, berating me for traumatising their children, and nothing I could say would placate them.

Johnny put a hand on my back and ushered me towards the exit. 'Come on, pet, we're not wanted here.'

'You don't say. Let's go to Westbourne Green, and hope they don't follow.'

'Oh, we can do better than that,' he said with a twinkle in his eye. 'Let me treat you to a cup of tea and a private park, eh?'

I was still wary of Johnny. That sticking plaster on his arm worried me. But the braying parents were a much more immediate concern, and at least he was offering a method of escape.

'Darling, you know all the right things to say to a girl. Lead on.'

CHAPTER SIXTEEN

'I assume this means the end of Bad Dice?'

Ace and I followed Johnny past Warwick Avenue Station. My question was a little tactless, but I couldn't help remember Birch's remark about the band's lack of new material when we found Crash's notebook.

'Hard to say, pet. There's others who've carried on, you know? AC/DC, New Order, even Queen. But it's too early to think. Plus, Fox might have an opinion, of course.'

I hadn't previously considered what Fox might stand to inherit. 'Does she take over his music rights, then? Those must be worth a penny or two.'

'There's less than you might think. But I wouldn't want to upset her, you know. Maybe . . .' Johnny shook his head. 'Like I said, there's a lot to think about.'

We were chatting comfortably so I decided now was a good time to slip my real question into the conversation. 'What happened to your arm, by the way?'

He looked confused, then said, 'Oh, the plaster. Changing a guitar string, can you believe it? The thing whipped up and cut me. Not deep but it bled like billy-o. That's why I normally have my tech do it,' he added, laughing.

'Why didn't you this time?'

'I was worried where Crash was, you know? Sure, you remember I phoned you. Nothing de-stresses me like fiddling with the guitar.'

It was a plausible explanation but was it the truth? Johnny was hard to read. I'd already seen that his cheery and gregarious demeanour hid a more serious side, and while I've never been on a music tour, I've performed in enough travelling theatre productions to know that you don't survive fifty years on the road by being happy-go-lucky.

We passed a side road of shops, Choudhury's the grocer among them, and then entered the Crescent proper; a long, gentle arc of beautiful white-fronted houses with columned porticos. As we mounted the steps to Johnny's place I remarked on the area's tranquillity.

He turned from the door and said, 'What's that?'

'I said it's so peaceful around here. This is a very lovely house.'

Johnny led us inside. I kept Ace on-lead; the dog might know this house but I didn't, and I feared if I unclipped him he might gallop upstairs and leap on Johnny's bed or go ten rounds with the loo roll.

'It wasn't always like this,' he said. 'Sure the BBC's

down the road but after the war it was hardly *des res*. It's only when the likes of muggins here stepped off the boat that they put the prices up.'

It was hard to believe this house had ever been cheap. Even the hallway featured a twelve-foot ceiling and miniature chandelier. Like Crash's houseboat, the walls were lined with gold discs, concert posters, and—

'Good lord, is that . . . you?' I asked, taken aback by a life-size statue of Johnny playing guitar. Hooks were attached all over its surface, holding hats and coats.

He laughed and slung his jacket over a hook erupting directly from the statue's forehead. 'A gift from the architect who did this place up. I could hardly say no, and then after a while I got used to it. Now, let's get a tea brewing.'

I had a sudden attack of concern. 'Johnny, are you sure? I don't want to impose, and after what's happened . . .' Here I was, gawping at his spacious home like a pint-sized Loyd Grossman, when it was Johnny who'd lost what must surely be one of his oldest friends.

'Nonsense, pet, it'll do us both good. Come on.'

He walked on through the hallway, but I was quickly brought up short by Ace who was intent on giving the bizarre hatstand a thorough inspection. I wondered if he could smell Crash. Waiting for him to finish, I noticed an occasional table piled with incoming post. The topmost letter was to this address, *FAO Mr Jonathan Ormond-Wiles*.

Ace's curiosity satisfied, we proceeded into the

kitchen and I quietly upgraded my description of the house from *spacious* to *palatial*. This was another large room, all chrome and marble, with vintage American diner signs hanging from glazed splashback tiling and a large breakfast bar. It looked out over a wide expanse of green, sandwiched between another row of houses opposite and accessed by a door towards which Ace was already pulling me.

'You really are tireless, aren't you?' I laughed, winding in the dog's lead and directing him to lie at my feet while I took a stool at the breakfast bar. 'Wait a minute and then we'll see Johnny's park. Although it looks like you've seen it before.'

Johnny turned from the kettle where he'd been preparing tea. 'Milk and sugar?'

'Just milk, thank you. Has Ace been here before?'

'Sure, a few times. It's a good runaround, lots of folk with dogs.'

'But not you?'

He shook his head. 'Too much work and then I'm often not here, you know.'

I did. It was why I hadn't taken in a dog of my own after my father died, because I knew I'd be out for auditions and rehearsals all the time. It wouldn't be fair on either of us as I'd be forever handing the dog off to another sitter.

Not for the first time, I thought how ironic it was that the people who could most easily afford this sort of house, like Johnny or my friend Tina with her country mansion at Hayburn Stead, were the least likely to spend much time in them.

He finished preparing the tea and sat opposite me, placing the mugs between us. 'It's a bad business, this,' he said quietly.

I remembered the notebook and the photos I'd taken. 'At least you won't be short of new material if you do carry on. Look at this.' I opened my phone's photo gallery and showed him the pictures. 'The police found a book of lyrics in Crash's safe. I'm told it's all new.'

Johnny's eyes almost popped out. 'Sweet Mary . . . in his safe, you said?'

'Not any more. The police took it for evidence but I snapped some photos before they took it away.' He raised an eyebrow at me. 'They didn't say I couldn't,' I protested, which was true but only because I hadn't asked.

'Can I see those?'

'Of course.' I handed him my phone and drank my tea as he swiped through them in silence. With perfect timing, I remembered Fox's cookie. I retrieved it from my pocket and began happily munching.

Johnny watched me sceptically. 'Tell me you're not eating dog biscuits, there.'

'No,' I laughed. 'Fox gave me this earlier, so I kept it for when I had a drink to go with it. Do you want a piece?'

He smiled and said, 'From Fox, you say? No, pet, you enjoy it.' Then he returned to looking at the pictures.

'Actually, I wondered if you could explain something,' I said. 'Keep swiping until the end.' He did, until he came to the page of random numbers and letters. 'This was on the last page, but it's gibberish to me. Is it something to do with his studio, perhaps? Who's this manager?'

He peered at the screen. 'Could be mix settings, sure. EQ and the like. What manager?'

I leant over and moved the picture on the screen, to reveal the name and email address underneath:

Don Christopher Management Ltd
dcm@top-emails.net

Johnny looked up and asked, 'Do you know who that is?'

My mouth was full, so I shook my head.

'Well, me neither. Maybe Crash met him at a party.'

'Oh.' I couldn't hide my disappointment. 'I thought perhaps you'd been writing new songs together.'

'Ha!' Johnny laughed bitterly. 'Chance'd be a fine thing. I've been writing by myself but this is all news to me.' He swiped back to the lyrics, reading them thoughtfully.

'Don't you think it's odd, keeping his notebook in a safe like that?'

Johnny looked up but didn't answer. Instead he said, 'Can I send these to myself, like? I don't trust the coppers not to lose the original.'

'Go ahead. I don't see what good they are locked up

in a police station.' I sipped my tea, pleased I'd had the impulse to take photos. New songs from Bad Dice really were more valuable than I'd assumed.

Ace barked, almost making me spill my tea. When I looked down I found him sitting upright, staring at me with his mismatched eyes, tongue out and expression hopeful.

'All right, all right,' I laughed. 'It must be at least fifteen minutes since you last had some exercise. Shall we take you in the park? Johnny, what do you say?'

I looked up as the guitarist passed my phone back. 'Thanks for that, pet. Come on, now, let's get the boy some exercise.' He took a keyring from a wall hook and opened the door to the rear garden with it. 'You can let him off-lead, it's all safe. Private park, remember.'

I didn't want to appear rude but I wasn't ready to take his word for it. Johnny had admitted he didn't have a pet himself. In my experience, people who've never had to worry about a dog bolting after a squirrel don't notice gaps and openings that to canine eyes might as well be lit with a neon sign. When we walked out, though, I saw that the park was truly private and fully enclosed. In addition to the row of houses opposite, more houses bound the top and bottom ends, ensuring the triangular green space was only accessible by the surrounding houses as a privilege for residents.

Satisfied, I unclipped Ace's lead and threw his ring. Johnny and I ambled across the grass as the Collie sped away, burning off yet more of his inexhaustible energy.

'Tell me about Crash,' I said. 'You two were obviously old friends, and he seemed quite normal for . . . well, for a rock star. Did you grow up together?'

'Sure, we were ten years old when we formed our first band. In Tullamore, for God's sake.' He looked wistful for a moment. 'Shaun got out first. One day when he was fifteen, straight out of the blue he said, "No! Enough." Packed his bag and caught the bus to Dublin that night. See, I thought he'd be back in a week.'

'But he wasn't?'

Johnny laughed. 'The fella went and got himself a job at the paper. He wrote to me, said come and join him. Well, I was doing nothing and hating every minute, so why not? Of course, when I got there, I found out he was the tea boy! We lived in one room with no heating until I could find a job. For a fair while after, too, you know.' Johnny smiled at the memory. 'But that was Shaun. Before he became Crash, like. Before all this.'

'Speaking of all this, if you don't mind me asking; how come you have such a beautiful place, while Crash was living in a houseboat?' His expression darkened, but I had to know. 'I mean, it's a very nice houseboat, but he was, well – no offence – he was rather more recognisable than you. Do your neighbours even know who you are?'

He looked at me with surprise. I winced, worried I'd pushed too far again. But then a deep, rumbling, full-body laugh built up and exploded like an erupting volcano from his big, broad frame. Even Ace, who'd once again dropped the ring at my feet, was caught off guard and cocked his head at Johnny.

'I shouldn't laugh, not with everything,' he said between laughs. 'But there are two things you must know. First, just because Crash is up front shaking his arse, doesn't mean he wrote the songs. Sure, we wrote a few together and he got producer cuts from a couple of the early records. But most of our songs, certainly all the big hits, they were mine. And in this business, it's your name on the songwriting that gets you royalties, not pouting at the camera.' He paused for a moment, thinking. 'Used to be, anyway. With the Internet now, maybe it's the other way around, after all. Anyway, then your man married and divorced the same woman over and over. You know there was a time when Fox took eighty pence of every pound Crash earned?'

I hadn't. 'That seems excessive. But surely he wasn't still paying, now they were married again?'

'No, but historical, like. Never so good with money and the business side of things, was Crash. Not that Fox is much better, with her plants and rainbows, though she'll be right enough now. God bless her.'

A silence fell upon us as we walked. It wasn't uncomfortable, but it carried a certain weight that neither of us felt ready to lift. I certainly didn't think it was my place to move the conversation on, considering this man had today lost his oldest friend.

Then Johnny laughed again and said, 'You were asking if my neighbours recognise me. Probably not, it's the truth. But I don't know who they are either. They've

153

obviously got money and there's plenty of that washing around Little Venice, but it's still London, you know? A few weeks ago, I saw a removals van and realised what's-his-face from breakfast telly lived five doors down. You know, your man with the hair? Never seen him until that day.'

Ace returned with his ring, but as I bent down to take it, I overbalanced and stumbled, almost falling flat on my face. Johnny caught me and I looked down to see his hand gripping my arm. Or two hands gripping two arms, thanks to a slight blurring in my vision.

'I'm terribly sorry,' I mumbled. 'I feel a bit dizzy.' At least that's what I tried to mumble but I could tell from his expression that he struggled to understand me. That made me think of something else, something that felt important, but my head was spinning too much to think straight. I held onto his arm, hauled myself upright and took a deep breath. A moment later I took another, and slowly but surely the world steadied around me.

'I'd better take Ace home,' I said. 'Perhaps we both need some rest.'

'Grand idea,' said Johnny, smiling sympathetically. 'Everyone's had a long day, pet.'

We returned to his house, where I clipped Ace back on-lead and led him out to the street. The evening was drawing in and I suddenly felt very hungry. Had I eaten anything since breakfast? Had Ace? I couldn't remember. Wobbling slightly, I walked back to Blomfield Road and down to Crash's houseboat to feed us both.

Constable Wright had other ideas.

'Sorry, madam. Off limits, by order.'

'But Crash wasn't . . . wasn't killed in there,' I said, noticing with some alarm that I was slurring my words. 'Said that this afternoon, remember? Need to . . . feed the dog . . . get some clothes. Jigsaw.'

'Are you quite well, madam? What clothes?'

I rattled Ace's lead, then regretted it as I almost lost my balance and clutched at the policeman to steady myself.

'Dog sitting! God's sake . . . don't you remember? Call Fletcher . . .'

'The superintendent has left for the night, madam. I'd advise you do the same and sleep it off.'

Stupid boy! I couldn't make him see straight, though to be fair I was having trouble doing that myself. I resisted the temptation to shove the constable in the water because who would look after Ace while I warmed a cell for the night?

I swallowed my anger and trudged back to Warwick Avenue Station. At least at home I could relax and find something to eat, far from trouble.

I almost fell asleep on the Tube and missed my stop, but I fought the urge because I didn't want to risk Ace getting away from me. I wondered if he'd ever been on a train before. He boarded happily and sat at my feet but didn't seem at all relaxed. His head was in constant motion taking in the Saturday night crowd.

Finally, we emerged from Sloane Square Station onto

the King's Road and the fresh air gave me a second wind. Something nagged at me, something my mind was trying to make me notice or remember about Johnny. But I was too tired and it wouldn't come. It would have to wait until morning.

Turning into Smithfield Terrace, my thoughts were cut short by an unexpected sight. The dizziness returned as I walked down the road, and I couldn't be entirely sure I was seeing right but it looked like someone was having building work done. Seeing the assembled scaffolding, I wondered if I should pop round and ask them for a recommendation.

Then I recognised my own house.

A sign hung off one of the bars but I couldn't read it. The scaffold covered the frontage, taking up much of the pavement, and I couldn't seem to find a way through to my door.

'Guinevere, my dear. Could I have a word?'

I turned too quickly, stumbled, and steadied myself on an upright pole as I faced the Dowager Lady Ragley. She wore her customary black frock with white cuffs and stood on the far side of the scaffolding outside her front door. Her hair was scraped back in a tight bun, accentuating her severe expression.

'Good evening . . . lady,' I slurred. 'Who . . . did you do this?' I hadn't meant it to come out like that, but I was having difficulty forming words.

The Dowager was about to respond when she saw Ace, who first cocked his head at her, then without breaking eye contact cocked his leg up a scaffold upright.

The normally composed widow practically vibrated with indignation. 'My dear girl, this abomination was erected by one of the rudest men I have ever encountered, and I once dined with the late Australian ambassador. When I asked him what he was playing at, well, I won't repeat his exact words. But he insisted I should "call Darren" to clear up the matter.'

'Must be . . . misunderstanding,' I tried to reassure her. 'Darren . . . said no. Shouldn't be . . . scaffold.'

'There most certainly should not be scaffold,' agreed the Dowager. 'Their van blocked the road for an hour, and the noise! Radio blaring, men shouting, and who ever imagined a Pole would know such Anglo-Saxon language? On a bank holiday weekend, no less!'

There was nothing I could do about it at this time or in my current state. 'No, of course . . .' I said, trying to soothe her. 'Call . . . tell him off, yes. Misunderstanding. Could you show me . . . front door?'

She finally noticed my shambolic state and looked appalled. 'Guinevere, are you *drunk*? Dear, oh dear. Whatever would your father think?'

'No! Tired . . . anyway, Daddy drunk plenty . . . but no! Just . . . door. Wherezit?'

I felt a tug on my hand and looked down to see my arm outstretched; at the end of it, my hand holding Ace's lead; and at the end of that, a tricolour Border Collie leading me through a canvas-lined tunnel in the scaffolding. I recognised my own front door at the tunnel's far end and gratefully followed Ace while the Dowager returned to her house, muttering with disapproval.

It took a couple of minutes of wondering why my key didn't work to notice I was trying to open my door with Crash Double's keyring. Laughing at my silly mistake, I found the right keys, opened the door and fell inside.

The right keys. That felt important but I couldn't think straight. I closed the door and collapsed against it.

CHAPTER SEVENTEEN

Ace woke me again the next morning, standing next to the bed and whining plaintively. After shooing him away I glanced at the time. Quarter to nine! I shot out of bed, immediately regretting it as the world dizzily rotated around me. Thankfully, it cleared after a few seconds of holding on tight to the door frame and with bleary eyes I led Ace downstairs to the garden.

'Guinevere, my dear. I trust you've recovered since last night. Did you hear about this terrible business in Little Venice? A rock musician!'

In what was either a remarkable coincidence of timing or a remarkable display of patience, the Dowager Lady Ragley stood looking over the fence into my garden, her pinned-back hair as immaculate as her ivory cuffs. Had she even been to bed? I hadn't brushed my hair, let alone my teeth, and stood barefoot in my pyjamas with a plastic bag ready in hand while Ace went to the toilet.

'Really, my lady?' I said innocently, not wanting to

feed her salacious hunger for gossip. 'How curious. As it happens, this dog belonged to someone who died in Little Venice yesterday. We live in such dangerous times, don't you think?' I quickly bagged up Ace's business and made to return inside.

'Two? Two deaths?' she spluttered as I hurried back in. 'Is that what you're saying?'

I closed the patio doors, leaving her bewildered. I hadn't actually said it was a different person to the 'rock musician' but I enjoyed imagining her spending all day searching in vain for a mysterious second death.

The last thing I heard before the double glazing cut her off was a faint cry about builders. Hazy memories of the night before began to resurface. Hoping I might have dreamt the whole thing, I flung open the curtains in the front room and looked out. No such luck; the scaffolding was still there, as solid as the pavement on which it stood. Feeling miserable, I closed the curtains and returned to the kitchen.

Making coffee for myself and breakfast for Ace, I grimaced at the state of the countertop and remembered ravenously scoffing toast before collapsing into bed. The kitchen was the one room I'd managed to keep in good and tidy order while caring for my father, but now it was a mess of breadcrumbs, butter smears, opened loaves and unrinsed kitchenware.

While Ace ate his kibble I wiped down the surface, loaded the dishwasher and tied off the open loaf. Feeling a little more organised and righteous, I decided to unload the rest of my frustration on Darren the builder and took out my phone to call him.

There was a text message from an unknown number waiting for me.

> See for yourself and leave H alone
>   I sent this to the cops too
>   – L

It included a link, which took me to a page of video recordings. Each thumbnail image was of Howard Zee's face, sometimes smiling, sometimes calm, sometimes sweating with exertion on his houseboat set.

L for Latesha Michaels. She'd got a bee in her bonnet about his alibi, and no doubt the video of Howard's class from Friday morning was somewhere in here. How did she get my number? I didn't recall giving it to Howard.

I really wasn't in the mood, so I closed the message and phoned Darren. I didn't expect he'd answer this early on a Sunday but I could leave a disgruntled voicemail.

He did answer, though.

'Hello?' said a gruff male voice with the unmistakeable tone of someone who had been woken from a perfectly good lie-in.

'Darren, it's Gwinny Tuffel on Smithfield Terrace. I don't know why you sent someone round to erect scaffolding yesterday but you need to take it away again. I declined your estimate so there's no reason for it to be here.'

'What are you talking about? I've already booked out the time, I start on Tuesday.'

'But I can't afford you. Why do you think I sent that emoji of money flying away?'

He sighed. 'I thought you were being funny, making a joke about the cost. You said you wanted me to start as soon as possible so I booked Mateusz.' He muffled the phone and I heard voices in the background. It occurred to me that he might have a whole family there and I'd woken them up. I felt slightly guilty about that but this had to be dealt with. He returned to the phone and said, 'If you'd wanted to decline you should have said so explicitly.'

'If I'd wanted to proceed I *would* have said so explicitly. You can't assume someone has agreed to have work done without checking.'

'Listen, you'll have to pay for the scaffolding, regardless. It's already up and whether they pull it down now or next week makes no difference. Mateusz's crew has done the work and they'll expect to be paid. Then you'll have to pay all over again when you find someone else to do your frontage and, by the way, good luck finding someone cheap enough to save that money compared to me. Plus, I'll have to charge you for at least one day of cancelled time anyway because I've already booked out the week to do this for you. So, do you still want to cancel?'

I felt frustrated, deflated and not a little extorted. Darren's quote was high enough to use up a substantial chunk of my savings. Every builder claims nobody else can do it cheaper, but the work really did need doing and if I wound up having to pay half of it anyway as a kill fee, then pay another builder the same amount again, he was right; I'd be even worse off.

Someone would have to pay me for dog-sitting Ace, I decided, whether it was Crash's lawyer, Fox Double-Jones or the damned residents' association. And I still hoped that Bostin Jim could negotiate my original fee for *Mixed Mothers*, regardless of recasting. If I could win both of those battles, I'd be OK. More or less.

'Fine. Have it your way,' I said, and went to brush my teeth.

Staring in the mirror at my red-rimmed eyes, I tried to understand what had happened last night. In the cold light of day, the idea that I'd been exhausted and hungry didn't hold water. I might not jog the streets of London every morning like Howard Zee, but I was in reasonably good shape and no stranger to spending all day on my feet. True, Ace had the boundless energy reserves of any Border Collie but I'd kept pace with him.

So what was it, if not weariness? It had been a very long time since I'd felt so disorientated and fuzzy-headed. In fact, not since—

The last time I smoked dope.

I'm no innocent prude. You couldn't be in show business thirty years ago without encountering drugs of all kinds and I doubt it's any different now. So yes, I smoked a little, and once or twice tried something stronger, but nothing ever took. Marijuana made me sleepy and hungry, which would explain stuffing my face last night. Other drugs just made me feel horrible, or rather made me feel like I became a horrible person, which had been confirmed whenever I'd remained sober while in the company of others buzzing off their heads. For decades, a drink or two had been my only vice.

Well, that and jigsaws. But they couldn't arrest you for driving after finishing a tricky thousand-piecer.

I tried to retrace my steps. Crawling into bed after scoffing toast; before that, a soporific Tube ride home; before that, slurring my words at Constable Wright; and before that, it all started with me stumbling around Johnny's private park.

Right after he'd made us both tea.

Had he spiked it? But why? He hadn't tried to take advantage of me; in fact, despite Crash's warnings, Johnny had been a gentleman. I didn't recall an odd taste or anything at all unusual about the tea, except . . .

The cookie I'd eaten with it. The one from Fox's tray which she'd warned me not to give to Ace.

I groaned, feeling very naive. Of course. Celebrity gardener Fox Double-Jones secretly grew cannabis, probably in the unseen locked room on her houseboat, and had baked some into the cookies she was eating when I visited. To cope with Crash's death? Or was eating loaded biscuits a regular habit? It would explain her mellow demeanour. Either way it seemed an innocent mistake, with no nefarious motive and no harm done besides the butter smears on my kitchen countertop.

But what if it wasn't?

Had Fox hoped the cookie would disorientate me to stop me asking awkward questions? If I'd eaten it right away I'd have been reeling much earlier, perhaps even before I'd got round to mentioning her late-night leap over the fence.

Now another question formed in my mind, adding a new piece to this strange puzzle: what if Crash had been poisoned?

There were no injuries on his body; nothing to indicate he'd been attacked. But poison wouldn't leave a mark. A killer could simply wait for him to die, then throw his body overboard without a struggle. It would also explain why nobody saw or heard anything. At six in the morning anyone could stand on their deck with a coffee, seeming completely innocent while patiently checking the coast was clear.

Did that mean Crash had definitely been killed on someone else's boat? Or could it have been done in his own home after all? The killer might have called round for an early chat before Crash left for Dublin, spiked his coffee then tossed him out of the French windows without making a mess or leaving any trace of blood.

No matter where it happened, it would have to be someone Crash knew. He was mindful of his privacy at the best of times and I couldn't believe he'd invite a stranger in for coffee at six a.m. It would also explain Ace being at home; he'd either been left there when Crash visited the killer or locked inside when the killer departed.

The puzzle piece that continued to elude me was motive. Money? The singer wasn't as broke as he'd claimed, with thousands in cash to hand and a premises he rented out. But nobody else knew that . . . did they?

Only one person I could think of in Little Venice fitted the bill. Someone who knew Crash; whom he would have readily visited or received at home early in the morning; who gained financially from his death; and with easy access to poisons.

Fox Double-Jones.

I was due to meet Birch at eleven for our regular Sunday walk, but I felt so lethargic after the night before that I considered calling it off. I didn't need to look in the mirror to know I had bags under my eyes and the energy to do anything about it was in short supply, but I felt obliged to make up for the lack of Sunday dinner. Besides, he appeared in no hurry to turn his own blue eyes my way so he'd have to take me as he found me.

While attempting to perk myself up with another coffee, I texted the former policeman to say I'd be a little late. Then I saw the message from Latesha Michaels again and it gave me an idea.

You can add yoga to the list of things that aren't really 'me'; many years ago, Tina tried to recruit me as her classmate but half an hour of what felt like a sadistic game of Twister convinced me I wasn't cut out for it.

Nevertheless, that was a long time ago and she still

swore by it. I could at least hope it would put a spring back in my step. So, five minutes later – after double-checking the lounge curtains were well and truly drawn – I placed my laptop on a bookshelf and stood facing it in my underwear ready to watch Howard Zee. Ace watched me with unabashed curiosity from the sofa but that didn't bother me; Sabre, our family's German Shepherd, had a habit of following people into the toilet if they didn't close the door quickly enough. There was no privacy with dogs.

Latesha's link contained dozens of videos going back several months. As she'd said, there were two from Friday morning, one starting at six and another at seven. I played the one that started at six, figuring I might as well check Howard's alibi while trying to inject some life into my tired body.

As the video began, I was once again impressed by his professional set-up and presentation. No wonder her company saw potential in him. I wondered idly if they'd add maintaining the beard to his contract; I'd heard of clauses that banned actresses from cutting their hair or mandated that leading men spend a minimum number of hours every day in the gym. It sounded exhausting.

Things started easily enough, with deep breaths and stretching. I had to cheat a little; the last time I could touch my toes without bending my knees was thirty years ago. We progressed to sit-ups, toe-touching and holding out an arm or leg while trying to stay balanced. So far, so good, though I was already beginning to sweat.

By this time Ace had come off the sofa and decided to join in, doing his own version of stretching on the carpet beside me.

When Howard asked me to stand on one leg and stretch out the other while touching it, I started to worry that perhaps I wasn't in such good shape as I'd thought. Finally, after a position that made me hop, stumble and almost crash into the TV stand – which sent Ace leaping back onto the sofa – I admitted defeat. Muscles I didn't even know I possessed felt stretched in ways never intended by nature and I was sweating all over. Was this meant to feel good?

'Don't worry, boy,' I said to Ace, breathing heavily. 'At least we got near the end, eh?'

I touched my laptop to see exactly *how* near the end and whimpered when I saw barely fifteen minutes had elapsed. I skipped ten minutes ahead to find Howard doing press-ups, his muscular arms flexing and bulging. It wasn't hard to see why he might attract an audience of older women, particularly if their husbands had lost interest now that they'd produced the expected two-point-four children. I skipped again, and again, grimacing each time as the exercises reached far beyond anything I was capable of, until I suddenly reached a black screen showing a countdown timer. I went back to see what I'd missed, and found Howard declaring a break at the forty-five minute mark. He turned off the camera, and the view changed to a five-minute countdown. I skipped forward until that was over, at which point Howard reappeared with a towel around his neck and smoothie in hand, sitting on a stool and talking to the class. They were also visible now, smiling women in little boxes at the bottom of the screen.

The first question was something about chakras and my attention quickly drifted. It was horrible to think that at the very moment this was being recorded, Crash was dying nearby. In fact, if Lucy's mysterious climbing man was the killer then Crash had already been dead for almost an hour by now.

Could that man have been Johnny? Crash's death might cause a surge in Bad Dice record sales, and from what the guitarist had said most of the royalties would go to him. True, he was already loaded, but money is a powerful motive. His story about a guitar string sounded fishy, too. If he'd really cut himself while climbing the gate, and Lucy heard him cry out—

The doorbell rang, startling me. I turned to answer it, then remembered I was still barefoot in my underwear. Ace had already leapt off the sofa and ran into the hallway. The bell rang again and I hurried after him.

'All right, hang on,' I called out, grabbing a raincoat from the coat rack and hastily tying the belt around my waist. If the Dowager Lady Ragley insisted on calling at odd hours she'd get what she got and that was that.

In the split second it took to open the door, it occurred to me that the Dowager normally preferred to intercept me as I left the house. And it wouldn't be the postman on a Sunday morning. So who . . . ?

'Blimey!' exclaimed a wide-eyed DCI Alan Birch, retired.

CHAPTER EIGHTEEN

'Sorry, ma'am – said you'd be late – thought I'd call – save you – ah, that is—'

Birch turned a shade of red and averted his eyes. Not before I noticed he gave me a quick up-and-down, mind you. Ronnie and Ace wagged tongues at one another across the threshold.

I stood in the doorway, momentarily frozen as I realised I was sweating, still tired, *sans* make-up and currently resembled a street flasher. Oh, well. Birch would indeed have to take me as he found me.

'It's not the eighteen-hundreds, Birch. There's no need to be scandalised by my ankles,' I said, refusing to be embarrassed. 'I was just getting ready, so wait in the lounge and I'll be down shortly.'

Despite my bravura, I wasn't about to shed the raincoat in full view, so while he made his way to the sofa I hurried upstairs with it still tied around me. I'd expected Ace to stay with him and Ronnie, but instead the Collie followed me and waited on my bed as I dressed and put on a face.

Ten minutes later, with Birch's complexion returned to a normal colour, we strolled through South Kensington while I explained my theory that Crash had been poisoned.

'Plausible,' he said. 'Hard to imagine Fox hefting Crash up and over the side of a boat, though. An accomplice, perhaps?'

'I wouldn't discount her on the basis of strength. You should see her throw bags of compost around on telly. But you're right that it would have been easier for someone like Johnny.' I told him about the plaster on the guitarist's arm.

'Hmmm. Suspicious. Would he have access to the poisonous plants?'

I thought back to Fox's cabinets. 'Yes, I think so. She practises giving her tour on local residents, and the key is kept in a nearby jug so it's not a closely guarded secret. He'd have to have got inside the boat without her knowing, though.'

'And while Fox is already there, too. Tricky.'

'The question I keep coming back to is motive. The one person who had any real argument with Crash was Lucy Kwok, but would she really murder him over the Canal Carnival?'

'People kill for less every day, I'm sorry to say. But first let's find out if Crash was poisoned. I'll talk to Fletcher, see what she thinks and if they've checked for toxins yet.'

We entered Kensington Gardens and let the dogs off to run around. Ace tried to herd Ronnie again, but the Lab remained oblivious, being far more interested in the bushy-tailed squirrels darting in every direction. The Gardens looked lovely, as they always do in spring, with trees starting to leaf and flowers budding among the bushes and dewy grass.

Ace finally tired of trying to get Ronnie's attention and ran to me with an expectant look. I dutifully took the disc from around his neck and threw it.

'What if Johnny got that cut not from climbing over the gate, but from heaving Crash over the side of a boat?' I wondered.

Birch shrugged. 'Possible, but as you said, motivation's tricky. Crash and Johnny have had plenty of disagreements over the years, that's well documented. All in the past, though. Killing him now feels twenty years too late.'

I remembered that last night I'd been close to understanding something about Johnny, something about his behaviour, but I couldn't pin it down. By now we were approaching the Long Water and both dogs' tongues were happily panting, so we called them to heel and clipped on their leads.

'Jealous lover?' Birch mused. 'What if the feud between Crash and Lucy was for show? They were having an affair, Fox found out, slipped him some poison.'

'But why not simply divorce him again? Apparently, she took him to the cleaners the first two times, claiming almost all of his income.'

'True enough. Second divorce came about when he

shacked up with a Swedish model, who then dumped him anyway. Got a great album out of it, mind you. All heartbreak and bitterness.'

Once again the former policeman's tastes surprised me and I was glad of it. Talk about hidden depths.

'That reminds me,' I said, pulling out my phone. 'Let me send you those photos of Crash's notebook, with the new lyrics. I showed them to Johnny yesterday and he said he'd never seen them before. He didn't even know Crash was writing new songs.'

Birch smiled wistfully as I opened the photo gallery. 'Shame we'll never get to hear them now. Still, lyrics are better than nothing.'

But something strange had happened.

'I don't understand,' I said, distracted.

'Turn of phrase. I mean even if we can't hear Crash sing them, there's enough previous material to imagine—'

'No, not that,' I interrupted. 'The photos. They're not here.'

I scrolled through my gallery, wondering if I'd done something to make them show out of order, but the notebook was nowhere to be seen. I tried looking in my Favourites folder, then remembered that most of the recent pictures in it were candid photos of Birch I'd snapped while dog walking. Hearing a sort of strangled cough over my shoulder, I quickly scrolled down to save us both our blushes, but again: nothing.

'They were here yesterday. I showed them to Johnny, in his kitchen.'

'Beg pardon?'

'We were having a cup of tea,' I said defensively. 'He was amazed to see the new lyrics and asked if he could send them to himself. Of course, I said yes and gave him my phone . . .' I groaned. 'Ace distracted me while Johnny was holding it. Could he have deleted the pictures when I wasn't looking? Why would he do that?'

'Innocent mistake?' Birch ventured.

'Poppycock. He and Crash might be getting on, but they're no Luddites. Not like us!' I almost cried with frustration. 'What is it about this bloody notebook that's so valuable?'

Birch reached for my phone. 'May I?'

I let him take it, feeling rotten. I should never have let Johnny handle my phone but even with that cut on his arm, I hadn't been sure he was up to no good. Now, though . . .

'Look this way, ma'am?'

I did, to find Birch holding up my phone with the screen facing me. Then he tapped a few things and handed it back.

'There you go. All present and correct.'

He was right. The notebook photos were there, even including the last page with the technical recording codes. I stared at him in amazement.

'Not quite a Luddite myself,' he smiled. 'They were in your Recently Deleted folder, but it's locked behind facial recognition. Johnny couldn't access that, so wasn't able to purge it. I restored them.'

'I only understand half of that but I could kiss you all the same,' I said with delight, this time sparing him no blushes as I swiped through the photos. 'Next time I need help with a file that mysteriously disappears, I know who to—*oh*!'

'Beg pardon? Something else wrong?'

I stared at the photo of the page with the recording codes, and below those:

Don Christopher Management Ltd
dcm@top-emails.net

'Crash's solicitor said he rents out a place on Penfold Mews to a boutique management firm,' I explained.

'Is there much call for managing boutiques?'

'No, it . . . never mind. What are the chances it's this company? You're the music man, have you heard of them?'

Birch peered at the name. 'Does ring a bell, now you mention it. Where's Penfold Mews, then?'

'Let's find out.'

I opened my phone's map and searched for the street, expecting to be whizzed halfway across London. Instead, the pointer merely hopped north a small way . . . to a street in Little Venice.

CHAPTER NINETEEN

Finding Penfold Mews was easier said than done. Even with a map it took five minutes of searching before we located the road entrance because it was literally a street within a street; an old, narrow road that ran between two larger thoroughfares north of Warwick Avenue Station, tucked away out of sight.

Walking down its cobbled surface, my heart sank at the lack of any signage. 'Probably a residents' by-law,' I said. 'Should I call Mr Patwari again and ask which house it is?'

Birch gave me a disapproving look. 'Sunday, remember. Besides, he'd want to know why you're asking.'

Ace began pulling on his lead, which was unusual. Border Collies are all keen as mustard to get wherever they're going (even when they don't actually know where that is) but they train to heel well and Ace had quickly adapted his pace from Crash's long legs to mine. He hadn't forged ahead like this before.

'Something's got Ace's nose,' I said, giving his lead some slack. 'Let's see where he takes us.'

The dog moved directly ahead. Was he going to lead us straight out the other end of the street to a smelly rubbish bin? Then again, this didn't seem like an area where rubbish was left on the street, smelly or otherwise.

Ace veered left towards a nondescript door with a buzzer, where a card affixed inside its small windowpane informed us this was the home of 'DC Management'. There was no other indication of who was inside but it was enough.

'I remember now that when I asked Johnny to recommend a builder, Crash almost said something but stopped himself. I wonder if he was going to suggest whoever converted this place but realised it would blow his secret?'

'Why keep it secret is the question,' said Birch. 'Hiding assets in case of divorce, perhaps? As you said, he's been rinsed before.'

'Whatever the reason, I'm guessing Crash's scent lingers here and that's what Ace caught. *Good boy*,' I said, slipping the Collie a quick treat from my pocket. He panted with excitement, looking from me to the door with his tail going ten to the dozen.

Birch pressed the buzzer but there was no answer. He tried again. I strained to hear any reaction or sign of life from within, but it was quiet as a church.

I decided to be cheeky and try the door. It was locked. Pressing my face to the glass, all I could see inside was an unlit set of stairs leading up. Mews houses commonly have a garage space at street level with the living space starting on the first floor. Crash had presumably converted the house upstairs to office space but left the garage as it was.

Ace suddenly reared up on his hind legs and began scratching at the door. I pulled him away, but sympathised with his eagerness to get inside.

'Can I help you?'

We turned to find a slim young man standing behind us. I suppose we did look a bit suspicious, although having the dogs gave us good cover.

'Oh, we were out for a walk and thought we'd call on Mr Christopher,' I said. 'Have you seen him lately?'

'This is a respectable street, you know.'

'I'm sure it is,' I said, floundering a little. 'But, um, we're old friends of his. From the music business.'

He looked me up and down with a scepticism bordering on outright hostility.

'All right, you got us,' said Birch, laughing. 'Not showbiz types at all, of course not. Look at us! Terrible cover story.' Before I could protest, he continued, 'Truth is, here on behalf of a client. To collect a debt, if you get my meaning.'

The young man softened slightly. At least Birch looked the part.

'If you mean you're debt collectors, then yes, of course I do.'

'Good. So, seen him lately?'

'Never.'

'Here much, are you? Might come and go when you're not around.'

The young man indicated a house on the other side of the street. It was a hairdresser's, with the garage space converted to a shop frontage.

'That's my shop, so I'm here all day long and I've never seen a soul go in or out of that house. Don't know why he bothers, what with the rents around here. Maybe that's why he can't pay his debts.'

With that he turned and walked to his door, taking a set of his keys from his pocket. I suddenly remembered my own escapades the night before, mistakenly trying to open my front door with Crash's keys, and gave an involuntary squeak.

'The keys were for here!'

Birch looked puzzled. 'Come again?'

'Remember the old keys found in Crash's safe? I assumed they were an old set from before he changed the houseboat locks. But why keep old keys if they didn't fit any more?' I pointed at the mews house. 'I think they fit this door, instead.'

'Suggests he's had the place a while. Is it likely, though? Very recognisable man.' He turned to the hairdresser's house, where a light had come on in the upstairs rooms. 'Surely even that chap would know him.'

'He'd have to see him first. Perhaps Crash visited when nobody else was around and he knew he wouldn't be seen. If he brought Ace with him, it would explain why he's so keen to get inside.'

'Very plausible,' Birch agreed. 'Another thing to ask Fletcher.'

His loyalty to his old superintendent was admirable, but I was getting a little tired of it when she wouldn't take our suggestions seriously. Still, there was no sense in starting an argument.

I opened the final notebook photo again, noted Don Christopher Management's email address, then sent them a short message from my phone asking about their connection to Crash. Did they even know he was their landlord? Surely they would, being in the same industry. They might even know why he was so keen to keep this place hidden from family and friends, though I didn't mention that in the email.

Returning to the photo, a puzzle piece tentatively clicked into place in my mind. Not the management company, but the lines above it: what Johnny had said could be studio recording settings. Given his attempt to delete the pictures, I was no longer inclined to believe him. Instead, I had a new idea of what they might really be.

'Birch, I see a computer in our future. Let's get back to the canal.'

CHAPTER TWENTY

If I'd thought Crash's death would bring the Carnival to a halt and dissuade people from attending, I couldn't have been more wrong. Today was even busier, the tragedy seemingly forgotten by everyone clustered around the Pool.

The people gathered outside the residents' access gate hadn't forgotten, though. It remained locked, and presumably wouldn't open to the public again, but they wouldn't be dissuaded.

We pushed our way to it, helped once again by the dogs clearing a path. I spied Constable Wright still standing guard outside Crash's front door, which could be a problem after our unceremonious ejection yesterday.

'Hey, it's the angry drone lady!' shouted a voice in the crowd. All eyes turned on us as I fumbled with the key, trying to unlock the gate before embarrassment overtook me.

'You owe me a replacement,' called another voice.

The bearded young reporter whose drone I'd whacked pushed his way towards me with a furious expression. 'I've reported you to the police!'

'Why don't you use the money you made from that video?' I shot back, suddenly angry. 'I should be asking you for royalties!'

The reporter advanced. 'Do you have any idea what those things cost? The article fee doesn't even begin to cover it!'

Perhaps sensing the tension, Ace moved in front of me and snarled at the young man.

'Even her dog's vicious,' he called to the crowd. 'Shouldn't be allowed!'

'I suggest you step back, sir,' said Birch, taking a step forward himself. Before it developed into a proper stand-off, though, a loud voice behind us cut through the noise.

'Now, then, what's going on here?'

I practically fell through the gate as Constable Wright swung it wide open. Birch and the dogs followed, and we backed away onto the residents' path, leaving the constable to argue with the angry young man.

'Quick!' I whispered to Birch, realising that for the first time since we'd stepped onto the path, nobody was looking at us. While everyone focused on Constable Wright, I hurried to unlock the door to Crash's houseboat. We tumbled inside, and after closing the door behind us I made for the stairs. 'Like you said before, hardly breaking and entering when we have a key, is it? Besides, I still need to collect my things from in here. But we'll deal with that later.' I led the way up to the second floor and Crash's studio.

'You said he really was working on new music?' Birch asked.

'He was, yes. But it's not the music I'm interested in.' I sat at the desk and unlocked the computer with the password. Then I clicked on the folder called *Johnny*, and was confronted with another password box. 'I tried to open these folders before, but couldn't get in. I already tried *equilibrium* and it doesn't work.'

'Others all the same, I assume.' He pointed at the three other folders named *Fox*, *Howard* and *Lucy*.

'Yes, but now I think the answer was under our noses the whole time.'

On my phone, I opened the photograph of the last notebook page and zoomed in on the strings of numbers and letters. 'I thought this was some kind of technical gibberish, and Johnny said they were settings for the recordings Crash was making.'

'Looks like a funny way to go about it.'

'Well, I wouldn't know. But listen: I'd guessed "Roulette" was a stage name, but I didn't know Johnny's real name. Until I went to his house, where I saw a letter for "Jonathan Ormond-Wiles".'

'That's right. Family of bankers, I believe.'

'Oh, so not the poor farm boy he'd have us believe? That's interesting. But now look at this first line.' I pointed to it:

JOW-1000T-434206913IAFCLSHER

Birch's eyes widened. 'You're thinking "JOW" is for Jonathan Ormond-Wiles. Could be a coincidence?'

'I don't think so. Look at the others.' There were three other lines underneath the first. They read:

FDJ-600W-411276138PSHGCKSRS
HZ-800M-916942461SDGFPUASN
LSK-500T-549134347ICNESOPXC

'Fox Double-Jones, Howard Zee and Lucy S. Kwok,' I said. 'You haven't met Howard yet, and Lucy is the Carnival organiser whom you so gallantly helped off the barge yesterday.' Birch nodded, oblivious to my gentle reproach. 'Still think this is a coincidence?'

'Point taken. But what are they?'

I directed his attention to the computer screen, still asking for a password to the *Johnny* folder.

He smiled, understanding. 'I'll read that first line out for you.'

I typed it in as he did, and hey presto, the folder opened.

It didn't contain much: a spreadsheet and several more recordings. I opened the spreadsheet. It was damaged somehow, like the recording from Thursday, and many lines were filled with garbled text and symbols. Not all, though. There was enough to see what looked like a pattern: weekly dates going back a little over two years, with '£1,000' listed alongside each of them.

'What's going on here?' I wondered aloud. 'Some kind of regular transaction? If Crash was paying Johnny a thousand pounds every week, maybe he really was broke, after all.'

'Some exceptions, though. Varying amounts.'

Birch was right. A few dates listed '£2,000'. I leant closer to the screen, looking for a pattern. The amounts varied, but only between one and two thousand pounds. The dates . . .

'There, look,' I said. 'The dates are weekly but sometimes they skip a week, and the following date is always two thousand pounds.' I scrolled down the sheet to double-check. It was impossible to say for certain with the missing lines, but what we could see fitted that pattern. 'Crash and Johnny are bandmates living less than half a mile from each other. Why would they need to skip a week?'

'Touring? Could be dates when they were on the road.'

'But surely then they'd be even closer, wouldn't they? Let's listen to these recordings.'

I opened one of the audio files. It began with mechanical clicking noises, then after a few seconds of hiss we heard a muffled, low-quality recording of someone playing an acoustic guitar and singing. The tune sounded familiar but I couldn't place it.

'Do you recognise this?' I said and turned to look at Birch. He was listening intently. Behind him I saw Ace sit up from his bed, ears pricked and alert. 'Oh, is this Crash singing?'

Birch nodded. 'Young Crash, at that. Voice hasn't been that light in years. Singing "Spin the Lady", an early hit. Doesn't sound like Johnny's guitar playing, though. Maybe it's Crash by himself. Old recording.'

Screeching static suddenly blared from the speakers, and Ronnie's ears pricked up to match Ace's. I lowered the volume, hoping there might be more to hear, but the static continued until the end of the file.

'So much for that one. Let's try another.' I opened a second file, *Red Riding Hood*, and we heard much the same thing; young Crash, playing another song by himself in between long bursts of static. Birch confirmed it was another of the band's hits and while a third file wouldn't open, its file name was apparently the title of yet another chart-topping song.

'Are they all like this?' I wondered. 'What does it mean?'

But the last recording file, which did open, was different. It began with the now-familiar static burst, then cleared into Crash talking with Johnny. This time, even I could recognise their voices.

[Static]

Johnny: '—*believe you. This isn't proof.*'

Crash: '*Don't talk rubbish, man. Any fan will know the truth as soon as they hear it, and then you won't be able to cover it up any more.*

186

Really, I couldn't believe my luck when—'
[Static]
Crash: *'Think how much hiring experts would cost you. Besides, you're coining it in every year. Cheaper to pay up and then nobody else has to know.'*
Johnny: *'How do I know you won't go to the press anyway?'*
[Static]
Johnny: *'I've a mind to throttle you right here. Toss you over the side.'*
Crash: *'Oh, Johnny. You're not smart enough to get away with it . . . and your Da can't help you now, rest his soul.'*

The recording ended. Birch and I were both stunned.

'Damning,' he said. 'Practically a confession from Johnny. Surprised he'd allow that to be recorded.'

'He might not have known,' I said, and explained the one-button recorder Crash had used on me when he first showed me around. 'I had no idea he was recording until he played it back. It's faulty now, presumably thanks to whatever happened to the computer between then and me arriving. But at the time it worked like a charm.'

'Crash secretly records Johnny making threats. Keeps it on his computer in a password-protected folder. Why?'

I thought about what we'd just heard. 'Johnny wasn't the only one making threats, was he? "Pay up and nobody else has to know", Crash said. And Johnny was obviously afraid of Crash going to the press about something . . .' The answer struck me like a thunderclap. 'Oh! Silly us, we've got this the wrong way around. Crash wasn't paying Johnny a thousand pounds every week. Where did all that money in the safe come from?'

We looked at one another and simultaneously said, 'Blackmail!'

'This explains what I saw on Thursday,' I said. 'As I came out of Fox's boat, Crash and Johnny had their backs to me, arguing. Johnny took something from his pocket, but when they turned around it was gone.'

'Gone straight into Crash's pocket.' Birch nodded. 'Thursday, you said?'

'Yes, when Crash showed me around. This might also explain why Crash doesn't employ a cleaner. He wouldn't trust them not to snoop about.'

Birch pointed to the first few letters of the password. 'JOW-1000T, see? Jonathan Ormond-Wiles, one thousand, Thursday. A grand every week, in return for keeping a secret. Nice little earner.'

'It fits your idea of the missing dates being when they were on tour, too. There's no privacy on the road, so no way to keep the payments a secret. Better to wait until they're home, then pay double to catch up. And speaking of doubles . . .'

I closed the *Johnny* folder and clicked on *Fox* instead. Once again, the computer demanded a password. 'Read me the Fox one.' I typed it in as he did and the folder opened.

'FDJ-600W,' said Birch quietly. 'Fancy blackmailing your own wife for six hundred quid every Wednesday.'

'I'm sorry, Birch. This must shatter your illusions of Crash.'

'Not many left after almost forty years in the Met,' he said, but despite his brave face I could tell it hurt. He'd been a fan of Bad Dice for years but in the space of two days the singer had first been murdered, then revealed as a blackmailer.

I shuddered, remembering how I'd taken an immediate liking to Crash, largely because of his obvious love for Ace. He'd fooled us all.

The *Fox* folder contained another spreadsheet and several picture files. The spreadsheet was even more damaged than Johnny's, but it confirmed that Crash was collecting similar payments from Fox. The picture files were also in a bad state; only two would open and all they showed was part of Fox's houseboat from a high angle. The rest was bright green digital static.

'Shot from here, do you think?' said Birch.

I stood up and looked out the windows. The same view I'd seen the other night when recording on my phone, but bright and sunny. 'Yes, although it's zoomed in a lot. I wonder what he saw?'

'Impossible to tell from these. Something on her boat?'

'Oh, of course,' I said, remembering my morning hangover. 'It's the drugs. Fox is baking cannabis into cookies, and I think she's growing it in a spare room she doesn't show to the public.'

'Serious thing to have over someone. Consuming is a slap on the wrist these days but growing plants is a different matter. Dealing, even?'

'I hadn't thought of that. What a scandal that would be, the celebrity gardener dealing weed from her houseboat. If we're right, it would be a strong motive for her wanting Crash out of the way.'

Birch grunted. '*If* we're right. What's in the others?'

In the *Howard* folder was another spreadsheet, noting eight hundred pounds every Monday. Unlike the others, this one had a separate column for another day; every Wednesday, for five hundred pounds.

'Why do that instead of a single payment of thirteen hundred?' I wondered.

'Search me. What's in the photos?'

Most of them wouldn't open, and those that would were badly damaged. They appeared to be pictures of newspaper pages and screenshots of websites. I could make out the words 'scandal', 'reputation', 'substantial sum', and 'gave no comment', which could all have applied to many different things. Beyond that it was all indecipherable stripes of bright colours, like a TV set gone horribly wrong . . . apart from a blurry name on one photograph that looked like 'Vick'.

'Oh! It's Howard,' I said.

'Well, yes. Folder's got his name on it.'

'No, on the other recording. The one from Thursday. I'd hardly spoken to him when I first listened, so I didn't recognise his voice.'

I found the file on the computer desktop and played it again.

[Static]
Crash: '—*could have phoned, you know.*'
Howard: '*Not likely. Listen, we just want to talk. She—*'
[Static]
'*—very generous offer to resolve this once and for all. At least—*'
[Static]
Crash: '*—making your own generous offer to the likes of Vicki—*'
[Static]
Howard: '*—serious. Nine o' clock, all right? Don't be late.*'

'So Howard's involved in a scandal of some kind with a woman named Vicki, involving a "substantial sum". . . and he invited Crash to meet her? How odd.' I made a mental note for later, to search online for anything about Howard and a woman named Vicki.

'So far, all three of them had motive to kill Crash,' said Birch.

'Yes, and to want these files destroyed. I'm sure now that the damage to this computer wasn't accidental. Especially with that gold disc over the safe being askew.'

Birch nodded. 'Killer broke into the premises, disabled

the computer and attempted to crack the safe.'

'But they *didn't* break in, did they? There was no forced entry, so they must have taken Crash's keys after killing him. Then they did half a job on this computer and couldn't get into the safe at all. Why go to all that trouble if you weren't going to follow through?'

'Fair point. Interrupted, maybe?'

'But by whom? If someone else had come in on Friday morning and seen the killer, surely they'd have said something.'

'Unless the witness is now blackmailing them, too.'

My head spun with all these possibilities, so I turned to the final folder.

'Lucy Kwok, five hundred, T for . . . oh, of course. Thursday again.'

'Could be Tuesday, though.' Birch suggested.

'I don't think so. Lucy called at Crash's place on Friday morning, shortly after I arrived. She was rather cagey about why.'

'Um . . . Friday doesn't begin with a T.'

'No,' I explained patiently, 'but she said she'd called the night before, on Thursday, and got no answer. Crash was probably out walking Ace.'

I looked over at both dogs, dozing together on Ace's bed. That was a mistake because they immediately pricked up their ears.

'Let's quickly look at Lucy's folder before this pair get restless again.'

But then I heard the front door open. The dogs hadn't

pricked up their ears because I looked at them; they'd heard someone at the door long before us humans, and now leapt to their feet.

'No, *stay*—!' I hissed, but it was too late. Ace and Ronnie bolted past us and galloped down the stairs, barking. Birch and I ran after them, and halfway down the stairs came face to face with DCS Fletcher. Again.

'Superintendent,' I said, forcing a smile. 'We must stop meeting like this.'

CHAPTER TWENTY-ONE

'Nobody was outside the door when we came in,' I said, which was technically true. Constable Wright stood behind DCS Fletcher, looking simultaneously embarrassed and angry while Ronnie and Ace both circled around his legs. 'Also, I need to collect my possessions. After all, I can't stay here.'

The superintendent remained unimpressed. 'No, Ms Tuffel, you most assuredly cannot. In fact, I'd be grateful if you'd hand over your keys to this property.' I did, reluctantly. 'Thank you. Now, have you collected all your possessions?'

My cheeks flushed a little, thinking of the barely started jigsaw on the coffee table. 'Not yet. I was distracted by something we found upstairs that I think you should see.' I began climbing the stairs again.

'Stop there,' said Fletcher. 'Tell us what to look for and we'll find it ourselves.'

I ignored her and continued up. 'Impossible, I'm afraid. You'll see why.'

She and Birch, plus the dogs, crowded into the second-floor studio after me. I quickly showed Fletcher the files we'd found, explaining my blackmail theory.

'There's one folder remaining,' I said. 'Birch?'

He read out the password to the *Lucy* folder.

'Where did you find these passwords?' asked Fletcher. 'You should have given them to us.'

Birch cleared his throat. 'Matter of fact, you already have them. Notebook you found in the safe. Gwinny took photos.'

Fletcher reddened and glared at me. 'Ms Tuffel, I've overlooked your prior actions out of respect for your father, but this is too much.'

'Steady on,' said Birch, stepping in before I could respond. 'You've had the notebook since yesterday, but you didn't find this, did you? Gwinny's the one who figured out they were passwords. Without her you'd be stumped.'

I sat a little straighter in the chair, pleased that he was on my side this time. Fletcher certainly wasn't pleased, but at least she took Birch seriously.

'Sometimes, Alan, you can be infuriating.'

He nodded. 'Not the first to say it. Surely won't be the last.'

Before they could descend into an aphorism-off, I said, 'Shall we see what Lucy's been up to?' and opened the spreadsheet inside the folder. It confirmed the payments. 'Look here, though. These dates start three years ago, earlier than the others. Perhaps Lucy was the first person Crash blackmailed.'

'Must be something serious if it got him started down this path,' said Birch. 'What are the other files?'

There were two. One was an image, garbled enough that all we could see was part of the canal path at night, taken from a height. The second was another damaged recording. I played it:

> [Static]
> Crash: '—*fool me of all people, Lucy. Rock 'n' roll lifestyle [muffled]*'
> Lucy: '*So now what? [muffled] tell the police you'd have done it already.*'
> Crash: '*I still might. Unless of course we can come to a mutually beneficial—*'
> [Static]
> Crash: '—*small price to pay, don't you think? Sure and you must [muffled] already.*'
> Lucy: '*You scheming [muffled]. If you breathe a word of this to anyone, I'll—*'
> [Static]

'Good heavens,' I said when the recording ended. 'No prizes for guessing what was cut off there.'

'That sounded different to the others,' said Fletcher. 'Muffled, with lots of background noise. Like it was recorded outside.'

196

I nodded. 'If it was before this second floor was built, Crash wouldn't have had the easy recording set-up. He might have used his phone, in his pocket.'

'What was she so concerned about him coming to us about?' Fletcher mused.

'I don't know, but that's all of them. A rogues' gallery of blackmail victims, all with secrets to keep and a motive to kill Crash. Why now, though? This has been going on for years, with people happily paying up. Well, maybe not so happily. But what changed?'

'Something to do with the Carnival?' Birch suggested.

'Or maybe that was a convenient cover. Everyone expected Crash to be away for a long weekend anyway, and if his body hadn't surfaced during the opening ceremony none of us would be any the wiser. They'd be scouring bars in Dublin for him, not dredging Little Venice.'

Fletcher shook her head. 'You're leaping to conclusions again, Ms Tuffel. This material is damning, but it doesn't prove Mr Donnelly's death was murder.'

I could hardly believe my ears. 'After all this, you still think it was an accident? He was blackmailing four people!'

'Three of whom have alibis for the time of death,' said Fletcher, consulting her notes. 'At six o'clock Friday morning, Ms Double-Jones was on a video call with her daughter in Tokyo; six a.m. here is three p.m. there. Ms Kwok was at home with her husband, and you'll recall even volunteered information about someone she saw leaving the canal. Mr Zimmerman ran an online class, then went jogging; his colleague sent us an archived recording to confirm the class and he can be seen on CCTV footage of the surrounding area. We haven't been idle in checking the facts,' she added with not a small amount of hostility.

'What about Johnny Roulette?' asked Birch.

'Mr Ormond-Wiles is the one person with no corroborated alibi. He was asleep at home by himself, although several neighbours did see him an hour later.' She flipped her notes shut. 'The fact is that even if Mr Donnelly was killed, which I don't believe he was, it was most likely a random mugging.'

I tried to take this all in. 'Johnny told me he hardly ever sees his neighbours. But now, on the day he needs an alibi, suddenly they can vouch for him? Have you considered he might have deliberately made himself visible to throw you off?'

'He was having tea in his garden, Ms Tuffel. Hardly the stuff of criminal masterminds. The point is, combined with preliminary results from the pathologist, we don't believe this was murder.'

Birch's moustache twitched. 'Preliminary results?'

'Water in the lungs.'

The superintendent looked very self-satisfied by this revelation, while Birch looked crestfallen.

'Why is that bad?' I asked, confused by their reactions. 'Doesn't it just confirm he drowned?'

'It means he was alive when he hit the water,' Birch

explained. 'Dead men don't breathe.'

'OK, so maybe someone whacked him over the head and threw him in.'

'But there are no wounds on the body, remember?' Fletcher was being unbearably smug, and it made me so frustrated that I couldn't resist.

'Well, I think he was poisoned.'

I might as well have suggested Crash was killed by the Mafia by the look on Fletcher's face. Undeterred, I told her about Fox's drug-laced cookies and collection of poisonous plants.

'Hmmm,' she considered. 'We searched Ms Double-Jones's boat yesterday and didn't find any cannabis. But even if you're right, she didn't poison her husband.'

'She literally has a cabinet filled with deadly plants,' I protested. 'And she's clearly adept at cooking them into food.'

'As Alan said, dead men don't breathe. If Mr Donnelly had been poisoned and then thrown in the water, there would be nothing in his lungs.'

'Suppose he wasn't dead? She might have given him just enough to paralyse him.'

Birch intervened. 'Poisons don't really work like that. Even if they did, paralysis would also stop him breathing.'

I scowled, furious he wouldn't back me up, then turned to Fletcher. 'What do you mean, *if* I'm right about the cannabis?'

'There might be an innocent explanation. Perhaps you had a funny turn.'

'A funny turn?!' I leapt to my feet, which was a mistake because Ace also leapt to his, anticipating yet more exercise. But I was incensed. 'I might say the same of you! There's a man lying in your morgue whose death was unexpected, whose manner of death is unexplained, and who was blackmailing at least four of his neighbours, one of whom is an expert on poisonous plants and stands to inherit his entire estate, including this very boat. How can you be so blind? Look at this!'

I pulled out my phone and showed her the video I'd accidentally taken of Fox leaping over the fence on Friday night.

'Now, isn't that suspicious? Doesn't it at least merit investigation?'

She regarded me with a sceptical look. 'You say you took this?'

'Yes!'

'On Friday night?'

'Yes!'

'So more than twelve hours after Mr Donnelly died, then.'

'Well . . . OK, yes! But what if Fox was disposing of evidence?'

'What evidence? Evidence of what? Her alleged cannabis plants? Really, Ms Tuffel.'

She began talking about alibis and autopsies but I'd heard enough. I returned downstairs and clipped Ace's lead on when the Collie followed me down. Birch hesitated on the top step, his loyalties split. I gave him a single raised eyebrow, then turned and stomped out onto the path, startling Constable Wright.

DCS Fletcher had taken my keys to Crash's boat, but not to the access gate; that was Howard's, and still in my pocket, so I unlocked it and walked through. The crowd had finally gone, presumably giving up when they realised the police presence was here to stay.

Turning to lock the gate behind me, I was pleasantly surprised to see Birch step out of the boat and hurry in my direction. I softened a little and waited for him.

We walked in silence, Birch very sensibly understanding that I was in no mood for small talk. Instead of heading for Rembrandt Gardens we crossed the Grand Union bridge and turned down Delamere Terrace, heading for Westbourne Green. The Green was much larger than the Gardens and also well out of sight of both DCS Fletcher and the Little Venice houseboats, one of which I was convinced held a murderer. We stepped onto the grass and let the dogs off to run.

As usual, Ace began herding Ronnie and as usual the Lab remained oblivious. I envied him such calm but simply being here in the park with the dogs, and Birch, was helping my blood pressure. I took several deep breaths and wondered if I should take up yoga for real.

Birch finally spoke. 'Fletcher's just doing her job,' he said apologetically. 'Can't go off half-cocked chasing after a killer who might not exist.'

'I disagree, especially when someone like Johnny has no alibi. He's familiar with Fox's boat and would know how to get into the locked cabinet. If only we knew what he was being blackmailed for, we might also have a better clue as to his motive.'

'Still, bit unfair to call Fletcher blind. *Ronnie, no!*' He ran after the Lab, who was trying to climb a tree to get after a squirrel.

'Bah. Blind, deaf and—'

I stopped dead in my tracks as an elusive puzzle piece finally fell into place.

'Oh, my goodness,' I cried out. 'He's deaf!'

'No, just obstinate,' said Birch, dragging his black Lab away from the tree. 'Red mist descends when he sees a squirrel.'

'Not Ronnie. I mean Johnny Roulette.'

He looked confused. 'Johnny can't be deaf. He's a musician.'

'Beethoven was deaf as a post,' I protested. 'I don't think Johnny's lost all his hearing. He hides it very well, but in hindsight it's obvious.' I thought back to when I first met Johnny, then to seeing him in the park and his kitchen . . . 'Several times now I've stood behind him, or he's looked away when I said something and he didn't respond normally. Even the first time we met, Johnny wasn't facing Crash and didn't seem to hear him say my name. It explains so much.'

Birch puffed out his cheeks. 'Suppose it's possible. Surely by now he knows the songs well enough to play without needing to hear.'

'Could it be what Crash was blackmailing him over?

The recording talked about a "scandal" if the fans found out. Being exposed as deaf could spell the end of his career. That's more than enough motive for murder.'

'Might also explain why he deleted the photos. Perhaps Crash was planning to record new songs without Johnny. So you don't think it was Fox, after all?'

'Or perhaps it was a team effort,' I said, as a very different thought took shape in my mind. 'I should talk to the grieving widow again.'

CHAPTER TWENTY-TWO

The Carnival was in full swing, the noise easily travelling from the Pool to the residents' area. We approached Fox's barge, with its roof plants and bright rainbow colours, and found the main door open.

I handed Ace's lead to Birch. 'Stay here, in case Johnny Roulette or anyone else comes to see Fox. Keep them occupied until I get the truth out of her.'

'Right you are.' He gripped Ace and Ronnie's leads. 'If she tries to run, she won't get past me and this pair.' I doubted Fox would try anything of the sort, but I let Birch have his manly moment.

I stepped onto the boat and peered through the doorway but couldn't see anyone through the mass of plants and flowers. I knocked and called out, 'Hello? Fox?' No answer. If she was out visiting someone, surely she wouldn't leave her front door wide open?

I decided to act like a local and stepped inside, treading carefully around the pots and plants. How Fox could move around without knocking things over all the time I didn't know. Mind you, my own house was similarly cramped with my father's files, old *FT* copies and whatnot, and I managed. Fox probably knew the place well enough to navigate by muscle memory.

Unfortunately, so did her boat cat Lilith, about whom I'd forgotten until I felt something brush against my leg. I instinctively recoiled and stumbled over a stool, wincing as a plant pot crashed to the ground with a heavy thud. Thankfully it missed both Lilith and my foot by a hair's breadth. The cat sped away as I cursed and picked up the plant, wondering if I could scoop up the soil from the floor before Fox came in.

'Gwinny? What on earth are you doing?'

No such luck. I looked up to find her standing barefoot in a bathrobe, ready to thump me with a bright yellow watering can.

I raised my hands in surrender. 'I knocked, but there was no response so I came in to wait for you. I didn't think you'd be asleep at this time of day.'

She placed the watering can on a shelf. 'I—well, I haven't been sleeping much.' She said it implying grief, but I wondered if it was more of a guilty conscience. 'Why are you here?'

'Can we sit down? I think we need to talk. Before the police get involved.'

'The police are already involved. What are you talking about?'

A muffled *thump* sounded from the back of the boat.

Fox rolled her eyes and called out, 'Lilith, whatever you're doing, come away.'

But Lilith had retreated to her high bookshelf spot. I could see her eyes shining out from behind the cacti.

'Who's back there?' I said, not needing to ask why. Barefoot, bathrobe, too preoccupied in the bedroom to answer a knock at the door . . . 'Oh, darling, please tell me it's not Howard.'

Fox's disgusted reaction reassured me she wasn't completely doolally, but that left only one likely option; her partner in crime.

Sure enough, Johnny Roulette emerged from the bedroom with a small green bathrobe barely covering his wide body.

'Ah, Gwinny, is it,' he said with resigned nonchalance. 'How are you, pet?'

'Jonathan, what are you doing?' Fox admonished. 'It could have been anyone.'

He shrugged. 'Who is it we're keeping secrets from any more? The mean bastard's gone and nobody else cares. Wouldn't you say, Gwinny? Live and let live, isn't that right. We only get one go-around, you know. Man's time on earth is short and the heart wants what the heart wants.'

Overwhelmed by this barrage of clichés, I took a moment to gather my thoughts, took a deep breath, then plunged in.

'I know Crash was blackmailing you. Both of you.'

Fox and Johnny exchanged wary glances but said

nothing. I didn't want to name Crash's other victims; that would be their business to sort out with the police.

'Which means you both had a lot to lose and the opportunity to do something about it.'

'How—?' Johnny began, but Fox interrupted him.

'Jonathan, shush. Gwinny, why are you talking such nonsense? I think you should leave now.'

I held firm. 'Now that I think about it, Johnny wasn't the least bit surprised yesterday evening when I reacted badly to one of your cookies. I expect he knows all about the drugs in your spare room. Am I right, Johnny?'

'Spare room?' he repeated, seemingly confused. 'Sure you've lost me there. A few edibles and the odd spliff, so what? There's no harm in it.' He smirked. 'You were a proper sight in the park, though.'

'I'm glad you find it amusing. But while there may be no harm in imbibing, I'm reliably informed that actually growing cannabis is taken somewhat more seriously.' I turned to Fox. 'Serious enough for you to pay Crash six hundred pounds every Wednesday.'

Johnny turned open-mouthed to Fox. 'You what, now? I'll kill him. Well, I would have. You know what I mean. Fox, pet, say it's not true.'

Fox's expression turned from offence to confusion, then finally resignation. 'I'm afraid it is. Or, at least, half of it is.' She rounded on me. 'You're not as clever as you think. Yes, Crash was blackmailing me but it wasn't drugs. That spare room is where I keep Lilith's cat litter and dry my laundry. I'm not growing anything in there, and you can ask the damn police if you don't believe me. They went over the whole boat yesterday and found nothing.'

Johnny took Fox's hand. 'Then what for, pet? The nerve of him!'

Seeing their intimacy, more puzzle pieces fell into place for me. '"The spirit is willing, but the flesh is weak." That's what Crash said when I asked him about you living separately. I thought he meant he wasn't capable any more, but perhaps he was talking about your infidelity? Did he threaten to divorce you, this time, rather than the other way around? There'd be no question you were at fault. You'd be left high and dry.'

'He knew about us?!' Johnny spluttered. 'All this time, he didn't say a damn word!'

Fox squeezed his hand. 'He didn't care, love. He just wanted the money and I couldn't risk being cut out of his will.'

'To hell with his will! I've got more than enough for both of us.'

'But for how much longer?' I said. 'Even a rich musician like you must feel the sting of paying a thousand pounds every week.'

Johnny scowled at me. 'Now listen, I don't know what you've heard—'

'Everything, Johnny. Unlike you, and that's the problem, isn't it? You're going deaf. Are you really writing new songs? You may know your old songs well enough to play them without hearing the stage monitors, but recording and learning new songs would be much more difficult. Was that why you tried to delete those photos from my phone? Perhaps you couldn't bear the thought that Crash was writing new songs without you.'

Now it was Fox's turn to look aghast. 'Jonathan? Is this true?'

The guitarist looked frozen, like a deer in headlights. Then, to both Fox's and my surprise, he threw back his head and laughed heartily.

'Stage monitors! You should get out more, Gwinny, you and your pet copper. It's all in-ear, now, and I can hear fine with a pair of those plugged in.' He turned to Fox. 'I tried to keep it secret but Crash found out.'

'Was he really going to record new songs without you?' asked Fox.

He dismissed the idea. 'C'mon, who else would put up with his nonsense? No Roulette, no Dice. Crash knew that.'

'He also knew that Bad Dice is your life. I may be a music ignoramus but even I know the money these days is in touring, not record sales. You wrote the hits, but that's in the past. Without concerts your income would dry up.'

'It doesn't make sense,' said Fox. 'Jonathan's right, if he was forced to retire, people would stop paying to see them. It would have ruined Crash, too.'

I hadn't considered that, but it was easily explained. 'Even without Johnny's payments, he was still raking in other blackmail money. Plus, Johnny bowing out might have allowed Crash to record his new songs without a scandal. I'd say that's more than enough motive.'

Fox looked confused. 'Motive for what?'

'Killing Crash, of course. You poisoned him, didn't you? And then Johnny threw him in the canal. Was it in here? Or did you visit his boat on Friday morning at six o' clock?'

I wasn't sure what reaction I'd anticipated but *giggling* certainly wasn't on my list. That's what they both did, though; after a moment of shock, Fox and Johnny looked at each other and sniggered.

'Friday morning?' said Fox. 'I already told the police, I had a video call with Ellie in Tokyo. I was nowhere near Crash, let alone poisoning him.'

'Convenient that you happened to get up so early on that day, isn't it? Poison takes time to act. You could have administered it before calling your daughter.' I turned to Johnny. 'How's that cut on your arm? Guitar string, indeed.' He tried in vain to cover the sticking plaster with the tiny bathrobe's sleeve. 'It was you that Lucy Kwok saw climb over the access gate around six on Friday morning, wasn't it? She heard you cry out in pain because you slipped and cut your arm . . . in your haste to escape after throwing Crash in the water.'

Before he could protest, I continued, 'You have no alibi until an hour after he was killed, when you were seen at home. But you live less than ten minutes away. When you called me from Dublin on Saturday morning, asking where Crash was, were you trying to deflect suspicion?'

'You stupid woman,' said Fox, her amusement turning to anger. 'First of all, I'm hardly a stranger to getting up early after thirty years of TV and gardening. Second, use your eyes. Why do you think Johnny snuck away without wanting anyone to see him? We're not all celibate like you, Gwinny.'

'Sure and I was here with Fox all night, then left before she called young Ellie. I went straight to the gate and climbed over,' said Johnny. 'I admit it, that's how I got the gash on my arm. But I didn't even look at Crash's place as I went by, and it was before six.'

'You can't prove that,' I said. 'You could have disposed of Crash first, then climbed over the gate after six like Lucy said.' I remembered that she hadn't been completely certain about the time but Johnny didn't need to know that. 'There are no CCTV cameras along the path.'

'But they're on the traffic lights, aren't they? If the police check them they'll see me strolling across by the junction house, and before six o'clock. There's your proof.'

DCS Fletcher had said they confirmed Howard being out jogging with those same cameras. It was plausible Johnny would be on them, too.

'Well – perhaps you doubled back,' I protested. 'You know this area as well as any resident. It would be easy for you to evade the cameras, return to Crash's boat and kill him. Fox leapt over the fence the other night, you could have come in the same way.'

'Not this again,' Fox sighed.

'Don't deny it, I have you on video.' I turned back to Johnny. 'And with Crash dead, I bet your old records will shoot back up the charts.'

His face darkened. He got to his feet and closed the distance between us, looming over me. I regretted not bringing Birch along, but I refused to be intimidated and stood up to face the guitarist.

'Lord knows how you found out about the blackmail, but I swear on my mother's grave I didn't lay a hand on him, and Fox here will swear likewise. We don't need to hide ourselves any more now, and you've nothing but supposition and innuendo. So I think you should do as Fox asked and leave us alone.'

We glared at one another for a long moment, but he was right. I had a theory that fit the evidence but no proof it was anything more than coincidence. Without a confession the police couldn't act, and it was clear these two wouldn't crack easily. I backed away towards the door, not wanting to turn my back on him.

'Mind the plants,' said Fox. 'You've done enough damage.'

I cursed inwardly and hurried up the stairs.

CHAPTER TWENTY-THREE

Seeing my expression when I left Fox's place, Birch suggested we have a drink on the open top deck of the Pool's café boat. The Carnival was winding down for the day, so getting a spot was easy and the dogs were welcome. Both now lay under the table, eagerly accepting occasional strips of sliced ham from the pack in Birch's pocket, while I despondently stirred a tepid cup of coffee.

'Lucy was both right and wrong,' I said. 'She did see someone climbing over the gate, and Johnny admits it was him. But he was leaving Fox's place after spending the night and he insists it was before six.'

Birch nodded. 'Safe to assume he's not lying when CCTV from the road junction will prove it easily enough. Perhaps Crash was killed earlier than we thought?'

'I don't see how. He texted me at six on the dot, remember?' I clenched my fists in frustration. 'I was so convinced! Johnny was being blackmailed by a man he trusted, over something that could end his career. He admits climbing over the gate and the cut on his arm proves it anyway. Plus, he and Fox were having an affair and she knows poisons.'

'Can't say I'm surprised they want to move on, though,' said Birch. 'Everyone's blackmail secrets would have died with Crash if you hadn't found those passwords. Convenient for all.'

'I imagine that's why the killer tried to break his computer. Kill Crash, bury the truth and nobody need ever find out. Until we come along and royally mess up that plan, anyway. Now their secrets are out.'

'Not entirely. Still no idea what he had over Howard or Lucy. And much as I'm sure Fletcher would want to find out, they're under no obligation to tell her.'

I sipped my coffee, thinking. 'We know Howard is involved in a scandal with a woman named Vicki. On the recording it sounds like he owes her money. Could she be a loan shark? Does he have gambling debts?'

Birch smirked. 'Ironic to be blackmailed by a casino-themed band, then.'

'That would probably appeal to Crash's sense of humour.' On my phone I searched for *Howard Zee scandal Vicki*. 'Pity we don't know her last name. It would make finding her easier.'

I scanned down the meagre search results, none of which seemed at all related, then mentally kicked myself. 'Oh, Zee is a stage name, isn't it? What did DCS Fletcher call him?'

'Mr Zimmerman,' Birch recalled instantly.

'That's right. OK, let's see . . .' I retyped it as *Howard Zimmerman scandal Vicki*.

'Any joy?'

I laughed at the headlines. 'Not unless Howard is actually a Hollywood producer accused of cheating on his wife with a pornographic actress called Vikki. With two Ks.' I clicked on a *Variety* link and read the story, which was accompanied by photographs. 'Actually, I'm not sure if that's her name or her bra size.'

Birch coughed. 'Doubt that's our man.'

'Of course not. Howard's a former English teacher and already divorced. There's no sign of him in these search results but I suppose that makes sense. If it was a public scandal he wouldn't be susceptible to blackmail.'

My phone buzzed with a text message from Darren the builder, reminding me to move my car tomorrow so he could begin work on Tuesday. I groaned, feeling the energy drain from my body.

'Problem?' asked Birch, feeding the dogs another strip of cooked ham.

'The builder,' I said, tossing my phone onto the table in disgust. 'He's going to cost me a fortune. But I daren't tell him not to bother because it might take weeks to find someone else who can fit me in and they'll probably cost even more, and he was very belligerent, and if I send him away now he might bad-mouth me to all the other tradesmen in town and then none of them will want to work for me anyway.'

'Take a breath, ma'am. Look here.'

It took me a moment to realise he meant it literally. I looked up to find him holding my phone with the screen facing me, like he had in the park. Once again it unlocked upon seeing my face and he held a poised finger over it. 'Say the word, I'll tell this chancer to buzz off. Dealt with plenty of his type in my time.'

'Oh, my goodness!' I shouted, startling him, the dogs and a young couple sat two tables behind us to boot. 'Birch, you're a genius. Watch this.' Then I slumped in my seat with my eyes wide open and a slack jaw.

'Christ!' he exclaimed, jumping to his feet and knocking over what remained of his coffee. 'Gwinny, you're having a stroke! Can you hear me? Look at me and try to focus! I'll call an ambulance!' He began jabbing at my phone screen.

'No, no, give it here.' I snatched the phone from him before he could cause trouble. I was flattered by his concern, not to mention that he'd actually called me by my name for once, but this wasn't the time. 'I think we've been looking at this all wrong.'

'Wrong how?'

I resumed the slumped posture and let my head loll about. 'Do it again. Point my phone at me and see if it unlocks.'

He did, and it did, but he remained confused. 'Isn't that what it's supposed to do?'

'Yes, exactly,' I said, my mind working overtime. 'Now what if a killer did the same thing with Crash's phone, before they threw him in the water? What if the

216

text I got at six o'clock wasn't sent by him at all?'

Birch perked up, finally understanding. 'Killer unlocked his phone and sent you a message, pretending to be Crash, so we'd think he was still alive.' His expression darkened. 'Means the killer knew you were coming here to look after Ace.'

'Yes, and that confirms it was probably one of his blackmail victims. I met them all on Thursday. Well, apart from Lucy. Howard introduced us on Friday morning, by which time Crash was already dead. But she's obviously close to Howard, so he might have told her the night before.'

Two memories, one distant and one very close, clashed in my head. I checked the previous messages on my phone.

'Crash texted me at half past eight on Thursday evening, to say he'd given Johnny my number. Nobody except the three of us knew he'd agreed to do that, so it must be real.'

'Unless Johnny's the killer. Could have been setting up his alibi.'

'But then why not set one up for Friday morning, too, when we all thought Crash had been killed? Johnny's the one person *without* an alibi at that time, remember.'

Memories nagged at me. Something about Friday . . .

'Lucy! The box!' I shouted, earning another loud *tut* from the young couple behind us. They got up and moved to a table further away.

Birch threw up his hands. 'You've lost me.'

I leant down and fussed Ace's ears. 'Lucy tried to visit Crash on Thursday night but he wasn't in. Then there's the box from Choudhury's.' I explained about the singer's habit of collecting a cardboard box from the grocer for Ace. 'He said he'd pick up a fresh one Friday morning before leaving for the airport. But Mr Choudhury hadn't seen Crash since Tuesday. I assumed he'd simply run out of time.'

'Maybe he did, in more ways than one.'

'Exactly. I think this confirms that Crash was already dead on Friday morning, and in fact could have been killed at any time after half-past eight on Thursday.' I felt a sudden surge of anger. 'No wonder Ace couldn't wait to relieve himself when I arrived. He'd spent all night alone on the boat with nobody to let him out.'

'We're dealing with someone smart,' said Birch. 'Smart enough to plan ahead.'

I nodded agreement. 'And willing to kill to keep their secrets. It makes me wonder if anyone else is in danger . . .'

As we pondered this, my phone rang with a call from an unknown number.

'Another celebrity dog-sitting enquiry?' said Birch, seeing the display.

'Let's find out,' I said, answering the call on speakerphone. 'Hello?'

'Is that Gwinny?' asked a woman's voice.

'Speaking, yes. Who's this?'

'Is Howard with you, for some reason?'

That stumped me. 'I'm sorry, what? Who is this?'

'Lucy Kwok, of course.' Evidently, not being immediately recognised was an alien concept to her. 'I'm scheduled for a private session with Howard but his door is locked, his phone goes to voicemail and nobody's seen him.'

Birch and I both turned to look in the direction of the houseboats.

'Lucy,' I said, 'find the police. They might still be at Crash's place. We'll be there in two minutes.'

CHAPTER TWENTY-FOUR

When we arrived at Howard's boat we found Lucy trying to peer through the windows, but they were all curtained. Muffled music sounded from inside.

'Why did you think he might be with me?' I asked. Lucy now wore a sporting top, leggings and trainers. A rolled-up towel carried under her arm completed the look, even though I had a hard time picturing her working up any kind of sweat.

'I already asked everyone else,' she replied. 'I've been too busy with the Carnival to keep track of people. This is my wind-down time, to recentre my energy.'

Remembering Howard's offer to me of a 'personal one-to-one session', I wondered again what kind of relationship he and Lucy had. Was Crash blackmailing her over an affair with the guru? That didn't fit with his threat to go to the police, though. Adultery was scandalous but not a crime.

'What's going on? Howard's not picking up.' Latesha Michaels, Howard's American business partner, approached and held up her phone as if to demonstrate the lack of answer. Other residents now began to gather, wondering what the commotion was for. A small crowd was even forming on the other side of the Blomfield Road fence, as people peered through the railings to see what the fuss was about.

'Aren't you both flying out soon?' I asked Latesha. 'Could he be renewing his visa at the American Embassy?'

'Howard took care of that weeks ago and we leave tomorrow. He should be here, and besides, he's never without his phone.'

'So much for tranquillity and escaping modern life.'

She either didn't get my meaning or chose to ignore me, instead stepping onto the deck and pulling on the door. It didn't open. She turned to the crowd and shouted, 'Someone call the cops! They need to break down this door.'

'I already called them,' said Lucy.

'Besides, we don't know for sure he's inside,' I pointed out. 'Anyway, I doubt he'd thank us for destroying his door if he's having an afternoon nap.'

'Afternoon nap?' Lucy protested. 'Impossible. My session should have started eight minutes ago.'

'That's right,' said Latesha. 'It's on his calendar. His last session before we leave tomorrow.'

Lucy reddened slightly. 'You can see his calendar?'

'Zabok+ is about to make Howard one of its leading brands. His business is our business. That's why I need someone to break down this door!'

One or two people standing in the road had begun to climb the fence for a better view, and there was still no sign of DCS Fletcher.

'For heaven's sake,' I muttered, handing Ace's lead to Birch. 'Take the dogs and keep those people behind the fence. I'll climb around and see if he's in.'

'Can you swim?' he asked cheekily.

'Such confidence you have in me.' I hauled myself onto the deck beside Latesha. Remembering how the Carnival sculptress had moved around her boat, I gripped the roof lip, placed a foot on the gunwale and swung myself out onto the water side. I looked over to see Birch approaching the fence, and the gawping climbers begin to retreat.

The music from inside became louder as I approached the saloon window. Holding onto the lip with one hand, I leant down and peered in. The curtains were open on this side, and apart from Howard's absence the room looked normal. His giant TV screen was turned off, but the camera and lights were in their usual place with some weights scattered around.

That gave me pause. I'd only been inside briefly but it had been tidy and ordered, and on the workout video I'd watched he carefully replaced every weight on the rack after use. But now two small weights rolled loose and the floor mat was askew. Nearby a plastic jug lay under a side table with what looked like the residue of a green mixture inside. One of his health smoothies, no doubt.

I pulled myself upright in time to see DCS Fletcher

finally approaching, with Constable Wright in tow.

'What's going on?' the superintendent called out.

'Lucy will explain,' I said and continued shuffling along the gunwale. Next was a window into the galley kitchen, with Howard's packs of protein and health supplement packs lined up against the splashback.

Beyond that, though, was a strange sight. I couldn't see much beyond the counter, especially from my precarious position, but on the floor lay what looked like . . . a pair of jogging pants? Howard's or someone else's? Were we interrupting a 'wellness' session with one of his clients? It would explain the loud music but it didn't seem likely Howard would have forgotten his appointment with Lucy.

A piercing whistle blasted my ears, startling me. One foot slipped off the gunwale and my fingers held on to the lip for dear life. The whistle was followed by someone shouting '*Where's your drone, Spider-Gran*?!' A tourist boat sped past on its way to Camden, carrying drunk Carnival-goers who shouted and jeered at me while filming on their phones. If I hadn't been clinging on to stop myself falling in, I'd have given them two fingers, but instead I had to be happy with merely staying dry and telling them to buzz off. I righted myself, caught my breath and resumed shuffling along.

'Seen anything?' Lucy shouted from the path, oblivious to my well-being. I looked over the roof to see her keeping pace.

'Something seems off,' I said, 'but no sign of Howard.'

'Well, get a move on, then.'

I fought the urge to growl at her and finally came to a window in the bow. Most boats had their bedrooms here and Howard's was no exception. The curtain was only half-drawn, leaving enough of a gap to see inside. It looked very much as I expected, with black silk sheets, a large mirror . . . and a hairy, athletic body, wearing nothing besides boxer shorts, sprawled on the bed.

Howard Zee lay unmoving, his eyes closed and head lolling towards the floor, with green drool dribbling from the side of his mouth.

CHAPTER TWENTY-FIVE

'Superintendent!' I called out. 'You'd better force the door after all. Howard's in there, but he's not moving.'

'No!' cried Latesha Michaels, with genuine concern. DCS Fletcher guided her back onto the path while Constable Wright prepared to force the door of Howard's boat.

Still looking through the window, I heard the crunch of splintered wood, a sudden increase in music volume from within (and an equally sudden silence when someone mercifully turned it off), then finally watched the police rush into the bedroom. Fletcher took Howard's wrist in hand, checking for a pulse.

In response, he sat bolt upright and vomited bilious green goo down her shirt.

Fletcher recoiled as Howard doubled over, coughing. He was obviously in distress and pain, but also obviously alive. I knocked on the window to get her attention and mimed sliding the window open. She came around the bed and opened it to talk.

'Sorry about your shirt. As I passed the lounge I saw a half-empty smoothie jug that had fallen on the floor, and the drink in it was a very similar colour to what you're wearing. You should take a look.'

'Much obliged, I'm sure,' she grumbled. 'Some kind of allergic reaction, no doubt. If he was having difficulty breathing, it would explain why he shed his clothes.'

'Don't you think it's more likely he was poisoned? First Crash, now this.'

She rolled her eyes. 'Why don't you come inside and we'll discuss it?'

'I'm an actor, darling, not a contortionist.' I gestured at the one-foot-square window opening. 'Besides, the boat's now a crime scene, isn't it?'

'Only if—look, never mind. I'll see you outside.' She slid the window closed as Constable Wright helped Howard up and placed a bathrobe around his shoulders.

I took the short way around the front bow and hopped onto the path to relay the good news to everyone. Well, not exactly *good*, but certainly better than the alternative.

'Not sure you'll be catching that flight,' I said to Latesha.

'What are you, nuts? This is all the more reason to get the hell out of here. Some psycho is killing people and I'm not sticking around so they can try again. I've been working on this deal for months.'

'Killing people?' said Lucy, overhearing. 'Wasn't this an accident?'

I shook my head. 'First someone killed Crash, most likely with poison, and now they tried to do the same to Howard. The question is, why?'

'What do you mean, poison? Crash drowned. The whole of Little Venice saw it!'

Fox and Johnny, now dressed, had come to see what was going on. Johnny rolled his eyes. 'Gwinny thinks someone poisoned Crash on Friday morning then threw him in the water. In fact, she thought it was me, because of this.' He pulled up his sleeve to show the plaster on his arm.

Lucy took a step backwards. 'It was you I saw climbing over the gate! Right after someone screamed!'

'For God's sake, I didn't scream. I caught myself on the railing and yelled, that's all. Besides, you should check your clock. It was before six and Crash didn't die until after that, right?' He looked to me for confirmation.

Birch approached and handed Ace to me. I gladly took him, thankful for something to do with my hands while I broke this particular news.

'Actually, I'm not so sure. I think Crash's killer faked the text message to me, and if so, it means he could have been murdered on Thursday evening.'

'Never found his phone, did they?' said Birch, backing me up. 'Killer might have taken it.'

'Well, then someone call the bloody thing and listen for the ringtone,' said Fox.

'The police already tried that,' I said. 'It's probably at the bottom of the canal. What matters is that everyone's alibis for Friday morning are now useless.'

'*If* this and *could* that and *probably* the other,' said Johnny in disgust. 'Such claptrap. You're obsessed, Gwinny, and it's not healthy, you know. Why would anyone kill Crash?'

It was almost like he was daring me to expose the blackmail in front of everyone, but I wouldn't. Fox and Johnny knew about each other, but nobody else knew the identity of Crash's other victims and I felt it best to keep things that way for now.

'Well, I can tell you Howard's out of the picture,' said Latesha.

'Because he had an allergic reaction to a health drink?' said Lucy. 'That doesn't make sense.'

'OK, first of all, no way is Howard stupid enough to mix in something he's allergic to. Someone tampered with his smoothie. But it doesn't matter because he had live sessions all Thursday night.' Latesha turned to me. 'You can see for yourself on the recording stream. So don't come at me with this murder nonsense.'

The police brought Howard out of the boat and sat him down. He took deep breaths, his head hung between his legs, looking seriously worse for wear. But at least he was alive. Latesha fussed around him. Everyone else dispersed, the emergency and excitement over. Fox and Johnny returned to her houseboat while Lucy took her towel and expensive yoga outfit back home.

'Damned good luck we all got here in time,' said

Birch. 'Another five minutes, who knows what the effects might have been?'

'That depends on what was actually mixed into his smoothie ingredients. But Latesha's right; if anyone around here knows their own allergies, or is careful about what they consume, surely it's Howard. Someone must have snuck into his kitchen and poisoned his ingredients.'

'Why, though?' he pondered. 'Doesn't seem likely to be related to blackmail. Something else that connects Crash and Howard?'

'Why don't we ask him?'

Now that Howard was no longer in danger of keeling over, the police had gone inside to check the boat, leaving him and Latesha alone on the deck. He smiled as we approached.

'Apparently, I should thank you, Gwinny. If you hadn't climbed around and looked in the window, I might be dead by now.'

'The superintendent thinks you had an allergic reaction,' I said. 'Is that likely?'

Before Howard could answer, Latesha said, 'I already told you, he's not stupid.'

'I'm not so sure of that.' He gently squeezed Latesha's hand. 'I don't have allergies, but I was obviously stupid enough to leave my door unlocked so someone could sneak in and tamper with my plants.'

'Plants?' said Birch, confused. 'Thought you were drinking a milkshake.'

'Smoothie,' I corrected him. 'Get with the times. Howard, what exactly happened?'

'I'd finished a quick workout and I had some time before my appointment with Lucy. It was to be our last ever, so I knew it would be an intense session. I made a kale smoothie to fuel myself before we started, and . . .' He shook his head, as if searching for a memory. 'I think I went into the lounge? I don't remember much else until I threw up on that policewoman.'

How 'intense' a session he and Lucy had in mind was neither here nor there for the moment. More immediate were two concerns. First, if it was a poisoned plant smoothie that had made Howard ill, Fox was well and truly back on the suspect list. The second concern, as Birch pointed out, was motive. What connected Crash to Howard besides blackmail?

'Your relationship with Crash,' I said, trying to impart as much meaning as I could without spelling it out. 'Is that something we can talk about in private?' I nodded toward Latesha, hoping Howard would understand.

He didn't. 'We have no secrets,' he said, squeezing her hand again.

'Even about . . . Vicki?'

He'd been pale already, but now all remaining colour drained from Howard's face.

'Who's Vicki?' asked Latesha warily.

'Someone Howard owes money to,' said Birch. He was bluffing a little, of course, but the recordings we heard between Howard and Crash certainly suggested that.

Remembering something else Crash said, I was struck with inspiration. 'I thought it might be gambling debts,' I said, 'but now I wonder . . . are you hiding out from your ex-wife to avoid support payments?'

Howard stared at me for a moment, then exhaled heavily and hung his head. His shoulders relaxed, as if he was glad to finally get it out in the open.

'How did you know?' he asked.

I glanced at Latesha, who was silently processing this news about her star-in-waiting. 'Crash said you'd moved here following a divorce. And I know that he's been, um . . . holding it over you for the past couple of years.'

Mild panic showed in his eyes. 'He told you that?'

'Not exactly. It's a long story. But I'm sure the police will want to discuss it with you in light of Crash's death.'

'He was the worst. Washed up, star fading and vindictive with it. But I didn't kill him! I was . . . too open with him when I first moved here. I thought a rock star of all people would sympathise but instead he saw me as a new source of money. Not like he was making any from his music any more.'

'Source of money?' said Latesha, quickly understanding the situation. 'Were you paying him off? Where is this ex-wife, anyway?'

'I actually don't know. She moved out of the old house and that's the last I heard. But Crash said he was in contact with her.'

'You should have come to me. We deal with gold-digging exes all the time.'

Howard smiled nervously. 'Well, she won't be able to follow me to the States, right?'

'If she does, she's gonna run right into our lawyers, and they don't mess around. You shouldn't worry about it.'

He squeezed her hand again. 'I was hoping you'd say that. I'm sorry.'

'This is all very therapeutic,' I butted in, 'but it doesn't explain why you arranged to meet Crash at nine o' clock on Thursday.'

The mild panic showed again. 'You said he didn't tell you anything.'

'Crash had a habit of recording things, including a conversation you both had on Thursday after I left. Parts of it are damaged but others are quite clear. The upshot is that you offered to make a "generous payment", Crash said you should pay Vicki instead, and you told him to meet you at nine.'

'Whoa, hold on,' said Latesha. 'Generous payment? I thought you were already paying him.'

Howard shrugged. 'I tried to buy him off completely. What else could I do? I wanted this over before I moved to America.'

That made sense. Handing over cash in person was one thing, but if Howard had to start wiring large amounts to Crash every week, it wouldn't take long for someone to notice and ask questions.

He turned to me. 'You misunderstand. We were going to meet at nine o'clock on Friday morning, not Thursday.

Now I know why he didn't show up, so I went jogging instead.'

'Hold on, though,' I said. 'By nine a.m. on Friday he should have been on a plane to Dublin anyway. Why would he arrange to meet you then?'

Howard shrugged. 'I don't know. He didn't mention that to me.'

This cast a very different light on things. It could mean that Crash never intended to fly to Dublin on Friday morning. Why lie? Was it somehow connected to his death?

DCS Fletcher and Constable Wright emerged from the boat. The young constable carried Howard's half-empty smoothie jug in a plastic evidence bag.

Fletcher placed a firm but friendly hand on Howard's shoulder. 'Mr Zimmerman, can I ask you to accompany me to the station and give a victim statement? It won't take long.'

'Why? I'm fine now. There's nothing I can tell you.'

'Even so, sir. For the record.'

'I'm coming with you,' said Latesha.

'Can I at least get dressed?'

Fletcher agreed and sent the constable to accompany Howard back inside the boat.

'Presume you're on board that Crash was murdered, now?' Birch asked the superintendent. 'Lucky this one didn't succeed, I'd say.'

Fletcher pursed her lips. 'There's no obvious connection between the two incidents, but I've seen enough to make an arrest for this one. Looking twice is fifty-fifty, as they say.'

I wasn't sure anyone said that besides Fletcher herself, but let it slide. 'Who do you suspect?'

'Only one person had means and opportunity,' she said, already striding back along the path. We all knew who she meant.

'Note that she didn't mention motive, though,' I said as we watched her approach the rainbow-coloured boat. 'Why would Fox want Howard out of the way?'

'Mind of a killer can be hard to fathom,' said Birch. 'Fletcher may not see a connection, but the blackmail gave Fox motive. Perhaps after that she snapped.'

'How does him blackmailing Howard give Fox motive?' asked Latesha.

I wished Birch hadn't mentioned that, but the cat was now out of the bag. 'Howard wasn't Crash's only victim,' I explained. 'He was blackmailing Fox as well.'

Latesha whistled. 'His own wife? OK, this I have to see.'

Now dressed, Howard emerged from his boat and we walked along the path together, following the sounds of Fox and Johnny protesting her innocence. DCS Fletcher finally led the widow out, with the guitarist hot on their heels.

He saw me and shouted, 'Is this your doing? I've a mind to teach you a lesson!'

He loomed over me, all bluster and pointed fingers. Johnny was a big man; if he decided to thump me, I'd know about it. I took a step back, and the space was immediately occupied by Ace. The Collie stood between us and barked angrily at the guitarist's raised voice. Then Birch reached out to block Johnny with a straight arm and gently but firmly pushed him back. For once I was glad of the former policeman's protective tendencies.

'Wouldn't advise that, sir,' he said quietly. Johnny glared at him but Birch held his ground. 'I expect the DCS has sufficient reason to make an arrest, and threatening others won't help Mrs Double-Jones's case.'

'Absolutely,' said Fletcher. 'One of the poisonous plants in her cabinet has had a leaf clipped. Good chance it'll match what's in that tampered smoothie jug.'

'But everyone knows where I keep the key to that cabinet,' Fox protested. 'It's hardly a secret.'

'Surely you'd have noticed if one of your plants was missing a leaf?' I said.

She turned to me and shouted, 'I've been kind of preoccupied with my husband's death, in case you didn't notice! If I was going to poison someone, do you think I'd use one of my own plants? How stupid do you think I am?'

DCS Fletcher pulled her away. 'I must remind you that you're under caution, madam. Anything you say—'

'Oh, shut up. I didn't do anything! Why would I poison Howard? I hardly know the man!' She turned back to me. 'Just like you! Think you're so clever but you don't really know me, or any of us! I hope you choke on your own self-righteousness!'

I was stunned into silence, which I suppose was the desired effect. Birch puffed out his cheeks as the superintendent led her to a waiting police car. Johnny accompanied her while Constable Wright guided Howard and Latesha after them. Within moments, we were alone.

'Rum do,' said Birch. 'Watch her on telly, you wouldn't think she'd say boo to a goose.'

'Who we are in front of a camera is often very different to reality. Even so-called factual presenters are still playing a part.'

'Do you think she did it?'

I pondered the question. 'Honestly, I don't know. She had motive to kill Crash and her alibi for Friday is useless now. But she's right; what motive does she have to kill Howard? He seemed as confused as anyone about why he was targeted.'

'Possible he wasn't the intended victim? Milkshake was meant for someone else?'

An idea formed in my mind. 'What if the killer knew Lucy was due to have a session with Howard and expected them to share the smoothie?'

'Bit thin, if you don't mind me saying.'

'It is, isn't it?' I conceded. 'Perhaps we can remedy that. Fox was right about something else, too: I don't know these people half as well as I'd like. Let's pay Lucy a visit.'

236

CHAPTER TWENTY-SIX

Number 30 Blomfield Road was a beautiful white-fronted home with a gleaming Audi parked in the driveway and a doorstep of immaculate checkerboard tiles. Looking at it with more than a little envy, I decided I should definitely get the number of Lucy's builder.

I rang the buzzer. Nobody answered. I buzzed again. Still no answer.

'She only left a few minutes ahead of us. Did she definitely come back here?' I asked Birch.

'Think so. Could have run in and back out again?'

'Not without changing first. Can you imagine Lucy popping to the shops in leggings?' He said nothing, but adopted the far-away look of someone trying to do just that. I nudged him and said, 'That's enough. You're literally old enough to be her father.'

Birch coughed, and I turned back to the door as it finally opened.

A handsome middle-aged man looked at me with an

expression bordering on disgust. He wore a standard weekend casual outfit of shirt, slacks, and pullover, though with the unexpected addition of a bright yellow domestic rubber glove on one hand.

'We're not religious,' he said automatically, putting paid to my initial thought that Lucy might employ a housekeeper. Then I wondered what kind of evangelists they got round here who brought their dogs along. Didn't seem practical.

'I'm Gwinny,' I said quickly as he made to close the door, 'from across the road. Well, sort of. I'm a friend of Lucy's. Sort of. Look, is she here? I'd like to talk to her, especially after what just happened at the boats. With Howard.'

That was the first thing I'd said that got a reaction and I wondered if he had the same suspicions about Lucy and Howard as I did.

'I'm sorry, are you . . . Mr Kwok?' I asked. He didn't look Asian but I wasn't about to judge.

'Obviously not,' he said in a tone implying he'd been asked many times before. 'Lucy kept her maiden name for professional purposes. But I'm her husband, if that's what you really meant to ask.'

That certainly told me. He hadn't invited us in, although with two dogs in front of him and what looked like a spotless house behind, I wasn't surprised. Perhaps he *was* Lucy's housekeeper, after all. A 'house husband', as they say. I didn't care, but if Lucy did, it might explain why she'd asked me not to call round.

'I assume you've heard about the recent attacks, sir?' said Birch, in the unmistakeable cadence of a policeman. Retired he may be, but I doubted that would ever leave him.

'Attacks? I know they pulled that singer out of the canal. What else has happened?'

'Oh, for God's sake, Geoff, haven't you got rid of them yet?'

Lucy appeared in the hallway behind him, still wearing her sporting clothes.

He looked back and forth between us. 'This policeman said there have been – I'm sorry, are you police? I assumed – but he said—'

'Yes, I'm sure he did, but he's retired.' Lucy approached, annoyed at both our presence and her husband's vacillating. 'I told you, Howard had some kind of allergic reaction to his smoothie, it's why I'm back early. Gwinny insists he was poisoned, though. She's an actress,' she added, as if that explained everything.

'He *was* poisoned,' I protested. 'The police, that is to say the not-retired ones, have arrested Fox. It looks like she added one of her toxic plants to Howard's ingredients. He might have died if you hadn't sounded the alarm.'

'Keep your voice down,' she hissed. Did they have children? Lucy seemed about as maternal as me, which is to say not at all.

'I'm not deaf, and I'm not stupid either, much as you might wish it,' said another voice from inside the house.

I didn't see anyone, but then Lucy stood aside to reveal an old woman standing directly behind her. Ninety if she was a day, the woman's back was bent and she used a stick for support, but her voice was clear and certain.

'I didn't want to worry you, *maa maa*,' said Lucy, glancing back to shoot daggers at me. 'It's nothing to do with us.'

'We-e-e-ell . . .' I pulled a face. 'I think Crash would have disagreed. Don't you?'

Daggers became longswords, and if looks could kill Lucy would have murdered everything within a fifty-foot radius.

'Oh, this sounds good,' her grandmother chuckled. 'Bring them in, I want to hear everything.'

Suddenly everyone spoke at once.

'No, I think it would be better if—'

'Absolutely not letting those dogs—'

'I just finished cleaning this floor—'

The old woman banged her stick on the ground. 'Then you can clean it again after they've gone, can't you? I'm not dead yet, so this is still my house. I want to know what's going on.'

Lucy deflated, admitting defeat. I actually felt a little sorry for her, knowing from personal experience the impossibility of defying a matriarch once their mind was set. My mother had been perfectly happy to let my father run the household, so long as he did everything she said.

Geoff stepped back and opened the door to let us in while Lucy and her grandmother retreated into the

240

lounge. Birch and I followed with dogs in tow. Ronnie wanted to sniff every inch of this new place, while Ace's head rotated this way and that to take in the environment. He didn't try to pull me in any particular direction, though, so I guessed he'd never been in this house before.

'Actually, could I use your bathroom?' I asked Lucy. 'All the excitement, you know.'

She reluctantly directed me upstairs. I handed Ace off to Birch and quickly went up, leaving them all heading into the lounge. I really did need to go, but I was also curious about this house now that I knew it didn't belong to Lucy. Presumably she was hoping to inherit, although I wondered why it wouldn't go to her parents instead.

Upstairs was as clean and sparkling as the hallway and frontage. Geoff could have made good money doing this for a living; I almost felt bad using the bathroom, it was so spotless. But telltale signs of the elder Mrs Kwok were everywhere. Helper bars mounted around the bath, a wet room floor conversion and a booster toilet seat folded away by the radiator. After ten years of caring for my own father, I recognised them all.

I finished and left, trying to leave the room as I'd found it. It was quiet up here; if Lucy did have children, they were either out or unrealistically well behaved. Mind you, if she'd had them young, they could have already left home.

I quietly opened the nearest door, just for a quick peek, and immediately regretted it when a towel fell on me. It was a cupboard, one much less orderly than the visible parts of the house. Towels, bedding, a couple of brooms, canvas bags and cardboard boxes were all messily piled on shelves or sitting on the floor. I hastily threw the towel back on a shelf, closed the door, and decided not to push my luck any further.

Descending the stairs, something in my memory began to surface. It came to me as I entered the lounge, which was another shining example of Geoff's handiwork, lined with bright paintings and photographs of canal boats.

'I'm surprised you don't live on the water, given how much you obviously love it,' I said.

'I did,' said Lucy coldly. 'My parents still do. But some of us take our responsibilities seriously.'

I felt another pang of sympathy for her as I recognised more signs; a low, soft and comfortable chair, which matched nothing else in the room, was the elder Mrs Kwok's daily sanctuary. On either side stood occasional tables piled high with magazines, books, a reading magnifier, remote controls for the television and DVD player, and more. As I watched, the grandmother moved a newspaper to reveal a tin from which she took a piece of shortbread.

She popped it in her mouth and said, 'Come on, then, start talking.'

'Wait a moment,' I said, and took my phone from my handbag. Lucy snorted impatiently.

Then I found the right place and held up my phone for her to see. I played the accidental video recording

I'd made on Friday night, cued up at the moment the hooded figure left Fox's boat and leapt over the fence.

'This is you, isn't it? That tartan canvas bag is very distinctive, and you're sprightly enough to jump over the fence like that.'

'Rubbish,' she said. 'It could be anyone.'

'I'm sure that was the idea, yes. I even thought it was Fox, at first, as it's her boat you're leaving. But I just saw that same tartan bag in a cupboard upstairs, and this is you wanting to avoid the CCTV cameras at either end of the road. Is that why you made such a fuss to the police about seeing someone climb over the gate? Because you didn't want them thinking too hard about people jumping the fence?'

'What do you mean, in a cupboard? Were you sneaking around?' Lucy's voice rose. 'God, you're as bad as—' She stopped herself before saying any more, but I knew she was going to say *as bad as Crash*.

Mrs Kwok's eyes darted keenly back and forth between us but poor Geoff looked bewildered.

'I'm sorry, I don't understand,' he said. 'None of this makes sense.'

'It does if you know that Fox is well practised at baking cannabis into biscuits. Are you enjoying yours, Mrs Kwok? Good for your back pain, I imagine.'

The old lady popped another piece of shortbread in her mouth and grinned.

Lucy glared at me. 'This has nothing to do with Crash's death.'

'Doesn't it?' said Birch. 'Criminal escalation's a common pattern.'

'Do you remember when we met, Lucy? We were with Howard and you froze up when I said that you must having an "interesting relationship". I was talking about Crash and wondered if you'd misunderstood me, thinking I meant Howard. But now I realise you were actually worried I knew about your relationship with Fox. Because that's why Crash was blackmailing you, isn't it?'

Geoff looked ready to burst a blood vessel. 'Blackmail?!' he cried. 'What the hell?'

Lucy didn't take her eyes from me. 'Why would he tell you? He hardly knew you.'

'That's true. But you're right, I'm as bad as Crash. I've found recordings of you pleading with him not to say anything about the drugs to the police. Or, I assume, your husband.'

'Nonsense,' Geoff said. 'Of course I know about the drugs. But blackmail? The impudence of the man!' He looked ready to murder Crash all over again, if he hadn't been already dead. 'How long has this been going on?'

Lucy hesitated before she answered. 'About three years.'

'On one of those recordings you also threatened to, um, do something very nasty if Crash told anyone. Did you run out of patience? Or money?'

She swept the accusation aside. 'We're fine for money, thank you for asking. I told you, I didn't kill him.'

'Who else was he blackmailing?' said Mrs Kwok suddenly.

I turned to her. 'What makes you think he was?'

'They never stop at one, young lady. I grew up in Hong Kong, you know.' I waited for her to elaborate, but she said no more.

'It's true,' I said, 'There were others.'

'If the police have arrested Fox for poisoning Howard, maybe she killed Crash as well,' said Lucy. 'He knew she was baking the shortbread.'

I wondered then if Fox had lied to me about her own blackmail, letting me make wrong assumptions. An affair with Johnny was one thing, but much as the police might often turn a blind eye, cannabis remained illegal.

'Where do you get it from?' I asked, suddenly picturing Lucy's attic converted to a plant nursery but dismissing the thought. 'Surely your grandmother wouldn't want to grow them inside her own house?'

'From a dealer, like everyone else,' Lucy said with an air of resignation. 'I buy it, I give it to Fox, she pays for half and bakes the other half into cakes.'

'And you do all this late at night, coming and going over the fence to avoid being seen. Does the money from Fox go towards paying off Crash?' She nodded, and I continued, 'But not any more. With him gone you can turn what was a monthly cost into a tidy profit.'

'Do you really think I'd murder him over a few hundred pounds?'

'People have killed for less,' said Birch. 'Family

circumstances aside, the police wouldn't look kindly on your actions. Selling to Fox is *de facto* intent to supply.'

'You seem like a woman who cares a great deal about her reputation and standing,' I said.

Lucy all but sneered at me. 'Some of us have a standing to care about.' She laid a hand over the elder Mrs Kwok's. 'But more than that, I'm needed here. I couldn't put that at risk.'

'Is that why you killed him? Did you use your familiar escape route to come back home without being seen?'

'No, it's why I paid his filthy blackmail money. The first I knew about his death was when he ruined my play, floating in the water. If you could prove otherwise, I'd be talking to the real police, wouldn't I? So I think you should leave, and be assured that if you tell anyone about this I'll deny every word of it. We all will.'

I saw Birch bristle at the implication he wasn't 'real police' but caught his eye and shook my head. He looked furious, but Lucy was right. There was nothing to tie her directly to Crash's murder. Not yet.

Geoff ushered us out, ensuring I didn't do any more 'sneaking around', and we found ourselves back on the street. From the junction bridge we looked out at the Carnival boats and colourful bunting in the Pool, all enveloped in the warm glow of a spring evening as the sun began to set. Could Lucy be the killer? Hers was the one blackmail we'd found so far that was actually criminal, giving her a strong motive.

'Ought to call Fletcher myself, send the knock-knock

boys in,' said Birch suddenly. He was still seething from Lucy's dismissal. 'They can flush it all away, doesn't matter. Easy enough to find traces with the right kit.'

'I don't think that would help anyone. It would immediately put her in the frame, but if she didn't kill Crash then the real murderer will still be walking free, and all you've done is prevent Lucy from taking care of her grandmother.'

'Not a matter of help. Matter of the law. Can't let people go around selling drugs with no consequence.'

I laughed. 'Birch, if that were true half of the glamorous showbiz world you're so interested in would be locked up. Besides, where's the harm? She's giving pain relief, not running a gangland empire. We don't arrest landlords for serving beer and that's no better.'

He snorted. 'Different, though. Legal.'

'By some quirk of history, not because it's any less harmful. Some might say it's worse.' Birch said nothing, but his silence spoke volumes. I tried to make peace. 'Can we at least hold off on telling Fletcher until we know more about what happened? Keep our powder dry, as it were.'

'Whatever you say, ma'am. We'd best be getting along, eh, Ronnie? Come on, boy.'

'Birch, wait—'

He didn't. Instead, he crossed the junction without looking back, heading for Warwick Avenue Station. I refused to chase after him; Ace looked terribly confused but stayed by my side. Besides, I still hadn't collected my things from Crash's houseboat.

There was no point attempting subterfuge this time, so I asked Constable Wright to call DCS Fletcher. She agreed to let me inside, but on the condition that he supervised me while I gathered my possessions.

'What do you think I'm going to do?' I complained to her.

'For all I know, you might unmoor the boat and pilot it down the Thames singing the national anthem. It's with the constable or not at all, Ms Tuffel.'

I relented and went inside with the young policeman following. I took the groceries from the fridge and my clothes from the bedroom, then returned to the lounge and the jigsaw of Little Venice. So much for my plan to finish it before rehearsals resumed on Tuesday; I'd barely started it on Friday and had made no progress since. I'd have to puzzle like a demon to even half-finish it by tomorrow. On the bright side, at least there wasn't much to break down. I disassembled the corner I'd built, returned the pieces to the flattened box, and put that in my tote along with everything else.

Then I took what I assumed would be my last ever look around the place, marvelling at how its casual messiness disguised an orderly and calculated blackmail operation. What would happen to Crash's studio? To his gold discs? To the upright piano? They'd all go to Fox, or perhaps her daughter Ellie if she was in prison by then. Would Ellie simply auction it all off?

I led Ace out into the cool dusk. Somewhere nearby, Fox sat in a police interrogation room with

Johnny watching. Howard would be there too, for different reasons. Meanwhile, Lucy was tending to her grandmother.

Crash's death really had thrown a wrench into everyone's lives, mine included, because DCS Fletcher was right: Birch could be infuriating sometimes. I doubted he'd ever stop thinking like a policeman, but a little flexibility now and then wouldn't hurt. I was annoyed with myself for not being more sympathetic to his view, but much more annoyed with him for making a mountain out of a molehill and flouncing off.

I crossed the road and finally followed in his footsteps to the Tube station.

CHAPTER TWENTY-SEVEN

This time I navigated my way through the scaffolding with ease, and there was no sign of the Dowager when I let Ace in the garden after feeding him. Then I fixed myself dinner, took it through to the lounge and reopened the Little Venice jigsaw on my puzzle table. It was only an ordinary coffee table, but I hardly used it for anything else, so I called it my puzzle table.

A bit like Fox calling Lilith her 'boat cat', I supposed. I hoped she'd be OK. Johnny would check on Lilith while Fox was at the station, wouldn't he? Then again, was that so important with cats? Fox had said the spare room contained her litter box.

My thoughts were interrupted by Ace leaping onto the sofa and curling up beside me. As he snoozed, I picked at my food and tried to focus on the puzzle, quickly rebuilding the corner section but knowing I'd never finish the rest before rehearsals resumed. If only I could turn the calendar back a couple of days! At least now

I could return to the puzzle whenever I liked. Fletcher couldn't confiscate my own house keys.

That made me think about the house we'd found on Penfold Mews that afternoon, almost forgotten in the subsequent excitement. Birch had said the name 'Don Christopher' rang a bell but I wasn't about to call and ask why. After stomping off like that he could jolly well sit and stew for a while.

Realising I was sitting with an empty fork in one hand and a puzzle piece in the other, staring into space, I conceded defeat and tossed the piece back in the box before quickly scoffing dinner.

With that out of the way I retrieved my laptop and checked my email, but nobody from Don Christopher Management had replied. It occurred to me that I hadn't hidden my identity in my email to them and wouldn't know how even if I'd wanted to. Had I made myself a target? What if the mysterious Don Christopher was involved in all this and thought I knew too much? Was that why Howard had been attacked? But everyone already knew I was asking questions. How much difference could an email make?

Everyone involved in this tangled business had an adopted persona. Crash pretended to be everyone's easy-going friend when in fact he was blackmailing four of his neighbours – including his own wife! – and using an alias to hide an expensive property that none of them knew about. Johnny let everyone think he was a poor farm boy from Ireland, despite his family apparently being well off.

Lucy's public face was that of an upstanding citizen, a straight-laced pillar of the community, but behind it was a woman who bought and sold drugs and had been left by her own parents to care for her ailing grandmother. Howard pretended to be a successful fitness guru but owed his ex-wife so much money that he was hiding in Little Venice, hoping to escape once and for all by jetting off to America. And while Fox outwardly played the celebrity wife, behind closed doors she was sleeping with her husband's best friend.

Would any of them kill to protect their secret?

Taking a different tack, I searched the Companies House website for Don Christopher Management Ltd. They were easy to find, but my excitement faded when I saw the company's registered address was in the British Virgin Islands. A tax haven. Was that normal even for small companies in the music business?

Then again, did I know for sure they were small? There were no other addresses listed, but perhaps the Penfold Mews office was one tiny outpost in a vast empire.

I wondered if it might be a front for illegal activity, but that would require some activity in the first place. The hairdresser insisted he'd never seen anyone use the house at all. There was no phone number or website listed, and the correspondence address for Don Christopher himself was the same house. The whole business was as circular as Ace's throwing ring.

I stroked the sleeping dog's head and wondered: what if none of this had anything to do with Crash's death?

Could DCS Fletcher even be right, and it was merely an accident? That would mean there was no connection to the attack on Howard. But then why would Fox poison him? He was due to leave tomorrow anyway. What did Howard know, perhaps unwittingly, that made him a target?

I returned to the page of his recorded classes and skipped through the Thursday night session to check his alibi. It was much the same as the Friday class I'd watched, with a similar progression from breathing and stretches to lifting weights and balancing on his big toe. Once again, after forty-five minutes he ended the session, set a countdown timer, then returned after several minutes to talk with the class. Drinking a vegetable smoothie, of course.

That feeling of routine and predictability made me wonder. Everyone knew where Fox kept her poisonous plants and the key. She'd pointed out the jug during the tour, complete with gloves to safely handle them. Everyone also knew Howard made health drinks and smoothies. You only had to watch one of his classes, or see his kitchen countertop, to know that sooner or later he'd whip up some horrid concoction of kale and fermented yak's milk.

What if someone was trying to frame Fox and get rid of Howard at the same time? Kill two squirrels with one garden rake, as DCS Fletcher might say. Could Howard's attacker be working for his ex-wife Vicki? No, that didn't make sense. Dead people can't pay their debts.

Unless it wasn't meant to kill Howard, but to frighten him into coughing up.

I opened a new search window, then hesitated. Earlier, when I searched for *Howard Zimmerman Vicki*, all I got were results about a film producer. I tried *Howard Zimmerman English teacher London* instead.

That returned plenty of results but about the wrong person; there had been a Mr Zimmerman who died suddenly a couple of years ago, much missed by his colleagues and students. I clicked through to be sure, and verified the tall, skinny man in the photos clearly wasn't the Howard I knew.

I decided to give it one more try and searched for *Crash Double Vicki*, figuring that perhaps Crash had discovered Howard's secret because he already knew Vicki. It was a long shot and even more tricky without a surname. Crash certainly knew women called Vicki; the most popular results were stories of him being seen at parties over the years with actresses and models of that name.

After the usual gossip, though, was a paparazzi story of Crash leaving a club with Vicki Richards, who'd apparently made headlines by accusing a TV director of sexual harassment when she was a teenager. I'd completely missed that story, and she didn't look like a celebrity, so I wondered how she was connected to Crash.

Searching for *Vicki Richards TV scandal* found some old newspaper stories. The director in question was a veteran of Saturday morning kids' shows. I try not to judge people by appearance but he certainly looked the predatory type, with a big mop of curly hair and large tinted glasses. I wondered if I'd ever met him at a party. If so, perhaps I had a lucky escape.

Nevertheless, this was all unrelated. Howard the wellness guru was nowhere in these results. To make sure I wasn't going mad, I searched for *Howard Zee fitness* and found some social media accounts. They were sparse, containing little besides promotions for his website and selfies of him in workout clothes. The photos didn't even show his face, focusing instead on his muscles. Simple vanity or, along with his stage name, another attempt to avoid his ex-wife?

'Come on, Ace,' I said, rubbing my eyes. 'Let's see if things look any better in the morning.'

I cleared away my dinner and let the Collie out for a late-night toilet, then we trudged our way upstairs. By the time I'd finished brushing my teeth and entered the bedroom, Ace was already curled up asleep at the foot. Envying him, I climbed into bed and stared at the ceiling, trying to sleep.

But my brain refused to slow down, trying in vain to make all these strange puzzle pieces fit into a complete picture. The harder I tried to stop thinking about it and relax, the more frustrated I became, and for what? Aside from looking after Ace for a while, none of this was anything to do with me. I had bigger problems, like learning my new, minor role in *Mixed Mothers* and wondering if I should let myself be laughed at in commercials for the sake of money.

I suddenly found myself wishing I could talk it out with my father. Crotchety old man he may have been but he maintained a good perspective on things that really mattered. What would Henry Tuffel do?

He would tell me to focus on my own happiness, of course. But that required knowing what I wanted in the first place.

CHAPTER TWENTY-EIGHT

While brushing my teeth the next morning, my mind continued swirling. The idea of Crash Double being a blackmailer still wasn't easy to get my head around, but it explained how he could afford to build that second-floor studio and fill it with expensive equipment. I hadn't thought about that at first because it seemed natural for a singer.

The corrupted recordings on his computer were maddening. Vital details were missing, details that might have revealed Crash's killer. I was now convinced it was one of his blackmail victims, but who?

Fox Double-Jones: three times wife, living close but separately. Was she really being blackmailed over her affair with Johnny, so as not to risk Crash's inheritance?

Or was it in fact over her now-revealed drug use?

Johnny Roulette himself: bandmate and lifelong friend, also living close by, in an expensive house to boot. By all accounts those two *were* Bad Dice, yet now their friendship stood exposed as a façade. Would Johnny kill his lead singer, and risk people not coming to their concerts, rather than pay up every week? He was surely making more than enough to pay for it from record and ticket sales, so why rock the boat? Did Johnny think he could do it all himself?

Something about that one bothered me but I couldn't put my finger on it.

Howard Zee: an ageing Lothario, divorced (presumably because of said Lothario tendencies) and so badly in debt he was forced to hide on a houseboat and take up an entirely new career. Howard said he'd tried to buy Crash off but the singer had been killed before they could meet. Now Howard himself had been targeted, but why?

There was a lie in there somewhere, too. I could feel it.

Finally, Lucy Kwok: imperious mistress of the canal, self-important would-be playwright, living a stone's throw from Crash. Was she having an affair with Howard? I didn't know for sure, and maybe it made no difference, but I did know about her blackmail. It made sense that she'd fear a visit from the police over her cannabis dealings, and Birch's reaction had reinforced how right she was.

But would she risk being taken from her grandmother to murder Crash?

Any of them could have done it, especially now we knew he was probably killed on Thursday evening. The only person with an alibi for that time was Howard, who'd been teaching a class.

Latesha Michaels wasn't in that class, though. Could *she* have killed Crash, to protect her business interest?

A fluffy tail beat a steady rhythm on the hallway floor, bringing me back to the present as I stood motionless with the toothbrush stuck in my mouth.

'All right, Ace,' I apologised. 'Let's get you toileted and think about what to do with the day, hmmm?'

The Collie wandered around the garden while I ate breakfast and considered what might happen to him. Would Crash's daughter Ellie be willing to take him halfway around the world to Japan? Emigrating a dog was a tedious and expensive task at the best of times.

My phone rang. It was Birch.

'Morning, grumpy,' I said. Perhaps not the best way to solicit an apology, but I was still annoyed with him. 'What's up?'

'Kept thinking about yesterday,' he said. 'Couldn't get it out of my mind.'

'Go on,' I prompted hopefully.

'Well, um. Perhaps you'd better come round to my place.'

My heart fluttered in anticipation. Was this the moment? A candlelit dinner, a springtime punt on the Thames . . . ?

'Uncovered something important about Crash Double. Easier to explain in person, you see.'

My flights of fancy crashed down to earth. 'Was there

anything else you wanted to say, Birch?'

After a moment's thought he said, 'No, don't think so. See you soon.'

It took some persuading to get Ace into my old Volvo. I was confused by his reluctance until I remembered that Crash didn't own a car, and whenever he went on tour he left Ace with someone in Little Venice. It was entirely possible the Collie had never set paw inside any vehicle besides a boat, so I tempted him with treats and reassurance. He quickly got the hang of it; driving to Shepherd's Bush, I looked in the mirror and saw him taking in the passing world with keen, mismatched eyes.

Birch opened his door before I could even knock and, after Ace and Ronnie had sniffed their hellos, he ushered everyone into the lounge where I saw a collection of Bad Dice vinyl albums lying on the floor next to his stereo. Birch knelt beside them, grunting as his knees popped, and Ronnie lay down with him. Ace joined me on the sofa, his pricked ear alert and twitching.

'So, what have you found?' I asked.

Birch passed me a record. 'Been bothering me since Penfold Mews. Tip of my tongue but wouldn't come until I played one last night. Early stuff, you see.'

I didn't, not entirely, but dutifully examined the album sleeve anyway. Worn and creased around the edges, it was old and well used. I half-remembered the cover art from many years ago. The title *Something is Rotten* was scrawled over a photograph of four young men, standing in a scrapyard. I recognised Crash Double and Johnny Roulette front and centre, looking stereotypically thin and sullen in wingtip collars and striped trousers.

'Good lord,' I said, laughing at the fashion. 'Birch, please tell me you never dressed like this.'

His cheeks coloured. 'Perish the thought. Now, back cover. Credits, bottom left.'

I turned it over. The sleeve back featured a track listing, more photos of the band posing next to wrecked cars and a block of small text.

Produced by Don Christopher for Wade Enterprises

Recorded at Regent Sound and Island Studios

Engineer: Tony Allom and Brian Humphries

Management: Nobby Wade, Wade Enterprises

All compositions by Johnny Roulette, except (3) and (7) by Johnny Roulette and Crash Double

All compositions published by Essex Music Int. Ltd

As I've said, music isn't my strong point. I was never the type to sit and pore over records in my bedroom, so whatever Birch was seeing sailed straight over my head.

'You'll have to be more specific. What am I looking for?'

He pointed at the first line of the credits. I reread it . . . and my mouth dropped open in surprise.

'Don Christopher! The management firm who

rent Crash's house on Penfold Mews. Which might be some kind of scam, by the way.' I related the company information I'd found last night, then looked again. 'It says here the band's manager was called Nobby Wade. So did they change to Don Christopher at some point?'

Birch smiled. 'No, they're still with old Nobby. Try again.'

I reread the credits but was no wiser. 'This record must be fifty years old. I'm surprised you could . . . um . . . well, what I mean is, jolly well done for remembering a detail like this.' I quickly moved on. 'They must be old friends . . . but wait a minute!'

'Yes?'

'When I showed Johnny the photo of Don Christopher's name and email address he claimed he didn't recognise the name.'

'And that was before he deleted all the pictures? Another lie, then.' He looked crestfallen.

'Oh, Birch. I know you love this band. It must be horrible to find out they're a bunch of rotters.'

'Can't hide from the truth,' he said, taking a deep breath. 'No matter where it leads.'

'Yes, and the lead we have to follow now is Don Christopher. I haven't had any response to the email I sent yet, though.'

'Doubt you will. I'm a big fan, remember? Read a fair amount about Bad Dice over the years. Enough to know these early albums were low-budget, self-produced affairs.'

'What does that have to do with the mysterious Mr Christopher?' I suspected I was about to get a musical history lesson.

'Well, for a start, the mysterious Mr Christopher doesn't exist.'

After a moment's confusion I understood what he meant. 'It's a pseudonym. So who is he really?'

Birch tapped his nose. 'Expensive chaps, producers. But back in the day, a band producing their own album looked amateurish. Made people think nobody was willing to invest in them. So when they did it all themselves, they used fake names.'

I was beginning to see the light. 'That way it looks like a record company *has* invested in them, which in turn persuades people they're worth listening to. Yes, that makes sense.' I might not know music, but everyone in showbiz understands the importance of a credible façade.

'Remember I told you what Crash Double's real name is?' Birch asked.

'Yes, it's come up a few times since his death. Shaun Donnelly.'

'That's right. Full name Shaun *Christopher* Donnelly.'

I looked at the credits, then at Birch's smiling expression, then back to the credits. 'Christopher Donnelly. Don Christopher,' I groaned. 'Now something else Johnny said makes sense – that Crash had "producer cuts" on some of their early albums.'

He nodded. 'Crash didn't write the big hits, but some

producers get a royalty on album sales. Johnny, too. Look here.' He took another record from the floor and passed it to me, pointing once again at the credits.

'*Producer: Willy Ormond*,' I read. 'Because Johnny's real surname is Ormond-Wiles, isn't it? The banking family, you said?'

Birch smiled, enjoying showing off his knowledge. 'That's right. Tales of being a poor farm boy are, ahem, embellished. Minor scandal when it came out that his parents funded Bad Dice for years before they were signed.'

'So even the band aren't the plucky underdogs their legend claims. But why would Johnny lie about not knowing who "Don Christopher" is? Does this mean that Crash rents the mews house to . . . himself?'

'Odd, isn't it?' he agreed, taking back the records and carefully replacing them on shelves near the stereo. 'Should take this to the DCS. Let her look into it.'

'Pfft,' I snorted. 'Odds are she'll say it's a matter of his estate, nothing to do with his death and we should forget about it.'

'Don't have much choice. Can't break into the place and snoop around, can we?'

'Why not?' I said, smiling conspiratorially. 'You said you know how to pick a lock.'

He frowned at me. 'By the book. That's how Fletcher likes things.'

'All right,' I sighed, conceding. 'Let's pay Little Venice one last visit.'

CHAPTER TWENTY-NINE

We bundled into my Volvo, once again tempting Ace in with treats, though he was more keen than before. Collies are nothing if not fast learners. Ronnie had already leapt into the boot without prompting, but looked pathetically bereft until I gave him a treat as well.

'I wonder how much the solicitor knows,' I said as we set off. 'About the management company, I mean.'

'Good question. You think it's not real?'

'It's real in the sense of being registered, and presumably pays rent every month. Mr Patwari even said he'd have to inform them about Crash's death. Does that mean he doesn't know Crash is behind it? Or was he pretending for my sake? Perhaps it's a scam or a tax dodge.'

'Money laundering. Lots of dirty cash coming in. Use it to pay "Don Christopher's" rent, it goes through the system, comes back to Crash clean as a whistle.'

I considered that theory. 'Mr Patwari wouldn't even need to be involved, would he? It could all be Crash, deceiving everyone. It seems he was very good at it.'

We fell silent as I turned onto the Westway. Then Birch said, 'Spoke to Fletcher last night.'

'Oh, Birch, no.' It hadn't occurred to me before now that he'd still have the superintendent's number but I shouldn't have been surprised. I envisaged a dawn raid on Lucy Kwok's house, with the police breaking down her door and terrifying her grandmother. Not that Mrs Kwok seemed the kind to scare easily. I revised the vision to include her whacking an unfortunate policeman over the head with her stick.

'Thought you'd want me to,' he protested. 'Asked about checking for poisons in the bloodstream. She said they're already testing, should have results this morning. Shows she's listening, see? Told you she's a good sort.'

I was relieved, but before I could thank him for not ratting out Lucy over the drugs, his phone rang.

'Ma'am,' he said, answering. No prizes for guessing who was on the other end. 'Hold on, driving. I'll put you on speaker.' He did, raising a finger to his lips to signal I should stay quiet. 'Go ahead.'

'You'll be pleased to know we received the toxicology report this morning and it confirms our hypothesis. Mr Donnelly didn't ingest poisonous plants at all. We found high levels of alprazolam in his blood.'

'That's Xanax, isn't it?' he said for my benefit. 'Like in his bathroom?'

'Correct. So you see, whether it was suicide or misadventure, his death has no connection to what happened yesterday with Mr Zimmerman.'

I protested silently but Birch waved for me to be quiet. 'Doesn't that make the attack on Howard even more suspicious?'

'If it even was an attack,' said Fletcher. 'We're not ruling out an accident there, either.'

'*House*,' I mouthed as we turned off for Little Venice.

Birch understood and (without mentioning me) told the superintendent about Don Christopher Management, the house on Penfold Mews and the possible scam of it all.

'Should take some uniforms. We, uh, that is Ronnie and I, can meet you there, show you which house. Break in if necessary.' He winked at me.

'Break in? What on earth for? Birch, I must say I think Ms Tuffel is exerting a bad influence on you.'

He bristled. 'Just trying to get to the bottom of things.'

'I warned you retirement wouldn't suit you. You're not a copper any more, Alan. I know Beatrice is gone, but you can't fill your days meddling in official business.'

The mention of his late wife incensed him. 'Uncalled for!'

'Is it? Anyway, assuming you're right and Mr Donnelly has an interest in that property, it'll all come out in the will.'

'Could be weeks away,' he protested. 'Trail will have gone cold by then.'

'There is no "trail"!' she shouted. 'I won't take a brigade of coppers to break down the door of someone's office because you think they have a funny name. Good day.'

She ended the call, leaving Birch fuming. This was

the closest I'd ever seen to him losing his temper. Being dismissed by his former boss was evidently a step too far and if she imagined bringing up Beatrice would help, she clearly didn't know him as well as she thought. He'd wear that wedding ring to his grave.

I turned into Blomfield Road, found a parking spot and turned off the engine. Birch stared out of the window, as below us the last day of the Carnival got underway at the Pool. People wandered along the paths, greeted heartily by the boaters. I saw Lucy darting about, organising things, eternally busy.

'Let's hope she doesn't summon another body from the depths, eh?' I joked, hoping to rouse Birch. It didn't work, so I stepped out and opened the boot to let the dogs down. He finally joined me in silence as we clipped on their leads, then crossed the junction bridge and descended the steps to the residents' path. As we reached the access gate, Howard was returning from a jog.

'You're obviously feeling recovered,' I said.

'Eighty per cent,' he smiled. 'Wild horses couldn't keep me, though. I fly out in a few hours.' A thought struck him. 'You know, Gwinny, this may be the last time we see each other, so thank you again for yesterday. I do wish we'd met under better circumstances.'

'I'm sure you're not the only one. Come to think of it, I should return your gate key.' I began rummaging in my handbag, but he waved it away.

'Won't need it, will I? Keep it, and consider yourself an honorary resident.'

He continued on, taking a wide berth – or as wide as the canal path would allow him to – around Fox's boat, where Johnny Roulette stood on the deck. The men exchanged scowls but nothing was said.

Curious about the guitarist's presence, Birch and I approached. We were greeted with a similar scowl.

'What are you doing here, Johnny?' I asked. No point beating around the bush. 'Is Fox still with the police?'

'She's right here, no thanks to you,' he grumbled. 'Coppers weren't willing to make an arrest and she's to meet Ellie at the airport later. Do everyone a favour and leave us alone.'

'Not yet, sorry. I want to know why you lied to me and deleted my photos of the notebook.' I decided not to mention we'd recovered them, to see how he might react. 'Birch here has all your albums, you see. Even the early ones produced by "Don Christopher" and "Willy Ormond".'

Johnny's shoulders sagged a little. 'It's band business and you've no right to be poking around in it. Don't you see it's over for us? No more concerts, no more tours. It was Crash who held the audience, there's no lie in that. But now maybe some West End eejit with more money than sense wants to make a tribute musical or something, right? Think how much those lyrics could be worth! And here's you, with them saved on your bloody phone.'

Fox emerged from the doorway. 'Tell her to go away, Jonathan. We have nothing to say.' Then she remembered he wouldn't hear her and tapped his leg to draw his attention.

'What's up, pet? I was just telling this pair to get lost.'

'Good. You do that.'

Fox retreated into the dark interior, followed by Johnny. Birch and I beat our own retreat, back down the path. Could we take the guitarist's word for it? Had he really acted out of caution?

Constable Wright maintained his guard outside Crash's houseboat, but as Birch still hadn't spoken a word since his phone call to DCS Fletcher, now didn't feel like a good time to ask after the superintendent's whereabouts. Much as she frustrated me, I hoped they wouldn't fall out completely. Birch and I had disagreed before but he was always quick to forgive, to the point that sometimes he barely acknowledged we'd argued. But those were disagreements about things like dogs, not his late wife. As for Fletcher's perspective . . . well, Birch had said she and I were similar, and if I do say so myself, I'm pretty good at holding grudges.

'Birch,' I began, 'I'm sorry Fletcher wouldn't listen to you, but—'

'Let's do it,' he said suddenly and marched off ahead.

'Do what? Where are we going?' I asked, hurrying after him. Ace thought this sudden burst of speed was enormous fun and I struggled to keep him under control as we mounted the steps back to the road.

'Penfold Mews, of course. Time we took a look inside.'

CHAPTER THIRTY

We walked in silence; Birch's mind was obviously set on something and I was hurrying to keep up. Finally, we turned onto the cobbled street of Penfold Mews and approached the house-slash-office of Don Christopher Management Ltd.

Ace eagerly sniffed the door, keen to get inside.

'It's still a bank holiday,' I said, catching my breath. 'Even if someone does work here, they're probably not in today.'

'Good,' Birch said, and rang the doorbell. Sure enough, there was no answer. 'Good,' he said again. 'Now, look here.'

He leant in close, with an air of secrecy, and took a small metal case from his pocket. 'Picked them up before we left.' He opened the case to reveal several thin, metal tools. Like a misshapen set of Allen keys, or—

'A lockpick set,' I gasped. 'I thought you were joking.'

The former policeman and I had flouted rules before,

certainly; distracting Constable Wright to get inside Crash's houseboat wasn't even the first time we'd snuck into a crime scene together. But this was a new level of mischief.

'Thought I'd use them to help Fletcher,' he grumbled. 'But she's too damn foolish to follow the evidence under her nose. Shouldn't have taken on this case, in my opinion. Rusty. I should have listened to you,' he added sheepishly.

'Yes, you should have, and not only about Fletcher. This is no less "illegal" than what Lucy and Fox are doing, you know.' He opened his mouth to protest, but I cut him off. 'Never mind that for now. Get to work, Raffles.'

He handed Ronnie to me, then inserted the tools into the lock and began to wriggle them around. I don't pretend to know the first thing about lock picking but Birch remained calm and collected, so I trusted things were going well.

Until someone said, 'Good morning.'

Not being well versed in the art of breaking and entering, I hadn't thought to keep lookout. Now I turned to see the young hairdresser approaching, with a takeaway coffee in one hand and a paper deli bag in the other. From behind me came a startled cough and the tinkle of metal tools falling to the floor. Whether Birch had dropped them out of surprise or thrown them down deliberately, I couldn't say.

'Morning,' I replied, trying to act natural.

Unfortunately, Ronnie had other ideas. Before I could take a firmer grip he surged forward, pulling his lead from my hand and bounding over to the startled young man.

'Ronnie, *no*!' I called, running over with Ace by my side. 'Come back here!' Normally the Lab was amenable to my commands, but not when faced with a delicious-smelling sandwich. He leapt up at the hairdresser, barking loudly, trying to grab the deli bag.

'I say, ham sandwich by any chance?' Birch called out, running over to tame his dog. 'Bit keen, sorry. No harm meant.'

'That's easy for you to say!' said the hairdresser angrily, spinning in circles and holding his breakfast up out of Ronnie's reach. This made the Lab jump even higher in his efforts and I foresaw disaster if this didn't end soon.

I dropped Ace's lead and thrust a finger towards the ground in front of his nose, trusting Crash's words that he was unlikely to run off. The Collie obediently dropped to the cobbles. Then I stepped between the hairdresser and Ronnie, admonished the hungry dog with the loudest '*Ah*!' I could manage and made a grab for his lead. It was enough to draw his attention, so I held his gaze while raising a rigid index finger to the sky. He froze in place, looking from my eyes to my finger and back again, then slowly lowered his head as I brought my hand down.

I gave Ronnie's head a fuss for obeying at last and turned to apologise, but the hairdresser was already incensed.

'I told you before, you're wasting your time at that house, and you can't even keep your bloody dogs under control! Now get away or I'll call the police!'

He retreated to his shop, grumbling, and we backed up to the management company's door.

'Reckon you've got a minute, tops, before he looks out of his lounge window, sees us still here and calls the police,' I said. 'Can you do it, or shall we scarper?'

Birch was already retrieving his fallen lock-pick tools. He gave an annoyed snort. 'Not letting a nosey parker like him get the better of me.'

DCS Fletcher might have called that 'the deer mocking the rabbit's tail', but I kept schtum and let him resume work while I watched the hairdresser's house for shadows that might betray movement on his upper floor.

A *click* sounded from the door. 'Are we in?' I whispered.

'Not quite . . . almost . . .'

I thought I saw a slight change in light through the window opposite. 'Any time today, Birch . . .'

'Gotcha,' he mumbled, and I heard another, more solid *click*. 'When you're ready.' He opened the door and stood aside.

'No time like the present,' I said, refusing his chivalry, and pushed him in ahead of me.

With the dogs weaving around our legs, we all tumbled inside and I quickly slammed the door closed. Feeling like a naughty schoolchild, I peeked out through its small glass pane. The hairdresser stood at his lounge window. Was he on the phone? Was he even looking this way? I couldn't tell.

'Don't use any lights,' I said to Birch. 'If he assumed we ran away, let's not give him reason to think otherwise.' The house interior was gloomy, but not so much we couldn't find our way.

I stepped back from the door and noticed something on the floor – or rather, the absence of something.

'How strange,' I said. 'Birch, what's wrong with this picture?'

He followed my gaze down. 'Not sure I follow. Nothing there.'

'Exactly. If this place was unused, wouldn't there be post piled up and waiting to be opened? Someone must have been here recently to pick it up.'

'Or nobody sends anything to this address?'

'I've never in my life set foot in a Domino's but they still shove a menu through my letterbox every week. I can't believe a business address five minutes' walk from Paddington doesn't receive junk mail.'

He shrugged. 'Fair. So despite what our friendly hairdresser says, someone's using the place. Perhaps coming at odd hours when everyone's asleep, like you said.'

I began climbing the stairs. 'Then let's hope our suspicions are correct and the someone in question was Crash Double, because if it turns out Don Christopher is real and decides to visit, we'll have a job explaining ourselves.'

On the first floor, in what would normally have been the living area, the theme of absence continued. The kitchen looked even less used than Crash's houseboat galley, although there was a mug drying on the sideboard and a water bowl on the floor. Ace tried to lap from it but as I had no idea what was in it, or how long it had been standing there, I snatched it up and emptied it into the sink. After refilling it with fresh water I let him drink, and Ronnie joined him.

'Not so unused after all, if there's a dog bowl,' I said.

'Only water, though,' said Birch. 'Any dog food in the cupboards?'

There wasn't, but I did find two packs of the same energy bars Crash ate. 'Why have a bolt-hole like this, but keep nothing in it?' I wondered.

The dining room and lounge were nothing more than plain walls and bare floorboards. No carpet, not even a rug. The closest thing to furniture was a blind that completely covered the window facing the street.

On the second floor, though, we finally got our answer. Like the rest of the house, the attic room wasn't furnished for creature comforts. But it did contain a desk, chair, filing cabinet . . . and a well-used dog bed in the corner. Another blind was drawn fully over the dormer window.

'Crash told me Ace suffers from separation anxiety,' I said. 'He must have brought the dog with him. No wonder Ace recognised the scent at the door.'

Besides a coaster, presumably for the mug downstairs,

the austere desk held two items: a closed laptop and a mobile phone, which was plugged in and fully charged.

'Now we know why the police didn't find Crash's mobile on his body,' I said. 'It was here all along.' Ace weaved around my legs, sniffing the desk and chair. I felt sorry for him, knowing that sooner or later he'd realise his human was never coming back again. I reached for the phone—

And jumped like a jack-in-the-box when it lit up and vibrated. Someone was calling!

I peered at the screen, hoping it would identify the caller. It did, but what I saw only further confused matters.

'Birch . . . why is Mr Patwari trying to phone Crash, when he knows perfectly well the man is dead?' Then I looked again at the phone and saw that I'd jumped too quickly to a conclusion. This wasn't the one I'd seen Crash use. It was smaller and lacked the distinctive photo case of Ace.

The phone stopped vibrating and the screen showed a missed call. Two, in fact. The one from the lawyer just now, and another from Lucy Kwok on Friday morning.

A puzzle piece clicked into place in my mind. 'It's his blackmail phone,' I said. 'Crash must have kept a separate number, so there was nothing incriminating on his regular phone. I bet that call was Mr Patwari trying to reach Don Christopher Management.'

'Explains why the phone is still here, too, rather than at the bottom of the canal. Killer never found it.'

'Let's see if the laptop can tell us anything.' I opened it, fingers poised to type *equilibrium*, but there was no demand for a password. It simply opened to the desktop.

'Curious,' said Birch, looking over my shoulder. 'Password at home, but not here?'

'Perhaps he never took this computer anywhere else? We're definitely in the right place. Look at that.'

As soon as the screen had lit up, a notification message appeared to announce a new email . . . from me. The email I'd sent to Don Christopher.

'No wonder I didn't get a reply. I was writing to a dead man.'

Unlike the computer at Crash's studio, this one was sparse and tidy. Its desktop contained four familiar folders, in alphabetical order: *Fox*, *Howard*, *Johnny*, and *Lucy*.

I opened *Lucy*. The contents were identical to what we'd seen before; a spreadsheet, a photo, and an audio file. The spreadsheet was a copy of the one we'd seen already but with one big difference: it was intact, with no missing or garbled entries.

'Copies of whatever was on the computer at his boat,' said Birch, looking over my shoulder. 'Killer damaged those, but didn't know about this computer.'

I gasped. 'Which means . . . oh, I don't want to say anything and jinx it. Let's just see.'

Like its duplicate, this folder contained two other files. I opened the photograph and was confused to see a freeze frame from the video I'd accidentally taken in

Crash's studio, showing the hooded Lucy leaping over the fence to Blomfield Road with a tartan canvas bag in hand. But then I noticed that the trees in this picture were shedding their leaves; it was the same scene, but taken at a different time.

'He saw Lucy, too,' I said. 'That's how he blackmailed her. Now, here goes nothing.'

I played the audio file. Ace's ears perked up at the sound of Crash's voice and I gave him a reassuring fuss as we listened to the undamaged recording.

> Crash: '—*know you can't fool me of all people, Lucy. Rock 'n' roll lifestyle [muffled]*'
> Lucy: '*So now what? [Muffled] tell the police you'd have done it already.*'
> Crash: '*I still might. Unless of course we can come to a mutually beneficial arrangement, that is. I mean, buying and selling drugs is a serious offence. So five hundred a week is a small price to pay, don't you think? Sure and you must [muffled] already.*'
> Lucy: '*You scheming [muffled]. If you breathe a word of this to anyone, I'll kill you.*'
> Crash: '*Now why would I do that? You keep paying, and I'll keep quiet. That's how it works.*'

Birch whistled softly. 'Blackmail material, all right. Credible threat, too. What's in the other folders?'

'Let's find out,' I said, opening them all.

Ten minutes later we tumbled downstairs, barrelled out the door and ran back to Little Venice as fast as our ageing legs would allow.

We had a killer to catch.

CHAPTER THIRTY-ONE

Ace and Ronnie naturally thought our sprinting (more like breathless jogging, if I'm honest) was the most fun they'd had all day. Their incessant bouncing almost tripped us several times as we ran to the canal.

We reached the junction bridge, and I heard Lucy's amplified voice announce that she would shortly reveal the winner of the 'best boat' prize. She stood on a barge in the centre of the Pool, watched by hundreds of people in the surrounding boats and crowded on the canal-side paths. I saw Mr Choudhury the grocer among them, smiling and applauding with everyone else. It was the last day of the Carnival and a jubilant mood filled the air.

We ran on, down to the residents' area.

Clinging to Ace's lead with one hand, I scrabbled in my pocket for the key as we descended the steps. I saw Fox and Johnny approaching from the other side, walking hand in hand. The guitarist was right; there was no need to hide their relationship any more.

Fox unlocked the gate and swung it open, then noticed me, Birch and the dogs hurrying towards it. She and Johnny leapt aside to avoid a collision.

'What the hell are you doing here?' Fox said.

'Explain . . . later . . .' I panted, hurrying through the gate.

We ran on, past Crash's houseboat.

The front door opened and DCS Fletcher stepped onto the path as we rushed past.

'Come on!' I called to her, gasping for breath. 'No time . . . to waste!'

We ran on, along the canal path.

Latesha Michaels stood by Howard's boat, looking every bit the glamorous transatlantic businesswoman with her LV luggage, oversized sunglasses propped on her head and casual chic travelling clothes.

I stopped. Ace obediently sat and looked up at me, tongue panting as he waited for the next game to begin. I envied him; if I could have stuck my own tongue out six inches to cool down, I would have.

Birch, Ronnie and DCS Fletcher all came to a halt behind me. Birch was puffing and wheezing, too, which made me feel the tiniest bit better.

'It's the Keystone Kennel Club,' said Latesha with disdain. 'Do you mind clearing a path? We have a flight to catch.'

At that moment Howard emerged from the boat, carrying a suitcase in either hand. Unlike Latesha, he looked much the same as always in a sleeveless shirt and cargo shorts, his sole concession to travel being a multi-pocketed jacket.

'What's going on?' he said. 'We're about to leave.'

'Sorry,' I said, still trying to catch my breath, 'But no . . . you're not.'

Latesha glared at me. 'I'm gonna give you five seconds to get out of the way and then I'm calling Zabok's London lawyer. This is harassment.'

'What *is* going on, Ms Tuffel?' asked DCS Fletcher. 'I have work to do.'

'Yes, you do,' I said. 'Like arresting Crash Double's killer.'

Latesha began dialling. 'OK, that's it. You are *so* getting sued, lady.'

'I wouldn't bother if I were you,' I said. 'I doubt your lawyer will want to defend Howard in a murder trial.'

Everyone froze for a moment. Then Lucy's voice carried from the Pool, announcing that a boat called *Tadeusz* had won the boat contest, and it broke the spell.

'You silly woman,' said Howard. 'Get out of the way.'

'Steady on, sir,' said Birch, stepping up. Those old habits really did die hard.

'Ms Tuffel, this is a serious accusation,' said Fletcher. 'What evidence do you have?'

I drew myself up to my full height, which was admittedly a good deal shorter than Howard, and faced him. 'I hoped to finish my jigsaw before rehearsals resumed, but Crash's death messed everything up. Last night I was annoyed about that and thought, If only I could turn the clocks back a couple of days . . .'

His eyes widened, and I knew he understood.

Then he shoved Latesha into us and made a run for it.

The American stumbled and fell, knocking me back into Birch, who fell into Fletcher, and we all collapsed in a heap on the path. Ace and Ronnie wagged their tails and licked our faces, united at last by the humans' highly entertaining new game.

By the time we'd untangled our limbs and got to our feet, Howard was through the gate and running under the bridge to the Pool, where the crowd stood shoulder to shoulder watching Lucy hand out the boat awards.

'He's trying to blend in,' I said, giving chase with Ace by my side. 'Don't let him get away!' I'd barely got my breath back from running down here, but if Howard escaped now we might never find him again. I hurried through the gate, about to follow him under the junction bridge when I had a better idea. Instead, I climbed the steps and ran onto the bridge, scanning the crowd from the high vantage point. I saw Howard right away, his bald head weaving between the crowd.

I was so busy watching him that I didn't pay attention to where I was going, and collided with someone standing on the bridge.

'Oh! I'm so sorry, I wasn't—' I stopped when I saw who I'd run into.

'You again!' said the bearded BuzzFeed reporter angrily, clutching his drone controller. 'If you've got a problem with the video, take it up with my editor. Leave me alone!'

'Really, it was an accident—' I began, then saw the controller screen and had an idea. 'Your drone has a camera, right? How good are you at flying it?'

He snorted. 'Third in the Shoreditch racing league. Why?'

I resisted the temptation to ask if the league had a fourth competitor and said, 'The man who killed Crash Double just ran into that crowd to evade the police. There, with the bald head.' I pointed in Howard's direction. It was hard to pick him out now, as he was further away and moving more slowly so as not to draw attention. 'Keep him in your sights and you'll have one heck of a story.'

He hesitated, but no reporter can resist a scoop for long. He turned back to the controller and a high-pitched buzzing sounded from the sky. I watched as the tiny drone swooped over the crowd, heading for Howard's position.

'Perfect! Stay out of reach, so he can't, um . . .' I tailed off, realising what I was about to say.

'Hit it with a ball thrower?' the young man suggested acidly.

I was saved from having to respond by Birch and Ronnie, who found me on the bridge.

'Where's Fletcher?' I asked.

'Giving chase,' Birch replied, pointing down into the crowd. Sure enough, DCS Fletcher surged through the crowd, with Constable Wright following in her wake.

I cupped my hands and called out, 'Superintendent! Look for the drone!'

Fletcher stopped and looked around, confused, then saw us standing on the bridge.

'The drone!' I shouted, pointing at the tiny flying device. 'We're following him!'

Understanding, she nodded and resumed pushing through the crowd. Several bystanders yelled at me to be quiet while they listened to Lucy. There's no accounting for taste.

But I wasn't done. 'Howard!' I called out at the top of my lungs. 'You can't get away! *Come back*! *Come back*!'

I couldn't be sure he'd heard me, but someone certainly did. Suddenly Ace leapt to his feet and bolted back across the road. 'Ace, *no*!' I called, but it was too late. I'd been so focused on watching Howard, and the Collie was normally so obedient, that I hadn't kept a firm enough grip on his lead. Now something had spooked him and he was running back to the safety of Crash's houseboat. Paralysed by indecision, I didn't know whether to give chase or trust he knew what he was doing.

Then I heard cries from below and looked down to see a ripple of people sway and move as a furry tri-colour shape weaved between them.

I laughed, remembering Ace 'dancing' with Crash. He wasn't running back to the boat. He was off to herd!

Lucy, the competition boats and most of the crowd had no idea anything was going on. The skipper of the

Tadeusz now had the mic, happily telling the crowd what an honour this was. I watched Howard slowly draw closer to the Westbourne Terrace Bridge. The drone dutifully followed, with DCS Fletcher and her policeman gaining on them both as fast as they could, but it was slow going through the mass of people.

Then, suddenly, Howard stopped moving. The skipper handed the mic back to Lucy and the crowd applauded again. Lucy motioned for quiet, and opened her mouth to deliver a speech . . .

But was drowned out by Ace barking. On the drone controller screen, I saw the Collie run in circles around Howard, clearing a space as the crowd backed away from this unknown dog. Howard tried to back away too but Ace was too fast and nipped behind him, then back around, herding him towards us, barking incessantly.

'Will someone shut that bloody dog up?!' Lucy shouted over the PA but people had stopped paying attention to her. They were all trying to see what was happening closer to home, craning their necks and standing on tiptoes.

DCS Fletcher finally caught up with Howard and he turned to shout angrily at her. The drone didn't capture sound, but it didn't take lip-reading to recognise a torrent of swear words. Then I noticed Ace sneaking up behind, the dog's body pressed close to the ground, while Howard's attention was elsewhere. He said something final to the superintendent, then turned to run – and came face to face with the Collie. Ace barked again, something I *could* hear even from the bridge, and the guru instinctively recoiled. Unluckily for him, the movement sent him stumbling over a knot of mooring rope on the path's edge.

Arms flailing and mouth agape, Howard Zee toppled between two barges and hit the water with a mighty splash.

CHAPTER THIRTY-TWO

We gathered in Crash's saloon. It seemed appropriate.

Howard Zee was outside, being checked over by an ambulance crew after he almost drowned in the cold waters of the Pool, under the watchful gaze of Constable Wright. DCS Fletcher had agreed to open Crash's houseboat to the rest of us so I could explain.

Fox Double-Jones and Johnny Roulette took the sofa. Lucy Kwok and Latesha Michaels brought stools from the galley area. I perched on the upright piano bench, under the gold disc that hid Crash's safe. Ace lay on his corner bed, worrying at the remains of the cardboard box Mr Choudhury had given me on Friday. Was that really only three days ago?

Birch and DCS Fletcher both stood in the doorway, with an exhausted Ronnie sleeping at their feet.

'He almost got away with it,' I said when everyone had settled down. 'Especially because *everyone* involved in this was hiding their true selves behind a façade. Nobody here is who they seem.'

Fox, Johnny, Lucy and Latesha all looked sideways at each other, but said nothing.

'Let's start at the beginning. Three years ago, Crash Double built his second floor to install a home recording studio. Whether he planned to spy on everyone, or if that was a bonus, we'll never know. But he did and that's how he first saw Lucy taking drugs to and from Fox's houseboat, climbing over the fence to avoid CCTV cameras.'

'What?!' Fletcher exploded. 'Ms Kwok, I'm afraid I'll have to—'

'Please wait, Superintendent. When you hear Lucy's tale you might be inclined to leniency.' I resumed the story. 'Crash confronted her, but not to make her stop. On the contrary, he was happy for Lucy to continue so long as she paid him hush money. That's how his blackmail operation began.'

Fox, Johnny and Howard all turned to look at Lucy. 'He was blackmailing you as well?' said Fox, incredulous.

Lucy returned the expression. 'What do you mean, "as well". . . ?'

'Crash developed a taste for easy money and expanded,' I explained. 'He discovered Fox and Johnny were having an affair and threatened to divorce her unless she paid up. Then he found out that Johnny—'

'I'm going deaf, all right?' Johnny interrupted. Lucy gasped. 'I was worried the press would find out and people would stop coming to the shows.'

Knowing what was coming next, Birch handed me

the laptop we'd found at Penfold Mews.

'You'd like us to think that's why Crash was blackmailing you, wouldn't you, Johnny?' I said. 'It's true you're losing your hearing and have been playing songs from memory for some time. But that's not a problem, because you wrote them . . . didn't you?'

I opened the *Johnny* folder on the laptop. 'Does Fox know? About the songs and the tapes?'

She clearly didn't. 'What songs? Jonathan, have you started writing again? That's wonderful.' His deadpan expression made her pause. 'Isn't it?'

The normally loquacious guitarist glowered at me in silence.

'All right,' I said, 'I'll tell her. You're right, Fox. Johnny told me he's been writing new songs for a while now. But Crash wouldn't record any of them or let him make them solo.'

'How could he stop him? I don't understand.'

I pressed Play and we all listened to Crash sing one of Bad Dice's early hits on an acoustic guitar. But this file was undamaged and included parts we hadn't heard before. Parts where Crash would play something different to the final version of the song, then stop and mutter, '*No, that doesn't work. How about this?*' before continuing with the song everyone knew. It finished and I played a second recording with similar contents.

Not knowing the songs well myself, it had taken Birch – who knew the band's discography from back to front and upside down – to understand what this meant.

It put Crash and Johnny's recorded conversation, about 'the fans finding out', in a whole new light.

Fox cottoned on quickly. 'That's Crash, from years ago. He hasn't sounded like that since their early albums. But it's like he doesn't know the songs . . .'

'Johnny told me the real money is in songwriting,' I said. 'That's where the royalties come from, how he made millions and bought the house on the Crescent; because he wrote all of the band's hits. Except it turns out that he didn't. Crash did, and they both knew it, but it couldn't be proven . . . until Crash found some old tapes in amongst all this mess.'

'They're fake,' Johnny insisted. 'You've seen his set-up, all those computers. The man could manipulate anything to sound like anything.'

I shrugged. 'Perhaps they are. I don't think so, but it doesn't really matter. What matters is that *this* is what he was really blackmailing you over, not your deafness. He threatened to release these recordings and sue for decades of royalties if you didn't pay him instead. A thousand pounds per week was quite reasonable compared to the millions you stood to lose, not to mention how your fans would react.'

Unsurprisingly, it was Lucy who zeroed in on the big question. 'I'm confused. If Crash wrote them, why did he let Johnny take credit for all these years?'

'Mr Ormond-Wiles senior was a successful banker who almost single-handedly funded the band's early days. Somehow, he convinced a young and naive Crash to assign the songwriting to his son Johnny, presumably in return for all the financial support their family gave Bad Dice. Crash came to regret it but was powerless to change anything until he found the tapes.'

Fox had been sitting next to Johnny, holding his hand. Now she withdrew and went to stand by the French windows instead.

'We each thought he was blackmailing us alone,' she said, 'When in fact it was all three of us. So much for him being broke.'

'Actually, it was four. Blackmail is, after all, why Howard killed Crash.'

'But how, and when?' asked Fletcher. 'Howard has alibis all Thursday night and Friday morning.'

I closed the laptop. 'When I came here for the weekend, I brought a jigsaw puzzle with me. A lovely painting of the canal, which I planned to finish over the bank holiday. But I'd barely started when Crash turned up dead and after that there wasn't time. Last night I thought to myself, *If only I could turn the calendar back a couple of days*. In a way, that was the breakthrough.'

Everyone glanced sideways at one another, probably thinking I'd lost my mind.

'Let's return to Thursday afternoon,' I said. 'Crash introduced me to most of you that day. He also warned me that Howard Zee wasn't his real name, but as I'm so used to people using stage names I thought nothing of it. There were other things I should have noticed, though, such as Howard not taking clients younger than forty.

Or that when Crash said to Howard, "I'll see you later," he wasn't being polite, he meant it literally. At nine o' clock that night, in fact.'

'No, that can't be,' said Latesha. 'Howard was in session, you know that. I sent you the recording.'

'You did, and I'll explain in a moment. When I arrived on Friday morning, I met Howard returning from a jog. We came in here and the moment I opened the door Ace ran onto the path, desperate for the toilet. Then Lucy called, looking for Crash. She'd tried the night before but Crash hadn't answered the door. She was trying to make her weekly blackmail payment, which was due on Thursdays.'

Lucy huffed. 'I thought it was strange when he didn't answer. There were lights on and Ace barked when I knocked.'

'Yes,' I said, 'because there *was* someone inside, but it wasn't Crash. Luckily for them, Ace's bark is worse than his bite.' The Collie pricked up an ear at the mention of his name.

'Next, Howard gave me a key to the access gate. Crash had changed his locks after a burglary and forgot to put one on the new keyring he supplied me. That's when I first saw Howard's studio set-up, which struck me as very professional. I didn't know how significant that would be. More immediately, though, Mr Choudhury the grocer told me that Crash hadn't called in that morning as he'd planned to.'

'Why is any of this important?' said Fox. 'Didn't you

say Crash was already dead by Friday?'

I nodded. 'Long dead, in fact. Don't you see? At first, we thought Crash was killed Friday morning because he texted me about getting a car to the airport. But that text was a fake. Crash didn't answer the door to Lucy on Thursday night, or call in at Choudhury's on Friday morning because he was already at the bottom of the canal. No wonder Ace was desperate for the toilet; by the time I arrived, the poor dog had been shut up in here for almost twelve hours.'

'This is rather circumstantial,' said DCS Fletcher. 'I still don't see how it led you to Howard.'

'You will. Later on Friday, I used Crash's computer upstairs and discovered the files had been badly damaged. But they'd been fine on Thursday afternoon. Crash himself had played me some music and even recorded me talking. Now those files were damaged and the computer was open on one side. I also found four folders, all locked with a password; one for each of his blackmail victims.'

I stood up on my tiptoes and moved the gold disc aside, revealing the wall safe.

'Inside this safe, the police found a notebook, which contained lyrics for Crash's new songs. I took photos, as a keepsake for Birch.' Judging by DCS Fletcher's expression she still wasn't happy about that, but Birch couldn't resist a smile. 'It turned out to be much more than that, though. The notebook also contained the passwords to those folders. Unfortunately, the contents were so damaged it was hard to decipher them. With

Howard, for example, all we really discovered was that he was involved in a scandal with a woman called Vicki.'

'His ex-wife, right?' said Latesha.

'I'm afraid not. He fooled you, me and everyone else with that story. You were his ticket out, you see. He'd begrudgingly paid Crash to keep the real scandal a secret and then along you came, promising big money in America with Ziggy+.'

'Zabok,' she corrected me.

'Whatever. The point is, Howard couldn't afford to let this chance go. But Crash threatened to expose his scandal if Howard didn't turn down the TV deal.'

'He didn't tell me any of this,' Latesha protested.

'Of course not. He had no intention of turning you down, or of letting the blackmail follow him across the pond and risk his shot at fame. Instead, Howard came up with a plan. Everyone knew Bad Dice would be playing in Dublin over the Carnival weekend, as they do every year. So he scheduled everything around that and used you, Latesha, as bait.'

I opened the laptop again, found the *Howard* folder and played the undamaged recording of their conversation from Thursday.

Crash: '—*didn't have to come here to discuss this. You could have phoned, you know.*'

Howard: '*Not likely. Listen, we just want to talk. She knows everything, and on behalf of Zabok+ Latesha is proposing a very generous offer to* resolve this once and for all. At least come and listen to her, will you?'

Crash: *'Don't you think you should be making your own generous offer to the likes of Vicki Richards? I tell you, if you try to leave now, I'll go to the press with the truth.'*

Howard: *'By then I'll be in the States with big money and big lawyers to fight you. So let's get serious. Nine o' clock, all right? Don't be late.'*

'None of that is true,' said Latesha, horrified. 'I don't know squat about a scandal, or paying Crash off, or anything.'

'I know,' I reassured her. 'When I mentioned it to Howard yesterday, you hadn't even heard of Vicki Richards, let alone made her a "generous offer". This conversation was a lie, designed to lure Crash to Howard's boat. He lied to us about meaning nine o'clock on Friday morning, too. I might have believed him, until I remembered that when Lucy called at the boat that morning, it was Howard himself who mentioned Crash's preference for early flights. He knew very well that he wouldn't be around at that time.'

'But Howard ran a class from nine till ten on Thursday night. I watched it myself.'

I smiled. 'Did he, though?'

'There was a live Q&A,' DCS Fletcher pointed out. 'I've seen the video in question. You can't fake that.'

'Then how do you explain his watch?' I said.

Met with a sea of blank faces, I continued, 'This wasn't a spur-of-the-moment killing. Howard had already begun making plans, and my coming here to look after Ace was the icing on the cake. Normally, Crash would hand his dog off to Fox. But not this time because she recently took in Lilith, her boat cat.' Fox turned from the French windows and I caught her eye. 'To spite Crash for the blackmail, I assume? Make him spend some of the money you were paying him on a dog sitter?'

Fox snorted. 'Stopped him coming round as often, too.'

'Yes, so you could spend more time with Johnny . . . like you did overnight on Thursday.' I turned to Lucy. 'It really was him you saw climb over the gate on Friday morning.'

'So Johnny killed Crash?!' she shrieked.

I sighed. 'No, and neither did Fox. Lilith's presence alone should have told me that earlier. If Fox planned to kill Crash, taking in a cat – which forced him to find a sitter, like me – would only have made things more difficult.'

Birch coughed. 'You could say that if not for the cat, Howard would have got away with it because Gwinny wouldn't be here.' Fletcher shot him an accusing look but he didn't apologise.

I continued, 'Two nights before, at nine o'clock on Tuesday night, Howard conducted and recorded an online session as usual – but it wasn't broadcast. Instead, for forty-five minutes Howard performed to nobody but the camera, all the time pretending an audience was watching. He ended it, as always, by calling a five-minute break before questions and discussion. During those breaks he normally replaced the video with a countdown timer.'

As if sensing we were approaching the heart of the matter, Ace stood up from his bed and padded over to sit by me. I fussed behind his floppy ear and continued.

'At 9 p.m. on Thursday, Howard opened another online session. But instead of doing it live, he played the video he'd recorded on Tuesday. The attendees had no idea; to them it was like any other class. But while they watched a recording, the real Howard prepared a drink for Crash. What was it they found in Crash's bloodstream, Superintendent?'

'Massive amounts of Xanax,' Fletcher confirmed.

Fox perked up. 'So it wasn't poisonous plants at all!'

'No,' I reassured her, 'it was plain old pills, stolen from Crash's boat when Howard burgled it weeks ago. Crash thought nothing had been taken because he kept such a stash of Xanax that he didn't notice one missing bottle. On Thursday, Howard presumably fobbed him off about waiting for Latesha and offered him a drink full of the stuff. It would have rendered Crash unconscious very quickly. Then Howard took his keys and his phone, which he unlocked with Crash's own face. Next, he checked the coast was clear and carried him out of the boat; easy enough for a strong man like Howard. Finally, he lowered Crash into the canal. No noise, no fuss.'

'Hence water in his lungs,' Birch explained for Fletcher's benefit. 'Unconscious but not dead. Um, until he drowned, of course.'

Fletcher was confused. 'But when we analysed Howard's smoothie maker, we *did* find poisonous plants.'

'He couldn't very well get back into Crash's boat for more Xanax with you guarding the place, could he?' I said. 'Howard expected Crash to stay submerged. And if he hadn't floated to the surface on Saturday, we'd have all assumed he went missing in Dublin instead. The body turning up threw a wrench in Howard's plans, which is why he tried to throw me off with talk about Crash having a "dark side" that might have led to suicide.'

'He was blackmailing people,' said Fletcher. 'That's dark.'

'But also a reason to keep living. So when things went awry, Howard thought if he could keep us chasing our tails for another day or two, he'd be long gone on a plane to LA before anyone worked it out. Fox was easy to frame, with her poisonous plants. The display case may be locked, but everyone knows where she keeps the key.'

Fox shrugged. 'The cabinet was to prevent accidents. It never occurred to me someone would deliberately take a plant.'

'But that's exactly what Howard did. He snuck onto your boat, clipped some monk's hood, mixed it into his smoothie then drank it before Lucy was due to call, knowing she'd raise the alarm.'

Lucy looked shocked. 'He could have died!'

'No,' said Fox. 'It was a tiny amount. Even if we hadn't found him, it just would have made him ill for a while.'

'But we're getting ahead of ourselves,' I said. 'After disposing of Crash, Howard next tried to delete the incriminating blackmail material. He probably thought it would be on Crash's phone, but it wasn't – though my number was, which is how he sent me the fake text on Friday morning and later gave Latesha my number. Right?'

She shrugged. 'I didn't think it was odd. Lots of women give Howard their number.'

'More's the pity,' I grimaced. 'Anyway, there was nothing on the phone. So he came here and let himself in with Crash's keys. Ace didn't mind because he knew Howard. Then he tried to break into the safe.'

'He didn't manage it, did he?' said Johnny.

'No. Howard knows his technology but the safe was beyond him, so he left it and replaced the gold disc. When I arrived the next morning, I noticed it was askew. Next, he went upstairs to Crash's computer and resorted to brute force, wrenching open the case and . . . disconnecting wires or something. I'm not a computer person. Whatever he did, it damaged the files very badly. It was around this time that Lucy called and saw lights on inside. As I said, someone was at home. But it wasn't Crash.'

'I was inches away from a killer,' Lucy breathed. I

half-expected her to start taking notes for her next play.

'Howard waited till the next morning, sent me that fake text, then tossed the phone into the canal. With the phone gone and the computer damaged he thought that would be the end of it . . . because he didn't know Crash kept a copy of all the compromising material, as well as a separate "blackmail phone", at a secret location on Penfold Mews.'

'At a *what*?' said Fox and Johnny in unison. DCS Fletcher had the decency to look faintly embarrassed. I allowed myself a smile, pleased to know that I could still hold an audience's attention.

'Crash used the blackmail money to buy a house where he kept backups of all the files, including physical material we found in a filing cabinet. He went there on Thursday evening to update it, including the recording of his conversation with Howard. It was the last thing he did before visiting Howard's boat at nine o'clock.'

There was a commotion from the hallway and Constable Wright brought Howard into the room, wrapped and shivering in a silver-lined blanket.

'Medics say he's fit for transport,' said the constable. 'Bit chilly, that's all.'

'Sit him down, he's not going anywhere yet,' said DCS Fletcher. 'We're getting to the good bit and I want to see his face.'

Maybe the superintendent and I did have something in common after all.

'Hold on, pet,' said Johnny. 'Go back a minute. What

was that about Howard's watch? Did it track his location or something? I know they can do that now.'

'Oh, it's much simpler than that.' I opened Howard's private streaming page on the computer and began playing the session recording from Thursday evening, turning the screen around so everyone could see.

'We've already watched these,' said Fletcher. 'The recordings confirm Mr Zimmerman's alibi.'

'Do they?' I fast-forwarded to the moment when the main session ended and Howard told everyone to take a five-minute break.

'He timed this precisely. The Tuesday night recording was made at nine o' clock, and on Thursday he began playing it back at nine precisely. After forty-five minutes, as always, he tells everyone to take a break.'

On the screen Howard approached the camera to shut it off. The screen changed to a five-minute countdown clock. I fast-forwarded again until the clock ran to zero . . . but then it remained on screen.

'I haven't paused it,' I said. 'During this session the countdown sits at zero for almost two minutes. I didn't think anything of it when I first watched. But Howard's sessions are normally very punctual, so why did this Q&A session start late?'

Everyone pondered the question, but nobody could answer.

Birch came to their rescue. 'Because Lucy was standing at Crash's front door,' he explained. 'Howard had to wait until she'd gone, which delayed him.'

'Indeed,' I said. 'But here's what really seals it.'

The screen flickered to life and Howard reappeared, to chat with his class.

'I don't see anything out of place,' said Fletcher.

'Nor should you. He's wearing the same clothes, he's drinking a smoothie and he's out of breath. Not from a workout, of course, but because in the previous half-hour he murdered Crash, dumped his body in the water, broke into his boat, then ran back after being delayed by Lucy.'

I glanced at Howard to see how he was taking this. He shot daggers back at me.

'During sessions he's too far from the camera to read his watch, but as he sits here for the Q&A we can see it clearly on his wrist. Big, bright numbers.'

Everyone leant forward, peering at the image.

'It says nine-fifty-two,' said DCS Fletcher. 'Which is correct, if the break lasted seven minutes.'

'That's right. Look, you can even read the date. The eighteenth, which was Thursday.'

Everyone leant back, disappointed.

'So what are we looking for? You said this disproved his alibi.'

I smiled and rewound the video by eight minutes. 'As I said, during the workout you can't read his watch. But when he finishes, and walks to the camera to turn it off for the break . . .'

I paused the video at that moment, with Howard's watch clearly visible as he reached to turn off the camera.

It read nine-forty-five pm . . . on the sixteenth.

Two days earlier.

Fletcher grinned and clamped a hand on Howard's shoulder. 'Bang to rights, Mr Zee. I'd say you're up spit creek without a chimney.'

I wondered if she knew she was the *only* person who'd say that. 'Hold on, though, Superintendent. You still don't know why he killed Crash.'

'Yes, we do. Blackmail, like you said. Makes perfect sense.'

Lucy shook her head. 'But what was the blackmail for? You said this Vicki woman isn't his ex-wife, so why would Howard kill Crash because of her?'

'Well,' I said, 'first you have to understand that Howard Zimmerman didn't kill Crash.'

The room erupted, as I'd known it would. I was enjoying myself.

'You just spent ten minutes telling us he did!' cried Fox. 'What are you playing at?'

'Remember I said that nobody here is who they seem? That pathetic man over there, shivering in a blanket, killed Crash. But he's not Howard Zimmerman.'

CHAPTER THIRTY-THREE

I had everyone's attention, especially 'Howard' himself. Until now there'd still been a chance he could talk his way out of it; DCS Fletcher had pointed out the evidence was circumstantial, and as Johnny said, you can manipulate all sorts of things on computers these days.

But now he was cornered.

'Crash told me that "Howard Zee" wasn't his real name. I assumed he was talking about the *Zee* part, shortened to make a stage name. But he actually meant much more. You see, the only English teacher I could find called Howard Zimmerman died a few years ago.'

'Was his death suspicious?' asked Fox.

'Not in the least. He also looked nothing like the Howard we know, and there was no hint of scandal around him at all, let alone with anyone called Vicki.'

'You're saying he took the dead man's name?' Fletcher asked. 'But why?'

'To escape the real scandal, of course. When Howard

said the mysterious "Vicki" was his ex-wife, we had no reason not to believe him. In fact, I foolishly gave him the opportunity to spin that lie in the first place and took his word for it. But I kept thinking about the recorded conversation between Crash and Howard. It strongly implied Crash knew who Vicki was and why Howard was hiding from her. So I searched for that connection . . . and found a woman called Vicki Richards with whom Crash had been photographed leaving a club.'

Howard groaned. He knew the game was up.

I continued, 'Two years ago, Vicki Richards was one of several women who accused a TV director of sexual assault in the 1990s. His name was Archie Gough, and he worked on a Saturday morning children's show where Vicki and her friends were audience regulars. They weren't even teenagers. Soon after they made the accusations, though, the director vanished into thin air.'

Everyone in the room turned to look at Howard, who struggled against Constable Wright's grip.

'The professionalism of Howard's set-up should have been a red flag. What would an English teacher know about things like camera coverage and studio lighting? But, like most people, I had no idea what Archie Gough looked like. TV directing isn't as glamorous as making films so there aren't many pictures of him online. Crash found one, though.'

On the laptop, I opened the photo of the newspaper article that had been too badly damaged to read when I first saw it. Now it was crystal clear, explaining the scandal around Archie Gough and featuring a photo of him with his big mop of dark hair and tinted glasses.

'This is why he didn't teach women under forty,' I explained. 'It ensured Vicki and her friends couldn't accidentally sign up and recognise him. His social media pictures are also cropped so you can't see his face.'

'But that picture looks nothing like him,' said Fox, peering at the screen.

'You're right. Howard is bald, has a luxuriant beard and doesn't wear glasses. But when I fell over playing with Ace in the Gardens, Howard came to see if I was OK. From that angle, looking at him upside down, it was almost like he was clean-shaven with a big bouffant of hair. I thought nothing of it, but later it made me wonder how easily he could change his appearance.' I turned to DCS Fletcher. 'Superintendent, when you found Howard unconscious in his bedroom, was there a contact lens holder on his nightstand?'

She nodded. 'There was indeed.'

'Enabling him to lose the glasses. And anyone looking closely can see he isn't naturally bald, but rather hides his hair by shaving his head. Constable, perhaps you could check his jacket for a passport?'

Fletcher nodded agreement and Constable Wright searched Howard's multi-pocketed jacket. Soon enough he found the waterlogged document and opened it carefully. 'Photo's a bit ruined.'

She took the passport and read it. 'The name's still

readable, though.' She turned it around to display the ID page. 'Wouldn't you agree, Mr Archibald Gough?'

Howard – or rather, Archie – growled. 'That silly bitch and her mates weren't angels, you know! Everyone just wanted to have fun! It was another time! People behaved differently!'

'They were underage girls, legally unable to consent,' I said. 'Their parents placed them in the care of people like you, trusting you to treat them like the children they were, not playthings for your wandering hands. And for all Crash's faults, he clearly felt the same way.'

I tapped the laptop. 'The first time I saw this spreadsheet it looked like you were paying him twice a week for some reason. But when I read the intact version, I saw that the second payments were nothing to do with you. They were payments *out*, from Crash to Vicki Richards. He gave her most of the money he took from you and refused to let you pay him off before escaping to America. So you killed Crash, hoping your secret would die with him – or that by the time it came out you'd be in Los Angeles with a team of expensive lawyers ready to defend you against any accusations.'

DCS Fletcher pulled Archie to his feet. 'Looks like your swan is fried, my son.' Oblivious to everyone's confused looks, she and Constable Wright frogmarched him outside. 'Archibald Gough, I'm arresting you on suspicion of murder . . .'

Her voice trailed away, then she suddenly poked her head back in the lounge to point at Lucy and Fox. 'Don't think I've forgotten about you two. We'll be having words later.'

'Don't worry,' I said when she left again, 'Birch and I will put in a good word for you both. Won't we?' I looked at him with a determined expression.

He hesitated, then twitched his moustache and smiled. 'Of course, ma'am. No harm done.'

CHAPTER THIRTY-FOUR

'They did what?' asked Birch as we strolled lazily through Regent's Park a week later. Ronnie was happily wearing himself out, chasing squirrels in vain.

'I'll show you,' I said. 'Hold your phone as if you're taking a selfie.'

He did, slightly embarrassed. I doubted the former policeman had ever taken a selfie in his life. Then I showed him what people lined up outside the Sunrise Theatre's stage door had been asking me to do; look into the camera and adopt an angry expression while pretending to thump them on the chin.

When I'd called Bostin Jim to relate these bizarre requests, he explained that thanks to the video of me whacking the drone outside Crash's houseboat, for a while at least I would be known everywhere as 'the angry old drone lady'. Hardly flattering, but apparently people had also connected it to Violet's video from the Carnival where we plugged the play, and within hours the first two weeks of *Mixed Mothers* had sold out. Jim had cannily used this leverage to demand I be paid my full original fee, and even got me bumped up the billing order to boot.

Swings and roundabouts.

Birch frowned. 'Can't say I understand it. But good that more people recognise you now. As it should be.'

I smiled at his flattery and almost pecked him on the cheek before thinking better of it.

'That reminds me, guess what else has gone viral?' he said, and played another video. It was the BuzzFeed reporter's video from his new drone, when it joined the chase at the Pool. In slow motion we watched Howard Zee, aka Archie Gough, back away from Ace and fall into the canal over and over again on a loop.

I'd already seen the clip on TV a few times, in places you'd expect, like *Graham Norton*, and places you certainly wouldn't, like *Newsnight*. But I let Birch have his moment of discovery and said, 'That'll haunt him in prison, I should think.'

I watched Ace herd the killer towards the water and smiled. I'd been concerned about handing the Border Collie off to a rescue, but at the last minute he was taken in by Johnny Roulette, of all people. The guitarist insisted he and Fox would work it out somehow. As for Fox, she and Lucy had got away with small fines over the cannabis after we defended them. The only person Lucy was 'supplying' besides herself was Fox, anyway. I don't know if my support helped, but the word of the Met's own DCI Alan Birch, retired, certainly did.

Crash's daughter Ellie had finally arrived from Tokyo on Monday afternoon as the Carnival boats were leaving. The Pool suddenly felt very empty without them. Ellie made sure I was paid for looking after Ace, Fox grudgingly thanked me . . . then made it clear they wanted to be left alone.

I understood. It wasn't so long ago I grieved for my own father. In some ways I still did because it never really leaves you; it just becomes a smaller part of you.

Latesha Michaels had returned to America empty-handed. After I ruined their cash cow, I suspect Zabok+ won't be calling my agent any time soon.

Speaking of cash, while I now had some money, I knew it wouldn't last. I still had to replace the reporter's first drone, for one thing, and after seeing the price I was even more grateful I'd be getting my full fee for the play.

Then there was the building work. With everything else going on, I'd forgotten all about it until I woke up on Tuesday to find Darren sitting on the scaffold outside my house, chatting and laughing with the Dowager Lady Ragley. Laughing! She'd even made him a cup of tea. Apparently, he was the fourth cousin twice removed of some baronet or other, which was enough for the Dowager to decide he was a good sort. 'Much better than those foreign chaps,' she'd said and I fought the urge to roll my eyes.

Which left one matter to clear up.

'Birch,' I said, as he threw a stick for Ronnie. 'Can we speak frankly?'

'Always.'

'Do I really remind you of DCS Fletcher?'

He wisely took a minute to consider his answer, as we watched Ronnie bound into the lake to cool off.

'Have to admit, thought you'd get along. Peas in a pod, all that. Not afraid to admit I was wrong, though.'

'That's not what I asked,' I said, nudging him. 'What sort of relationship did you have with her, when you were in the Met?'

He turned to me, offended. 'How dare you! Strictly professional. Beatrice was still alive.'

Rats! I hadn't meant it like that, but now I'd offended Birch *and* inadvertently summoned the ghost of his late wife. Well played, Gwinny. At this rate we'd both be in a care home before I got so much as a kiss out of him. Damn it, we weren't getting any younger and I couldn't play second fiddle to a dead woman forever.

'Birch, I'm sorry, I didn't—'

'I'm only teasing,' he said, with a twinkle in his eye. 'I knew what you meant. For the record, you're very alike. But relationship-wise, very different . . . I hope.'

To my surprise, he took my hand. His was softer than I expected, but something felt wrong. I glanced down and saw he no longer wore his wedding ring.

'There you are!' called out a voice behind us.

We separated, embarrassed at being caught in the act like teenagers, and turned to see Tina Chapel bearing down on us with a wide grin. Her Salukis, Spera and Fede, trotted elegantly by her side. She wasn't unexpected; I'd invited her to join us for a stroll, but we'd started without her because Tina is one of those people for whom time is an abstract concept.

From the corner of my eye I spied Ronnie leap out of the lake, shake himself off and run to greet the Salukis. Not wanting to get soaked, I quickly fussed them first then hugged Tina.

'Darling, it's so lovely to see you. You won't believe what happened last weekend in Little Venice.'

'Never mind that, you secret lovebirds,' she said with a wink. 'Now, we've got all afternoon. Tell me *everything . . .*'

ACKNOWLEDGEMENTS

The first thing I must say is that Little Venice is a real place, is quite lovely and you should visit if you're able. It's even good for you – research shows that regular use of the UK's canals and waterways for leisure saves the NHS over £1 billion per year.

However, many aspects of the Little Venice in this book have been thoroughly fictionalised for the sake of story (not least its murderous residents). And while the real Pool hosts a 'Canalway Cavalcade' festival every spring, to the best of my knowledge the celebrations have never included a dead body.

Sophomore entries in a series are always tricky, and this book was no exception. Striking the balance between recurring characters and new situations, between familiarity and novelty, was particularly difficult. As always, I'm indebted to my redoubtable beta readers for their feedback and notes.

Thanks also go to Jeremy Burge and his circle of

boating friends for help with matters on the canal; to Linda Stratmann for advice on poisons and paralysis; and to James Thomson for technical musings.

Thank you to everyone who bought, read, enjoyed, reviewed, and contacted me about *The Dog Sitter Detective*, particularly the dog lovers and rescue volunteers. The book even won the Barker Book Award for fiction, which I'm still a bit speechless about. When this series was announced I said I hoped readers would come to love Gwinny and her peculiarities as much as I do, and it seems you have. I appreciate every kind word.

I also appreciate some of the kindest people you could ever meet, namely my fellow crime authors. The crime writing community, and the Crime Writers' Association in particular, continues to be a source of great friendship and camaraderie.

The team working at and for Allison & Busby have been tremendously supportive. A hearty thank you to Fiona Paterson, Fliss Bage, Libby Haddock, Lesley Crooks, and Daniel Scott; to David Wardle for the amazing covers; Helen Richardson for her sterling PR work; and of course A&B supremo Susie Dunlop herself.

As always, my agent Sarah Such remains a voice of sanity and guidance in an ever more chaotic world.

Finally, I really couldn't do any of it without Marcia, who has the most important and difficult job of all: living with an author.

ANTONY JOHNSTON's career has spanned books, award-winning video games and graphic novels including collaborations with Anthony Horowitz and Alan Moore. He wrote the New York Times bestseller *Daredevil Season One* for Marvel Comics and is the creator of *Atomic Blonde* which grossed over $100 million at the box office. The first book featuring Gwinny Tuffel, *The Dog Sitter Detective*, was the winner of the Barker Fiction Award. Johnston can often be found writing at home in Lancashire with a snoozing hound for company.

dogsitterdetective.com
@AntonyJohnston